MURDEROUS DREAMS

Also by Susan Jane Wright

Box of Secrets

The Glass Lake

Fortune Favors the Dead

MURDEROUS DREAMS

SUSAN JANE WRIGHT

ROAN IMPRINT

ISBN 978-1-7390380-4-5 (Paperback Edition)
ISBN 978-1-7390380-5-2 (eBook Edition)

Editing by Roan Imprint
Front cover image by Mark Timberlake
Front cover design by Roan Imprint

Published by Roan Imprint
1500 14 St SW Suite 119
Calgary, AB T3C 1C9
Canada

Visit www.SusanJaneWright.ca

For my mother

THE HOUSE

Once this had been an elegant house with high ceilings and light filled rooms, full of traditional furniture and a stunning art collection that reflected the owners' globe trotting tastes.

Now everything, right down to the copper wiring, was gone, stripped away by dealers selling reclaimed architectural materials and scavengers looking to make a quick buck.

A grey mouse squeezed through the crack under the sheet of plywood guarding the front entrance. It skittered across the battered black and white tiles into the kitchen and hopped down the stairs to the basement, twitching its pink nose as it darted across the floor into what had once been a barrel-vaulted wine cellar.

It stopped and rose up on its spindly hind legs. What was this? Slumped next to a dusty white pilaster was a lump wrapped in a woven shroud.

The mouse approached. Deciding it was safe, it dashed across the cold brick floor and crawled onto the blanket, its tiny paws burrowing deep between the folds.

In two hours the body would be stiff with rigor mortis.

In ten hours it would be as cold as the brick floor on which it lay.

But right now the body was fresh, still warm, and that was enough for the mouse to doze off and dream.

CHAPTER ONE

AJ stared out the windshield as the mob poured off the sidewalk and engulfed the car. "Evie." He shook his head, "this is all your mother's fault."

"What?" I glanced at my law partner; he was half-serious. "My mom has been gone for years. How could this possibly be her fault?"

Outside the protesters clogged the snow-covered streets, blocking our progress. Even inside the car with the heater going full blast and the windows tightly closed, the noise of chanting and shrill whistles was deafening.

It was a bitterly cold Friday in January but nothing, not even minus 30°C with the windchill, could deter the demonstrators who swarmed like fire ants into the plaza at City Hall. Their objective? To force our client, Marc Hubert, to stop work on the Ballet House.

I glanced at my watch. We were late. We should be back at the office by now, not trapped in the car by a horde of screaming protesters.

AJ drummed his palms on the steering wheel, "Come on, come on." Then he hit the horn. Two sharp blasts.

"Jeez, AJ, don't do that! Let's not make them any madder than they already are."

Too late.

The mob turned and faced us like a pack of zombies spotting their next victim. A huge, burly man with a thick red beard muscled his way through the crowd, shouting obscenities and jabbing his placard in the air.

His thick black glove slammed onto the hood making the sideview mirrors shudder. His placard—SAVE THE RIVER—flashed across the windscreen. The sign snagged under the windshield wipers. The bearded guy yanked the placard free, it tore and bits of cardboard fluttered away on the wind like misshapen butterflies. Then the Viking of a man glared into AJ's window and shouted his name.

Stunned, I turned to AJ. "You know that guy?"

"No," came AJ's curt reply.

The prickle of unease I'd been trying to ignore grew. "We have to get out of here before they tear us apart."

"And where do you propose we go? We're boxed in." AJ sounded as tense as I felt.

We were twenty minutes away from the office. Ditching the car and walking in this weather was out of the question. Besides AJ would sooner abandon his first born (if he had one) than leave his precious MGB to the mercy of the mob. I slouched lower in my seat. Where are the cops when you need them?

As if on cue, a siren wailed in the distance. The mood of the crowd changed. The bearded man raised a bullhorn and the mob grew quiet, listening as he bellowed instructions. "Clear the street. Clear the street." Like the Red Sea, the crowd parted, allowing two cop cars to pull up onto the sidewalks. A police officer stepped out of the first car, pointing at us and sweeping her arm briskly through the air to wave us forward.

"About bloody time," AJ grumbled as he inched forward and slowly pulled away from the mob.

Half a block later I repeated the question. "So how is this my mom's fault?"

"What?"

"You said this was my mom's fault."

The tension left his face and he laughed. "It was nothing. I was just thinking that your mom and Sabine were friends—"

"Ah, so by your convoluted logic, Mom was Sabine's friend, Sabine is married to Marc, Marc is building the Ballet House and we've got the environmental contract, ergo, it's my mom's fault we got trapped in the protest. Tell me again, AJ, who did you bribe to get into law school?"

His smile broadened. We may have gone to different law schools, but AJ and I think alike. We're well versed in the Socratic Method, but in the real world we relied on logic coupled with instinct. That it works is uncanny.

The mob faded in the rear-view mirror as AJ accelerated. We were on our way back from a meeting at the Atelier, Marc's office. I adored Marc and Sabine, but what a pretentious name. They've lived in Canada for twenty-five years but they never stopped being French. AJ took great joy in butchering Marc's name (it's Hugh-Bear, not Hugh-Bert). I'd given up correcting him a long time ago.

It's not that AJ is an unsophisticated rube—he's heir to a global fertilizer enterprise—but he was raised in the country and falls back on his 'yes, ma'am' farm boy ways whenever it suits him.

AJ joined the firm a year after Keith Lawson and I ditched Big Law to set up our own boutique (read: small) green/renewable energy practice. The biggest challenge we faced when AJ became a partner was figuring out what to call ourselves. It's amazing how many different ways you can arrange three surnames. Finally Bridget, our admin assistant, took matters into her own hands and presented us with our new stationary. The letterhead read: *Braxton, Lawson, Valentine*. Voilà, the birth of BLV. Together with Madeline, our paralegal, we were—in my humble opinion—the best eco law firm in town.

Marc Hubert's Ballet House project was an important file for us. It would go a long way towards boosting our reputation nationally and internationally—assuming the protesters didn't burn it to the ground first.

AJ gunned the engine through an intersection. "Hubert is committed to protecting the rivers"—he meant the Elbow and the Bow—"you'd think that would satisfy them. Can't they find someone more despicable to harass?"

"They? You mean NEO?" Depending on who you talked to, NEO was a bunch of eco-terrorist fanatics or dedicated stewards of the environment. "Why should they trust Marc, or the City for that matter?"

He glanced at me with those ice blue eyes and I continued.

"It certainly doesn't help that Marc plunked the Ballet House right on top—"

"*Beside*, not on top."

"Okay, beside the Elbow River. City council pretends to be as green as green can be, they could have rejected the project, instead they said, sure, fine, be my guest."

When the City announced it was tearing down the Victoria Park bus barns, people hoped the land would be reclaimed for green space. Instead, it was slated for an even bigger building with even more hard surfaces. The

Ballet House became a flash point. Either you loved it, or you hated it. There was no in-between.

CHAPTER TWO

AJ roared into our parking lot as if he were competing in the Indie 500. He's done this every day since the start of the Crow Wars. One crapped on his seat two summers ago—his fault, he left the top down—and since then he's determined to make their lives miserable. He blasts into the parking lot, sending them screeching and wheeling into the small, wooded hill behind our office, then guns his engine one last time to show them who's boss. The crows squawk back, singularly unimpressed.

"Stop riling them up," I said as we entered the lobby, "or they'll be pecking our eyes out like in that Hitchcock movie."

"AJ," Madeline's voice, "crows are smart. you'll never win." She strolled down the corridor looking like Katherine Hepburn in her prime. Her attire, pleated camel slacks and an oversized white shirt, matched the no-nonsense look on her face.

AJ grinned, he has a soft spot for Madeline and her bird mania, we all do. "If you keep feeding them, they'll never leave."

"You silly man, what makes you think I want them to

leave." She turned to me and asked, "How is the infamous Marc Hubert?"

Unlike AJ, Madeline pronounced Marc's name correctly but with a clipped edge. She moved to Calgary from Montreal decades ago and like many French-Canadians becomes snippy if someone criticizes her Quebecois French, especially if that someone is a Parisian. Last year at a client appreciation event, Marc pointed out that the French word for the weekend is *le week-end* and not *la fin de semaine* which he said sounded pretentious. She's never forgiven him for it.

"Marc is fine," I replied. "Why do you ask?"

She gave me an enigmatic smile. "No particular reason. Just wondering."

When Madeline starts wondering about something, I get worried. She moves in powerful circles and has no end of suiters dropping investment tips (and lavish gifts) on her every chance they get. She may not be a member of the glitterati, but she's certainly privy to all their secrets.

"Madeline, have you heard something about Marc or the Ballet House?"

"It's nothing." She arched an eyebrow and wandered off.

Sometimes Madeline is beyond infuriating but it's pointless to press her for information. She's like a sphinx. She'd tell me when she was good and ready and not a minute sooner.

Keith called out from his office as I was banging around in the coffee room. "We're out of coffee. Bridget's run down to Seb's to buy some more... heaven forbid you have a caffeine meltdown."

I went down to his office. "How can you work in this chaos?" I waved a hand at the files slumped on the floor beside his desk and the law books heaped in messy piles on his credenza. For such a meticulous lawyer—I swear he can recite the lawyer's code of conduct from memory—his office looked like a hurricane had passed through.

"Never mind." I lifted a stack of files off a chair and set them on the floor before sitting down. Keith's face was ruddy and his eyes looked tired. "Why are you still here." It was just past six o'clock, early in the day for most lawyers, but Keith gets in at six a.m., which is really early considering he has to drive in from his acreage south of town. He's usually packed up and out the door by now.

He pulled his backpack up off the floor and began to rummage on his desk looking for something. I spotted a red topped Tupperware container and passed it to him. He nodded thanks and said, "Got a late start this morning, Claire's goat is sick. You think it's tough getting medicine into a baby, you should try a baby goat."

As Keith took me through the details—a spindly goat bleating and flailing, and Claire, his eight-year-old daughter, pleading with her dad not to let it die—I marvelled that someone who looked as hard and tough as the Marlboro Man could be so gentle.

Keith's smile faded after the goat story. "What's this I hear about you becoming a community activist? You're going to raise hell at some town hall meeting opposing a new development in Mount Royal?"

"Activist? Whatever gave you that idea?"

There was a soft rap on Keith's door. Bridget stood in the doorway with an enormous bag of Seb's artisan coffee on her hip and a sheepish look on her face. She's blue eyed and rosy cheeked and built like Rosie the Riveter. She could wrestle me to the ground in a heartbeat.

"Sorry, Evie," she said. "My fault. I meant to leave you a message. Sabine wants you to join her at a town hall meeting. They're trying to stop the McMansion going up next to her place."

"Really? I talked to Sabine a couple of days ago. She didn't mention it." Sabine and Marc practically adopted my sister Louisa and me after Mom and Dad died four years ago. We talked every week. Or rather, Sabine talked and I listened. Sabine was a patron of the arts and loved to gossip about 'the real story' behind the events I only read about in the papers.

Bridget shrugged. "The final approvals for the McMansion came through this morning, no one appealed, and that monstrosity, to use her words, is going ahead. She's ready to kill someone, starting with Marc."

"Hold on," Keith said as he stuffed the Tupperware container into his backpack and bounced the canvas bag on his desk to settle its contents. "Isn't Marc designing the McMansion? We can't represent Sabine against her husband, even if she despises the McMansion, he's retained us for the Ballet House. It's a—"

"I know, I know, a conflict. Look, she's an old family friend. I'll make sure she understands I'm only going along as moral support. The appeal period is over, she's out of time."

"That's not what Sabine thinks," Bridget said as she hoisted the bag of coffee up higher on her hip. "She was spitting mad on the phone. Yelling in English and French. I only caught half of it, but the word *merde* came through loud and clear."

CHAPTER THREE

Louisa was perched at the kitchen island reading the newspaper on her laptop when I arrived home. She was wearing a fluffy bathrobe and had a cup of coffee in one hand and a Danish in the other. She's the head nurse on the neuro ward at Foothills Hospital and had just come off two weeks on the night shift. She's always out of whack on her first day off, hence the bathrobe and woolly socks. Quincy was lying at her feet, eyeballs rolling around waiting for a pastry crumb to drop to the floor.

Louisa and her bull terrier moved in with me six years ago. It was supposed to be a temporary arrangement until she got back on her feet after her divorce from the odious Dr. Bob. But the days turned to weeks and the weeks turned to months and six years later they were still here. Which suited me just fine.

"Is it make-your-own for dinner tonight?" I asked as I hung my coat in the hall closet.

"There's a pasta casserole in the oven," she replied, glancing up from her laptop. "The Ballet House, isn't that Sabine's husband's project?" She turned the laptop toward me so I could see the story. It was accompanied by two photographs.

The first was an architectural rendering of the building. Despite all the hype that it would be Calgary's version of the Sydney Opera House, they looked nothing alike. Instead of fourteen tall, white shells, it had a flat roof festooned with strips of steel that floated like red ribbons, and was nestled in patches of pale green and rich yellow, the artist's representation of the riverbank and the sun I supposed. Other than some small squiggles flying up into the pale blue sky—birds?—there wasn't a living creature to be seen.

The second photo was packed with people. Angry people. It captured last week's protest at the Ballet House construction site. The protesters looked as angry as the ones AJ and I had encountered in front of City Hall. The same glowering faces, the same thrusting placards and the same red haired Viking of a man yelling into a bullhorn. Off to one side behind three impassive cops stood a handful of construction workers who looked like they'd gladly throw the protesters into a cement mixer.

"The mayor is calling for patience," Louisa said. "The river will be protected; we have his word."

"As if we haven't heard that before."

Louisa scrolled through the story. "The protesters are becoming violent. Someone threw a brick over the fence at the construction site. It caught a worker in the face. Broke 'poor Jerry's nose' according to the foreman. He wants the cops to lock 'em up and throw away the key." Her expression turned grave. "These NEO guys have been staging protests every Friday since last September. At the construction site and at City Hall. For four months. That's a lot of pressure on Marc... and Sabine."

Louisa and I had known Marc and Sabine for two

decades. We met them when they moved into the neighbourhood. Dad joked that their mere presence gave Mount
Royal a special cachet.

Mom and Sabine became good friends, but Dad and
Marc never really hit it off. It's not that they didn't like
each other; they just didn't have much in common. Dad
was an accountant and Marc was an architect. They didn't
speak the same language.

Neither did Mom and Sabine now that I think about
it. Sabine was an elegant Parisienne who'd settled in 'this
cultural backwater' because it suited her husband's career,
while Mom, a feisty Hungarian, immigrated to Calgary as
a young woman and was grateful for the chance to start
fresh in her new home.

———

After dinner the scent of shea butter and strawberries
floated out of the bathroom, Louisa was pampering herself
in the bath, I pulled on my running gear and strapped
Quincy into his long lead for his evening run.

"Which way?" I asked him as he dragged me through
the front door and down to the sidewalk.

Quincy chose the riverbank. We angled around the side
of the house and jogged down to the river pathway. Our
townhouse is in the inner city. One of six facing a wide
leafy street and backing onto the Elbow River. Before the
flood, our jog along the riverbank was a relaxing jaunt with
nothing more than a chickadee or a little fox bursting out
of the wolf willows to slow us down; but now, six months
later, the path was as unpredictable as a mine field.

Louisa and I had chipped in with the neighbours to
reinforce the riverbank and recreate the pathway that

had all but disappeared when the river crested and filled our basements with filthy sludge. The work was finally complete, but we still had to go slow to avoid the loose bits of cement and twists of chicken wire hidden under skiffs of snow.

"Damn it," I said as I stumbled over a jagged piece of concrete. My mind flew to the construction worker at the Ballet House who'd been hit in the face with a brick. Accidents are one thing, but assault was something else entirely.

"You know Quincy, the trouble with being a lawyer is we believe rational legal arguments will solve all our problems." The dog flicked his ear but didn't break stride as I prattled on. "We work with environmentalists every day. Most of them are quite reasonable, but these NEO guys... I'm not so sure."

Quincy lifted his snout, testing the air. We were fifty yards from our house, close to the homeless man's lean-to. It vanished after the flood and for weeks I worried that its occupant, a thin middle-aged man with iron grey hair, had drowned and no one knew he'd died. Then one day he showed up with a shopping cart jammed with bulky green garbage bags and the lean-to was back. Louisa and I rarely saw him, but when we did, he'd nod his head in a solemn hello. As Quincy and I jogged past the lean-to we scanned the snow-covered shack, but there was no one home.

"Quincy." The dog continued jogging like a little robot. He could keep this up for hours. "Is it just me or is life becoming more unpredictable?" He huffed. He had no idea.

CHAPTER FOUR

The first time I met Sabine, she was dressed as Cleopatra. A golden headpiece rested lightly on her head; its filigree strands caught in her jet-black hair. A shiny gold snake encircled her upper arm and her pleated gold cape whispered in the breeze when she opened the front door. Except for the cigarette dangling from her fingers, she was every inch the Queen of Egypt.

It was Halloween, I was sixteen and Sabine was going to a party. My mother had sent me over to be briefed on the care and feeding of Sabine's Persian cat, a cranky old girl called Jasmine. Sabine and Marc were off to Dubai the next day and Jasmine refused to set foot in a kennel.

"Evie, yes, yes." She pulled me into the foyer as I stammered out my name. "Marc," she called over her shoulder, "she's here." She continued speaking in rapid French, much too fast for my untrained ear.

Marc appeared around a corner in full costume. He was carrying a fluffy grey cat. "Hello Evie, meet Jasmine."

His accent was less pronounced than Sabine's. The cat sank its claws into the front of his tunic. He yelped and Sabine grabbed Jasmine, chiding it in French as she pried its claws out of the cotton fabric. I fixed my eyes on Marc's wavy black hair to avoid staring at his well shaped calves. He was wearing sandals with straps that criss-crossed up to his knees. Jasime hissed when Sabine thrust her into my arms and I prayed she wouldn't tear me to shreds.

"Julius Caesar, I presume." I stroked Jasmine's head. She flattened her ears; this did not bode well.

He laughed and with a grand sweep of his red cape said, "Mark Antony." He slid his arm around Sabine's narrow waist and looked into her eyes. "Cleopatra's one true love." Sabine raised her chin, a small smile on her lips, and blew a stream of cigarette smoke over his shoulder.

Now, roughly twenty years later Louisa and I were standing on the threshold of Sabine's beautiful home, a modern sprawling bungalow surrounded by evergreens and tall birch and oak tress in the best part of Mount Royal. The area had caught the eye of developers intent on demolishing the stately older homes and replacing them with expensive glass boxes three times bigger and four times more expensive.

Sabine greeted us with outstretched arms and kisses on both cheeks, telling us how young and beautiful we were. Louisa winked at me as if to say, this is why I love coming here.

We chirped back that she was as elegant as ever. This was true, other than her thick black hair which was now silver and pulled back into a high ponytail, the years had not changed her appearance. She was still tall, slim, and ele-gant, a former ballet dancer who looked stunning whether she was wearing a black leather motorcycle jacket or a sleek designer gown, preferably black, dove grey, or white.

Sabine led us through the house. Marc bought the place because it had 'good bones' and spent two years redesigning the interior until he and Sabine were satisfied. With no family they had ample space for sleek modern furniture, vibrant paintings and art glass that refracted the light pouring in through the tall, wide windows. It was exactly the kind of house you'd expect a ballerina and an architect to own. Calm, tasteful, elegant.

She insisted we have tea on the heated terrace. It was a frosty January day, but Marc refused to be trapped indoors by Calgary's long cold winters and installed four large outdoor heaters on each corner of the flagstone terrace. "It looks like the patio at Earl's," Sabine said with a sniff, "but it's toasty warm."

Jasmine the cat was long gone, replaced by a succession of Persians also called Jasmine. This one hated being inside when everyone else was outside so Sabine tied her to an iron hook-like thing protruding from the ground at the edge of the terrace. Jasmine immediately flopped down on the heated flagstones and started gnawing on the tether, determined to make her escape.

With a wide smile Sabine said, "Look how lovely you are. Your mother would be so proud. You two are like mirrors, so alike." Louisa and I have heard this many times. I'm sixteen months older than my sister but we have the same dark brown hair, clear brown eyes and slim jogger's build and we're often mistaken for each other. "But you, my darling"—she pinned her gaze on Louisa—"you look tired. You are working too hard."

Louisa rolled her eyes. "I'm a nurse, Sabine, we always work too hard."

"I don't think Jasmine likes her leash," I said.

Sabine tutted. "It doesn't matter what Jasmine likes or doesn't like. If she's outside, she must be tied up." Sabine poured tea into porcelain cups. Steam curled out of the spout. Sabine was serving a new tisane, something with six herbs. She'd introduced us to herbal teas long before it became fashionable.

Glaring in the direction of the house next door, Sabine shuddered. "Jasmine can't be left out here by herself. What if she goes next door? She'd be crushed by the machines. All spring and summer it will be nothing but noise and dirt. Why would anyone destroy such a beautiful house to build a McMansion? Pah! *Cupide!*" We must have looked bewildered because she added, "Greedy, showy. Stupid people."

Louisa and I glanced at the empty Georgian manor next door. Sabine's thick, spikey border of burning bush loomed over her sandstone wall. The last defence against the workers on the other side who would surely chop down the birch trees that cast a welcome shade over Sabine's manicured garden.

When the previous owner had died, his children put the house on the market. Within a week it sold at an astronomical price. Sabine was delighted at the prospect of new neighbours... until they slapped a yellow wire construction fence around the place. That's when she realized the house was doomed; slated for demolition as soon as the City approved the construction drawings.

"I will fight that monstrosity to my dying breath," she said, taking a delicate sip of tea.

Louisa and I locked eyes, Sabine can be a little histrionic at times.

"Have you met the new owner?" I asked.

"Some muckity-muck oil executive. He hired Marc to do the design."

"So you've seen the plans?"

"Of course I've seen the plans," she snapped. "The entire

community has seen the plans. It is monumentally ugly like a dentist's office or a 7-11 store." She spat out the words.

"But Marc—"

"Marc! Don't talk to me about Marc!"

I glanced at Louisa who had rescued Jasmine from her tether and was now stroking the cat in her lap. It purred so loudly I could hear the rumble in its throat over the chatter of crows in the trees. Louisa raised her eyes to meet mine. Her message was clear. *She's in one of her moods. No point arguing.*

For a moment we were quiet, listening to the crisp breeze stirring in the treetops and I wondered whether the birch trees on the other side of the Sabine's wall would be replaced. A massive house requires a deep, wide excavation to accommodate its extra deep basement. Madeline had a friend who was building a mansion with an eight-car underground garage to house his exotic car collection. His dream was crushed when the builder discovered an underground stream that made the structure unstable. Everyone likes pretty things, but these McMansions were over the top.

"How could Marc do this to me?" Sabine glared at the sandstone wall. "He says the house meets the City's requirements and now that the building has been approved the owner will not make any further changes. The man is a philistine."

It was unclear whether she was referring to Marc or the new owner. Jasmine yawned and stretched, her paw bumped Louisa's teacup, rattling it in its saucer. Louisa turned to Sabine and said, "I'm sure when it's finished it won't be so bad."

Sabine's eyes flashed with anger. "It's worse than you can imagine. They will dig to China. My wall will collapse so the wife can have her ridiculous yoga studio and butler's pantry. It is too much space for two people. They won't see each other for days. They must hate each other."

Then she reached out and touched my hand, her mood shifting again. Sweetly, she said, "My darling girl, you will help me kill that monstrosity once and for all." I sputtered that it was too late, the approvals had been granted.

Undeterred, she said, "I don't want you to sue them or Marc, although God knows he deserves it. You will come with me to the town hall meeting. Marc and the owner will present their bloated excuse for a house, once they see how much the community hates it they will back down."

Years ago when Keith and I were starting out we augmented our practice with some municipal law files. I knew how the process worked. If the City issued the development permit, that was it. The community could rage all it wanted; it wouldn't change the outcome.

Ten minutes later we were all back in the foyer. Sabine and Jasmine stood in the doorway waving goodbye. Louisa's car was halfway down the driveway when she turned to me and said, "You're toast. You know that don't you."

"Yep," I sighed. "Maybe I should send her an email and put it in bold, capital letters: MORAL SUPPORT ONLY!!!"

"Good luck with that," she replied. "By the way, I've never understood what they call her the Black Swan. Is it her moods?"

"I think it's because she was a principal dancer with the Paris Ballet before she gave it all up to marry Marc. Maybe she rose to fame performing Swan Lake."

"That would explain the swan part, not the black part; unless your thinking of the movie."

It wasn't until much later that I realized it didn't matter

what colour a swan was, black or white, they're extremely aggressive, especially when they're protecting their nest.

CHAPTER FIVE

The instant Branford Marsalis stepped into the soft glow of the spotlight on the darkened stage we fell silent, as if struck mute. The conductor flicked his baton and music, liquid and lazy, filled the Jack Singer Concert Hall.

Louisa snuggled deeper into her seat. "I'm so glad I came," she whispered without tearing her eyes away from the Grammy award winning saxophonist on stage.

"Me too," I whispered back.

Sabine replied to my 'moral support only' email with an offer of two free tickets to the Marsalis concert. She wasn't feeling well, Marc was working late—on Saturday night, I'd asked; it's the Ballet House, she'd replied—and she hated to see the tickets to go to waste. So here we were in the best seats in the house.

Marsalis swayed gently back and forth, his golden sax filled the air with seductive mellow tones, so rich you could almost see the notes hanging in the air. Coltrane, Ellington, Jarrett, they were all there. Finally after a standing ovation and an encore, the lights came up and the last note faded into a haunted silence.

As we shuffled down the row to the aisle, my eyes

scanned the room, then snagged on a familiar face. Marc was three rows down from us, a little further to the left.

"Louisa." With a sharp whisper I tugged at her arm.

"What?" When she turned to face me, her face was still aglow.

"Isn't that Marc?"

"Where?"

For a minute I thought I'd lost him but then he reappeared just past the end of our row moving slowly with the crowd towards the lobby. "There." I tilted my head. He was talking with young woman in a long, navy dress. He leaned in, she barely reached his shoulder, and she laughed at something he said. He pulled her hand into his arm and patted it as if to say, 'You're safe with me.' By the time we reached the lobby, they were gone.

As we shuffled to the front of the coat check line, I turned to Louisa. "You saw him, right?"

Louisa pulled her coat check ticket out of her pocket and told the attendant there were two coats on the hanger. As she slipped into her coat she said, "Yes, I saw him. I thought he was working late tonight."

"Did you see the woman with him?"

"What woman?"

"The small blond woman with the pixie cut. She seemed to know Marc very well."

"Are you sure? All I could see was Marc."

"Of course I'm sure. He was with someone young enough to be his daughter."

"Well, whoever she was, they're gone now."

We joined the throng of concert goers milling about on the cold sidewalk. Some fretted about whether their cars would start while others, still glowing from the Marsalis concert—he played that sax as if it were alive!—wanted to grab a drink at a nearby hotel.

Louisa linked her arm in mine and we walked down the block to the car. The moon was full, a brilliant yellowy orange, and shone bright in the dark night sky.

Louisa looked up, following my gaze. "A Harvest Moon," she said.

"No we've already had that; it's a Hunter's Moon. So named because it's so bright and stays so long in the sky that hunters can stalk their prey."

We found the car and she popped the door locks with her key fob. "You sound like Dad, pedantic." She dropped her head, pretending to doze off.

"I can't help it," I replied as I strapped on my seatbelt. "What was Marc doing here with another woman?"

"Before you become obsessed with her, remember he might not have been with her at all. Maybe she's a client or maybe she's just a stranger who bumped into him in the crowd."

"You didn't see how he looked at her." The warmth in his eyes, the gentleness in his lips. It was more than friendship.

Louisa began to unwedge the car from the curb, moving slowly back and forth a few feet at a time until she could free herself from the two bloated SUVs that had boxed her in. When we were clear she said, "Remember what Mom said when she first met Marc?"

I shook my head, no.

"She said only a fool marries a man who is six years younger than her; those six years are nothing when you're in your twenties, but just wait until you hit forty. She didn't trust Marc. Not only that—"

Mimicking Mom's Hungarian accent I finished Louisa's sentence, "Never marry a man who's prettier than you."

Louisa laughed. Mom emigrated to Canada when she was twenty-two but her Old Country beliefs remained strong until the day she died.

Quincy greeted us at the door with his ears flat and his tail wagging so hard he could barely stay upright. You'd think we'd been gone for days.

I clipped him into his harness and took him down to the end of the block for one last outing before bedtime. I wanted to show him the Hunter's Moon but it had disappeared behind a wall of thick, black clouds.

CHAPTER SIX

AJ tore his eyes away from the glittering estate homes whizzing by on Premier Way just long enough to say, "Tell me again why I'm riding shotgun to a town hall meeting that has absolutely nothing to do with me?"

Unlike many single men I've met, AJ can take care of himself, except when it comes to food. He hates cooking. I swear he lives on Ichiban noodles and cheese and pickle sandwiches. How he stays fit is a mystery. But then again, he's thirty-four, a year younger than me, and plays soccer to stay trim. I'd bribed him to come with me with the offer of dinner after the meeting.

He pivoted in the seat and stared at me, waiting for my answer.

"It's because you're a team player and tonight, the team, that would be you and me, are going to give Sabine all the moral support we can muster on a hopeless file that we couldn't take even if we wanted to because it's a conflict of interest."

"Ah," he said with a knowing smile. "I just figured it out. Keith is afraid you won't be able to control Sabine and wants me here as back up."

I sighed. "Yeah. That too."

Keith was called to the bar two years ahead of me and although we're all equal partners in the firm, sometimes he acts like the senior partner, or worse, my big brother. It drives me crazy. We've discussed it many times. I say he's overprotective, he says he's trying to save me from myself, I say that's patronizing and Louisa says we both need counselling. I can't tell if she's kidding.

"He's got a point, you know." AJ interrupted my thoughts. "The optics of us working *for* Marc on the Ballet House and *against* him on the McMansion aren't good."

He braced himself as I sailed around a sharp corner. We were now in the Estate District. The towering birch trees lining the boulevard were bare, no longer screening the enormous mansions on their double and triple lots. A couple of minutes later we turned onto Sabine's street.

"Is that her?" AJ asked as we pulled up in front of her house. Sabine was standing on the sidewalk in front of the McMansion—we all called it the McMansion now, even though the Georgian house was not yet demolished—she was with two men. The older man, short and stocky with wiry iron-grey hair, was pointing at the roofline. Standing beside him was a younger man, taller and thinner and nicely dressed. He nodded thoughtfully while Sabine rifled through her enormous black handbag, pulled out a note pad and scribbled something down.

AJ and I got out of the car and walked over to join them.

The house was hidden under an enormous orange tarp which appeared to be held together by yards of grey duct tape. The tape was peeling away at the corners and the plastic fluttered and rattled in the stiff wind. The whole thing had the air of an abandoned circus tent.

A few feet away in the corner of the lot lay the remnants

of a large white birch tree, its limbs hacked off and heaped in a messy pile awaiting the woodchipper. A large, dirty blue dumpster sat in front of the house, strips of wood and broken plasterboard poking out of the top.

Sabine tsked and said, "Everything is gone, the marble countertops, the bathroom fixtures, the brass hardware. All stripped away by the vultures."

I could hardly hear her over the sound of Caribbean music blasting out of what remained of the house. The older man said something in Sabine's ear, then walked up the front path and through the portico. Two minutes later, the music stopped and the screech of crows and the soft thrum of the city filled the echoing silence.

"This is Vincent," Sabine said when the older man returned. "He's from Martinique. And this is his brilliant nephew, Luke. He works with Marc and has absolutely nothing to do with this appalling excuse for a dwelling."

We learned that Vincent's crew was inside ripping out the asbestos, hence the orange tarps, and his nephew was an architect working on the Ballet House project.

Vincent grabbed Luke by the scruff of the neck and gave him a gentle shake. "Luke's finally moving up in the firm. He's been designing window mullions for two years."

"No, not that long." Luke looked a little embarrassed. "But longer than I'd like." He turned to his uncle and said, "Come on old man, it's past your bedtime, let's get you home."

Vincent said something in French and all three of them laughed.

CHAPTER SEVEN

Sabine adjusted her seat belt and slipped her notebook back into her leather handbag. She was dressed in black with a grey silk scarf at her throat. She looked like she was going to a funeral.

AJ lobbed a few polite comments at her from the back seat but they bounced away like wayward tennis balls and by the time we got out of the car in front of the Mount Royal community hall, our mood was somber. Residents poured into the low building, stopping to greet Sabine and pepper her with questions. They hoped she'd been able to talk some sense into her husband and the nightmare development would be scrapped.

A thin woman with short curly hair gripped Sabine's arm. She was a local television newscaster, now retired, who was still a force to be reckoned with. "Someone should remind Marc he still has to live in this neighbourhood when this is all over."

Sabine pursed her lips and veered off to sit with her friends while AJ and I took up our positions leaning against the back wall.

"It's showtime," AJ said softly, nodding at the door as Marc and the owner of the McMansion strode into the hall.

The head of the community association, a frail looking older man with a surprisingly rich voice, called for everyone's attention. "As you know, the City has approved the construction plans and demolition will begin shortly." The crowd shifted uneasily, their wet boots squeaking on the floor. "In the interests of being a good neighbour, the new owner, Sidney Foster, and his architect, Marc Hubert, are here to answer any questions the community may have."

"Good neighbour?" someone snorted. "He's doing a piss poor job of it so far." This elicited a wave of grumbles.

The owner stared grimly into the crowd—he looked like a well-dressed, middle-aged mobster stuffed into a suit two sizes too small—and Marc rose and directed everyone's attention to the large drawings lining the walls. Before he could say another word, the questions started to fly.

Gamely, he tried to answer them. The McMansion was so large because the owners had unique needs. Like what, the audience demanded. Like a yoga studio for the wife and a secure garage for the owner's classic car collection, oh, and they were movie buffs and the house had to be big enough to accommodate an in-home movie theatre.

That's when the shouting started.

Sabine's face was as grey as her scarf as she rose slowly to her feet. Everyone knew the Black Swan was married to Marc, the architect. They fell silent, giving her a chance to speak.

"Mr. Hubert," she addressed him in a strong clear voice as if he were a perfect stranger. "You are a renowned architect; your work is praised for its exuberance and its imagination. The jury that awarded you the Pritzker Prize called you a courageous architect who was not afraid to explore new ideas. Can you look these people in the eye," she took a deep breath then continued, "can you look me in the eye, and say this ugly, pedestrian box is the best you can do?"

Marc stepped back as if he'd been slapped, then squared his shoulders and said, "Madam Hubert, change is hard, I understand that, however, this is an elegant design that will enhance the neighbourhood and increase property values—" the crowd drowned out the rest with disgusted groans.

Sabine marched over to the wall, cast a furious glance at Marc, and ripped an architectural rendering off the wall. Still glaring at him, she tore the drawing in half and in half again. When she finished shredding it, she opened her hands and the pieces fluttered to the floor. Marc shook his head sadly, then turned to the new owner and said a few words in his ear. The new owner rose to his feet and they left, abandoning the architectural renderings pinned to the walls behind them. The drawings lasted less than five minutes before they too became a pile of confetti on the floor.

"Well, that was a fiasco," I said to AJ as we pressed through the crowd to collect Sabine, "I don't think it could have gone any worse."

Famous last words.

CHAPTER EIGHT

The snow squeaked under the tires as we pulled up in front of Sabine's house. It was dark, Marc was not yet home. Next door the McMansion huffed under its orange tarp, the plastic snapping like sails in a stiff gale.

"The front light is burned out again," Sabine said, absentmindedly. As she stepped out of the car the wind ripped the door out of her grasp and she almost lost her footing.

AJ leapt out of the backseat to catch her, but she managed to steady herself before he reached her.

"Sabine, will you be all right?" I leaned across the front seat and called to her over the howling wind. "We'd be happy to stay with you until Marc gets home."

The icy wind tugged at her hair, loosening a few silver strands which floated around her face making her look like a witch or a wild woman. "I'll be fine. Thank you both for coming with me. I do appreciate it."

AJ walked her to the front door and waited while she fiddled with the keypad and stepped inside. The lights in the foyer and the living room blazed on, casting a buttery yellow glow onto the hard snow-packed lawn. And she disappeared.

When AJ returned to the car, he climbed into the front seat and said, "About that dinner...?"

What dinner? Then I remembered my promise of a proper meal, something prepared in a restaurant, not by me (obviously), if he agreed to come with Sabine and me tonight.

"...it's been a weird night; we can take a raincheck."

"No, let's do it," I said. He may not want to eat, but I'm a stress eater and I was ravenous.

Soon we were settled in a big squishy booth at Browns. At the bar, clumps of rowdy men sat in twos and threes yelling at the hockey game playing silently on big screen TVs.

It took me a moment to get AJ's attention after the server had taken our orders but finally he pulled his eyes away from the screens and focused on me. "Did you know she was going to attack him like that?" he asked.

"Are you kidding? I'm no expert on the male psyche but even I know it's not a brilliant idea to humiliate your partner in front of his client and a mob that's dying to lynch him. She practically called him a sellout."

"She *did* call him a sellout." AJ pulled his phone out of his pocket and tapped a few buttons.

"Oh no you don't. I'm not going to sit here and watch you play with your phone."

He grinned and shook his head. "If you'd just give me a minute, I'm googling the Pritzker Prize. Marc flinched when Sabine mentioned it." After a moment he looked up. "Wow, it's like the Nobel prize for architects."

The server returned with my dragon bowl and AJ's fish and chips; when he asked for vinegar she hustled back to the kitchen to fetch it and he continued scrolling through his phone while he waited.

"Marc's won an impressive list of prizes that I've never heard of. The Aga Khan Award, the Wolf Prize. Listen to this." AJ raised his eyebrows. "'Hubert broke the aesthetic of modernism and post-modernism to create a stylistic language all his own.' And they say lawyers talk bafflegab, what the hell does that mean?"

After the server returned with his vinegar, AJ drizzled it on his breaded cod and slid his phone across the table to me. Marc's Wiki photo was at least ten years old, but he still looked much the same. Short closely cropped hair and a tidy beard, a strong nose and expressive brown eyes that warmed your soul when he smiled. He wouldn't be smiling at Sabine tonight.

All through dinner AJ and I replayed the meeting wondering if there was anything we could have done to avoid the epic level fail. I'd never seen Marc so angry. He's one of those smooth men who cajoles others into doing what he wants by making them think it was their idea all along. NEO had been harassing Marc for months but he'd kept a cool head, refusing to respond to accusations that would send other CEOs scurrying to the courts for an injunction. 'It's not necessary,' Marc had said. He would talk sense into them. How? As far as I knew he had no contacts inside NEO.

I nodded to the server, silently requesting a takeout box, then asked AJ what he knew about NEO and how they operated.

He set his coffee cup down on the wooden table. "They've been at City Hall and on site for five, six months, but they would have started their campaign at least a year before that."

"That long?"

"Sure, the minute Marc announced he was building the Ballet House in the River District he was on their radar. Stage one would be numerous interventions in any regulatory proceedings coupled with a comprehensive smear campaign on social media. Then they'd move to stage two where protesters from all over the country would descend on the site to amp up the pressure and turn public opinion against Marc."

As he spoke, AJ became more animated. "Their primary goal is to shut the project down. If that doesn't work, they focus on the architect, trying to force him to redesign the building, although how you'd design around the fragile river ecosystem is beyond me. But these guys are dedicated, they'll do whatever it takes to stop him."

I narrowed my eyes at him. "Since when are you such an expert on NEO?"

His face turned a deep shade of red; he stammered a few words that were drowned out by the yelling and shouting that erupted at the bar. Three men were hollering at the ref, even a blind man could see that puck was offside.

AJ turned away to look at the screen while I caught our server's eye and signalled, one bill, not two. She nodded and went off to fetch the point-of-sale machine.

"AJ, who is NEO? Who's doing the strategizing, picking the causes and coordinating the protesters? Do they have a head office or central committee or something?" The idea of long-haired environmentalists in flannel shirts and Birkenstocks schlepping into the office every morning didn't seem likely.

He coughed and asked whether he could cover his half of the bill. I said no, and repeated my question—who are they?

He pulled on his puffer jacket and adjusted his scarf

before replying. "NEO's a loosely knit organization with regional leaders or captains. Each region operates as an independent pod, deciding its own agenda and how to carry it out."

The server appeared and presented the machine. I pecked at the buttons and waved my credit card over it, trying to focus on what I was doing. Every one of these diabolical machines is different and I usually screw it up.

We were halfway to the door when the server stopped me and said, "Ma'am, you forgot your take-out box."

Of course I did.

Outside, the wind was so sharp it made my eyes water and I was afraid to blink lest my eyelashes stuck together. AJ and I hunched deeper into our coats while we waited for the heater to warm up. I pulled on my gloves and said, "You seem to know an awful lot about NEO."

He pointed to his phone which was lying on the centre console between the car seats. "Not me, the all-seeing, all-knowing internet."

CHAPTER NINE

It was past midnight by the time I returned home. I'd just stuffed my takeaway box into the fridge and was rummaging around looking for something non-caffeinated to drink when a floorboard creaked behind me.

"Whatcha doing?"

I yelped. "For the love of God, Louisa. You almost gave me a heart attack!"

She was wearing a long pink tee shirt, green plaid PJ bottoms, and a mischievous grin.

"And you," I scolded Quincy who stood quietly by her side, "you're just as bad. Why aren't you two in bed?"

She tapped the dusty red metal paint box she was clutching to her chest.

"You found Mom's paint set?" We'd been searching for it along with some other family memorabilia since the flood. We'd tossed everything that could be saved into boxes before the reno guys showed up to tear out the basement and some things, like the artifacts of Mom's life, had disappeared. Being the cynical lawyer that I am, I thought they'd been stolen but Louisa pointed out that no one would want our junk. As it turned out she was right.

She'd found the paint set at the bottom of a box labelled TROPHIES at the back of the closet in the spare bedroom.

I settled at the kitchen island and watched Louisa pour milk into a saucepan and set it on the stovetop to heat. She caught my scowl—I hate warm milk—and said she was making hot chocolate for the two of us.

Memories of Mom 'the artist' washed over me. "Did you find her art too? The nudes? Did you find her nudes?"

Louisa laughed. "Not yet, but I will."

When Mom turned fifty, she decided to explore her artistic side. It turned out she didn't have one.

"What were we, twelve, thirteen, when she painted her first nude male?" Louisa snorted, laughing so loud that Quincy leapt to his feet to see who was bothering her.

Mom signed up for the charcoal 'figurative arts' class not realizing that 'figurative' meant 'nude.' Nevertheless she stuck with it. A quitter she was not. Week after week she'd return home with drawings of Steve or Toby, each one worse than the last. Louisa and I would press our lips together and avoid making eye contact while Dad dropped double entendres. 'Now girls,' he'd say, 'your mother is just getting started. I'm sure it's harder than it looks.' Clapping our hands over our mouths to stifle our giggles, we'd flee the room.

After figurative art Mom moved onto watercolours (which weren't much better) until finally she discovered the *Alliance Française*. Sabine was an AF benefactor who met Mom at one of its French Café events. She took Mom under her wing—apparently Mom's accent was atrocious— and taught her how to carry on a conversation without butchering her pronouns and sentence structure.

"I spent the evening with Sabine," I said to Louisa who

was banging around in the cupboards looking for cocoa. "It was God-awful."

"Oh, is there a new avant-garde ballet in town?"

"No, not at the ballet; the town hall meeting about the McMansion. It got really ugly. Louisa, I've never seen her—or Marc—so angry."

Louisa stopped sprinkling shaved chocolate into the milk simmering on the element and took it off the heat. "Well, there's nothing you can do about it now so put it out of your mind."

After we went to bed, I stared at the ceiling for thirty minutes before giving up and grabbing my phone. I keyed NEO into the search bar, AJ had made them sound like a SEAL strike team, but all I got were links to *The Matrix* and random stories about financial institutions and rap artists.

Whoever these guys were, they stayed under the radar.

CHAPTER TEN

I f anyone can stomp in heels it's Madeline. She flung her navy wool coat, the Audrey Hepburn one, over the back of her visitor's chair and stalked off in the direction of the coffee room.

I trailed behind her. "Madeline, what's with you?"

"That—" she gestured out the coffee room window— and glanced at her watch. "It's eight-thirty in the morning, it's pitch-black outside, half the birds are gone and the other half are frozen."

"That"—my arm swept across the view—"is the golden hour, that wonderful peaceful time just after sunrise." She blinked at me as if I'd lost my mind. "You've still got your crows and your magpies and your chickadees...and..." I couldn't think of anything else.

Our building is sandwiched between the Elbow River on one side and a small, wooded hillock on the other. The woods are packed with wildlife. I swear Madeline has given every squirrel and fox and sparrow a name. Whenever she steps outside the crows make an awful racket, announcing that the food truck has arrived.

"Mexico," she declared. "Melvin can take me to Mexico

to see the toucans and motmots." Melvin was one of Madeline's many suitors. As a retired investment banker he could afford to take Madeline anywhere in the world, and he often did. She was telling me about Melvin's place, a luxury apartment in the Polanco district, when Keith strolled into the coffee room.

Slowly he poured himself a cup of coffee and in an unnaturally calm tone asked if I could spare him a minute.

"For you, always." I followed him as he headed into AJ's office.

AJ looked up in surprise when we sat down across from him.

"You look as bleary-eyed as I feel," I said to AJ, then rolled my eyes in Keith's direction. It was a signal. Keith had something on his mind and was searching for a way to broach it with us.

"So how's the goat?" I asked, hoping to rev Keith up the way you would a a finicky car engine. Otherwise we could be here all morning.

Baffled, he looked at me. "Goat? Oh, you mean Claire's goat. It's getting better; should be out of the woods soon."

I nodded. Another long pause. "Keith, is there anything in particular you'd like to talk about?"

He took a slow sip of coffee, then set his mug on the edge of AJ's desk and crossed his arms. "Take me through what happened last night."

"Marc called, right?" I asked.

"Indeed he did," Keith replied. "An hour ago. He was livid."

"What did he say?" I asked.

"He went up one side of me and down the other for doing such an outstanding job with Sabine. He didn't realize BLV was representing Sabine on the McMansion project as well as his firm on the Ballet House. He was particularly impressed with the way you allowed Sabine to attack him in front of his client."

Keith gets sarcastic when he's angry. It's one of his few flaws.

"Now hold on," I said, "We made it crystal clear to Sabine that we could not represent her because we represented her husband and that we were there only as moral support—"

"Furthermore," AJ cut me off, "Sabine went off like a rocket before we could stop her."

Keith looked from AJ to me. "That's what I thought and that's what I told him."

"How'd he take it?" I asked.

Keith replied that after Marc stopped shouting he admitted he'd expected Sabine to be furious, but not quite that furious.

I shook my head in disbelief. "Marc expected to be drawn and quartered but with a stiletto not a battle axe?" Was this kind of volatility typical of their relationship?

"Who knows," Keith said, "but his client is undeterred. They've got all the approvals they need and they're going full steam ahead with the design as is, otherwise they'll lose the building season. The McMansion will be demolished within the next two weeks."

I sighed. "Poor Sabine."

"Poor Sabine, indeed." That was Bridget. She popped her head in the door and said, "Evie, Sabine wants you to call her as soon as you're free."

"How did she sound?"

Bridget shook her head. "She's French, I have no idea."

Something tightened in the pit of my stomach. Marc may be calm now, but last night he was furious and I'd been worried, just a little bit, for her safety. Then I remembered something my mom had said, Sabine had a fierce temper. If Marc raised a hand against her, Sabine would reach for the nearest ashtray and deck him with it.

CHAPTER ELEVEN

"Evie, how are you?" Sabine's voice sound calm and sweet on the phone, the fiasco of last night apparently forgotten. "I'd like you to join me at a fundraiser for the Ballet House this Friday."

"Pardon? What?" This woman's mood swings were giving me whiplash. That was the other thing Mom had said about Sabine. She could go to DEFCON ONE at noon and be back to CONDITION NORMAL by dinner time.

"Um, how are you? How's Marc?"

"Fine, fine. Sidney Foster, our soon to be new neighbour, just pledged a large donation for the Ballet House, he's a very generous man, but we need more. Even with the boost from Sidney donations are dropping off, thanks to those idiotic NEO people. And the City won't give us its forty percent if the private donors fall short on their sixty. Apparently, the oil company executives are spooked, they've got environmental problems of their own, if you know what I mean."

"Sure, but why do you need me?" I certainly didn't have the kind of money Sabine was looking for.

"It's time to focus on their wives," Sabine replied. "These

women love the arts—or pretend they do—but they're worried about bad publicity. They will listen to you. You can assure them everything is fine. NEO is fussing about nothing. Then the pretty young things will convince their stodgy old husbands to open their wallets." Sabine gave a throaty laugh. "In the old days, men showered their women with diamonds and furs to keep them happy, now it's diamonds, furs, and a seat on the Opera board. It's all about prestige."

Great. Sabine wants me to shill for the ladies-who-lunch. I ran through a number of excuses, but it was hopeless.

"I'm sending you the details now." She rang off with a cheery goodbye, leaving me to curse at the dial tone.

Madeline stopped in the hall outside my door. "Whatever it is, it's not your phone's fault."

I explained what Sabine had asked me to do.

"Is that in your job description?"

"I tried to get out of it, but Sabine's like the Borg. Resistance is futile."

Madeline advised me to park myself at the bar and keep the martinis coming until the evening was over.

—··—

Just hours before the event, I was raiding Louisa's closet. I had nothing to wear. Red and green and purple sparkly dresses piled up on her bed. It looked like a glitter box had exploded. There must be some research somewhere on birth order that says the first-born child is tasteful and refined (Louisa would say prudish) while her younger sibling is a raging extrovert, happy to parade around in a fuchsia skinsuit if given half the chance.

Quincy eyed me quizzically as I draped yet another too

short, too skimpy, too something, dress across my body. Finally, in desperation I selected a curve hugging blue silk number, no sequins, slipped into shiny black heels and raced downstairs to the garage.

Louisa pulled in, waving and honking, as I pulled out. My heart was beating so fast you'd think I was attending a command performance with the Queen (who as we all know is dead, but I hadn't warmed to her son, so for me it's the Queen or nothing).

I'd been to the Calgary Golf and Country Club once before for Texas Scramble golf tournament, a work thing, and I was sure I could find it again. But everything looks different in the dead of winter, in the dark, and I arrived late.

The sound of laughter drew me upstairs to the dining hall. Sabine was standing in the middle of an admiring crowd, stunning in a white off-the-shoulder mermaid gown that grazed the floor. Her silver hair was pulled back in an elegant knot at the nape of her neck. A diamond necklace sparkled on her collarbones. She smiled at a short middle-aged man with florid cheeks and gently shooed him over to the Silent Auction table so he could place his bids. When she saw me, her smile became more sincere.

"At last," she said. "Evie, come. I want you to meet someone." That 'someone' was soon replaced by another 'someone' and another one after that until I'd met almost everyone in the room and assured them that the Ballet House was being built to the highest environmental standards. Finally, she took me over to the Silent Auction table where people scribbled down pledges of hundreds of dollars for a single bottle of Chateau Margaux and thousands of dollars for a luxury spa weekend in Sedona.

Marc caught my eye from across the room and gave me

an approving nod, whether it was for the dress or because I was working the room with Sabine wasn't clear, but knowing I had his approval boosted my spirits. He just had that effect on people.

Someone announced it was time for dinner and Sabine pulled me closer and whispered, "You're at table eight, I hope you don't mind, I've put you with the Symphony."

"That's a step up from the last fundraiser I attended. I shared a table with a bunch of morticians. Who, I might add, were surprisingly lively, not morbid at all."

Sabine steered me to table eight. "Robert"—she pronounced it the French way—"meet Evie Valentine. Robert is a percussionist; timpani, bass drum, cymbals, that kind of thing. For a small man, he makes a lot of noise, don't you my dear."

Robert flushed and ducked his head. He looked to be in his fifties, thin with round Harry Potter glasses and an unruly mop of wavy, black hair.

The remaining chairs were filled with an assortment of musicians who Robert introduced with reference to their instruments, Jennifer: flute, Graham: another flute, Bongani: trumpet, Adel: cello. By the time he went around the table I'd forgotten their names, but had perfect recall of their instruments, flutes, trumpets, cellos and oboes. Which was frustrating because you can't exactly ask Mr. Cello to pass the butter, can you?

Over the endive salad Robert told me his life story. He was from out east, Hamilton. The eldest of three children born into a raucous Irish family. His dad worked in the steel mills and his mother was a homemaker. He graduated in music from the U of T and followed his then-girlfriend out to Calgary where he landed a part-time gig with the Calgary Philharmonic. Eventually they brought him on fulltime and he'd been a member of the Symphony ever since.

When I said Louisa and I had seen the Marsalis concert a few weeks ago, Robert dropped his fork into his roast chicken breast sending a spray of spätzle into his lap. "Remember that piece where Marsalis stopped and waited? There was a beat, then boom, the drum? That was me!" Robert's eyes glittered as he relived the moment. "In rehearsals Marsalis said not many people get that piece." He glanced around the room until he spotted Marc sitting next to Sabine at the big donors table. "Sabine gets it. Marc never will."

Robert pinched the corners of his napkin together, lifted it out of his lap and unceremoniously dumped the cold dried-out spätzle bits onto his plate. "Most people don't know this but there's something wonky with the acoustics at Jack Singer." That was the main concert hall.

The other musicians chimed in. Yes, there's a lag as the sound travels across the stage. If you aren't paying close attention to the conductor, you'll come in too early or too late and have to scramble to find your place.

"That's why Robert is so proud of his Marsalis performance," the trumpet player said.

Robert's eyes smiled behind his owlish glasses. "That's why it's so important to finish the Ballet House. Sabine is doing a fantastic job raising the funds to do it right."

The woman on my other side touched my arm. "Robert is Sabine's biggest fanboy, aren't you Robert?"

He ignored her, glancing at the other musicians around the table. "We were all summoned to this event. Not that we mind." He gazed past me to Sabine's table. She and Marc were engaged in a lively conversation with a portly man in a bespoke tuxedo and his young, toothpick-thin wife. Sabine leaned in and whispered in Mr. Tuxedo's ear.

"Isn't she marvelous?" Robert gazed at Sabine until he was distracted by the waiter asking if he'd like coffee or tea with his chocolate cake.

The tinkling of a spoon on a glass, like windchimes, drew our attention to the head table. A slim young woman asked us to raise our glasses in honour of our generous hosts, Marc and Sabine Hubert.

After much cheering and clinking of glasses Marc rose from his chair. "Finally, the moment you've all be waiting for. It's time to announce the winners of the Silent Auction." The crowd fluttered with excitement, which was funny given that everyone here (except table eight) could easily afford to buy the bits of pottery or spa weekends they'd bid on.

Sabine told me silent auctions were so successful because rich people love the thrill of outbidding their wealthy friends. "That's why the big-ticket items go for double or triple their actual value."

"Quiet!" Robert shushed the trumpet player who retorted Robert was in cloud cuckoo land if he thought he could outbid the high rollers in this room.

Marc started with the winners of the low value items then turned the small mic over to Sabine who worked her way up through to the pricier items. Finally she turned to the last prize, the getaway spa weekend in Sedona, Arizona. She smiled as she gazed at the bid sheet, pausing for a moment before calling out the winner's name: Sidney Foster.

A thick-waisted, balding man jumped to his feet and approached the head table, laughing and waving to the applauding crowd. He looked vaguely familiar. Sabine passed him a gold envelope and he leaned forward to receive her kisses.

"Sidney," she said in a husky whisper that was clearly audible on the mic, "I love Sedona. Tell Brittany you're going on a business trip and I will come with you." Sabine tossed a seductive wink into the crowd, then glanced at a young woman in a skintight silver cocktail dress.

"Ooh," Robert chuckled. "That's Foster's third wife, she's not going to like that."

The crowd tittered. Sidney blushed and handed Brittany the gold envelope as he sat down. To her credit Brittany accepted it with good grace.

That's when I recognized Sidney Foster as the man with Marc at the town hall meeting. Sidney and Brittany were building the McMansion. The one with the oversized underground garage for Sidney's Lambo and thousands of extra square feet to accommodate Btittany's yoga studio and her home movie theatre. Sabine and Brittany were off to a great start.

———

Louisa was in her pyjamas in front of the fire watching a French detective series, no subtitles—she'd aced French in high school and university—when I came up the basement stairs. Quincy, lazy dog that he is, didn't bother to greet me at the basement door, choosing instead to give me a baleful it's-about-time look before dropping his head back down on his paws.

"How did it go?" Louisa asked, turning off the sound, not that it mattered, without subtitles I couldn't understand a thing. I kicked off my shoes and flopped down at the other end of the teddy bear couch. "Who was there, what were they wearing, what did you talk about?"

"Louisa"—I stifled a yawn—"I should have sent you in my place, you would have enjoyed it more."

"Yes, but I can't speak intelligently about sustainability or whatever the environmental equivalent is for a Michelin five-star restaurant."

"Three," I said. "The maximum number of Michelin stars you can get is three."

"Whatever."

I gave her a rundown of the evening, starting with Sabine's dress. "She looked stunning."

"She always looks stunning. She stays in shape; it helps to have a dancer's body."

"Marc looked like James Bond in his tux."

"Everyone looks like James Bond in a tux."

"No," I said, "not necessarily." Robert, the percussionist, had told me that most of the orchestra can't afford brand new tuxedos, they buy their tuxes used from a tux rental shop.

"Did you know the Philharmonic has full time and part time musicians?" I added. "I met a percussionist who used to supplement his income by working in construction and cooking in workcamps up north." Now that I thought about it, Robert was a lot tougher than he looked.

"Anything to pay the bills, I suppose," Louisa said.

Later as I shimmied out of Louisa's gown, I thought about Robert, who would do whatever it took to perform with the Philharmonic, and Sabine who would shamelessly flirt with the owner of the McMansion if it meant another donation to the Ballet House, and Marc who stood right next to her, smiling and clapping, while she did.

My mom, who grew up poor in Hungary, said people will do whatever it takes to get what they want.

CHAPTER TWELVE

As a rule, people don't race around our office with their hair on fire so when Madeline knocked on the lawyers' doors urgently requesting our presence in the conference room, my heart skipped a beat. Her face was very pale, but her voice was strong. "Marc Hubert has had an accident!" she said as she turned and raced down the corridor in the direction of the conference room.

AJ was already seated at the conference table by the time I got there. "What happened?" he asked. "Is it on the local news?"

Madeline shook her head, bringing up the big screen TV and scrolling through the channels.

Keith entered; brow furrowed with concern. "What's going on?"

"Holy cow!" Bridget's voice rang out from reception, "Someone firebombed Marc's building." She hurried into the room clutching her tablet to her chest.

"Is anyone hurt?" My first thought was of Sabine, which was silly given that she'd be safe at home. The realization that I cared more about Sabine than Marc should have surprised me, but it didn't.

Heads down, Madeline, Bridget, and AJ scrolled through social media and the online press while Keith and I debated whether it was too soon to check in with Marc.

Finally, we pieced together what had happened. Around two a.m. someone tried to torch Marc's building, a compact sandstone structure in Beltline. Marc's offices were on the top three floors, the lower two floors were leased to a nonprofit think tank, an engineering firm, and an IT company. The arsonist had hidden an incendiary device under a pile of cardboard boxes on the loading dock. When the device ignited it destroyed part of the loading dock and filled the building with thick, oily smoke.

"Do we know for sure the firebomb was intended for Marc and not one of the other tenants?" I asked.

AJ looked up from his phone. "The firefighters found the device in the corner of the loading bay that's reserved for Marc's exclusive use. Luckily, the building was empty at that hour, the cleaning staff had gone home and the alley was deserted."

Bridget pulled up a photo on her tablet and showed it to us. "Apparently this isn't the first time Marc's been targeted. Eco-terrorists have been tagging his building for months. Looks like they're cranking up the pressure."

"Eco-terrorists?" I glanced at AJ. "Like that giant Viking who attacked your car? Would NEO resort to firebombing?"

"He didn't *attack* my car, he just hit the hood."

"Yeah, with his bloody great fist and then broke his placard on your windshield." .

AJ reached for Bridget's tablet and scrutinized the tag, a blood red symbol painted on the front façade next to the main doors.

Quietly, he said, "Looks like ordinary graffiti to me. Listen, it's true NEO is vehemently opposed to the Ballet

House, the City should never have allowed Marc to build it that close to the river, even with mitigation measures, but let's not jump to the conclusion NEO's capable of arson. That's not their modus operandi."

"How would you know?" I asked.

Bridget interrupted before AJ could reply. With a frown on her face she said, "Why would they set fire to Marc's building when the construction site is miles away?"

"Bridget's got a point," Madeline said, setting her phone down on the table. "Up till now NEO's been protesting at the Ballet House construction site or City Hall, which really messes up traffic by the way. But setting a firebomb? The risk to human life takes this to a whole new level."

I turned to AJ who'd been quick to defend NEO earlier. "Are you sure this would be out of character for them?"

He pursed his lips, not offering a reply.

"Look," Keith said, "it's not our job to figure out who's responsible, the police will do that. We need to touch base with Marc."

A few minutes later I was back in my office scrolling through my contacts for Marc's phone number when my cell rang. *Sabine.*

"Sabine, I just heard, I—"

A barrage of words. Her French accent thickens when she's distressed. Something terrible had happened, no not the firebomb at the Atelier. Something else. Could I come around to the house at once?

Of course I could. Sabine was like my second mom. She'd always been eccentric, but lately she'd become more volatile. Livid with Marc one minute and flattering him the next. I couldn't help but think Marc was driving her instability. The pressure to finish the Ballet House on time was intense, but if he'd laid a hand on Sabine, so help me God, he'd pay.

CHAPTER THIRTEEN

Sabine flung open the front door and dragged me into the tiled foyer. I was breathless from sprinting up the driveway. "Did he hurt you? Are you all right?"

Cat hair covered her black cashmere pullover and white wool slacks, she was wearing no make up and her hair was falling out of a sloppy ponytail. Jasmine blinked lazily at me from the kitchen as if to say, look at her, she's a mess.

Sabine frowned. "Did who hurt me?"

"Marc. I know he's stressed. What with the NEO protests and you attacking him at the town hall, and now the firebomb at the Atelier. It's a lot, I get it, but that doesn't give him the right to take his frustration out on you."

Her face hardened. "Have you taken leave of your senses? Marc would never hurt me."

"Then what am I doing here?" She was right, I was losing my mind.

"Come through, come through." She waved me down the hall. "Marc will be home soon." She explained he'd been holed up with the police and firefighters since they dragged him out of bed at three this morning. All night long, she'd paced the floor, beside herself with worry.

Her agitation increased as we moved through the house. By the time we reached Marc's study, a cold, spartan room, very different from the rest of the house, she was vibrating with nerves.

"Sit, sit." She indicated a chair across from Marc's glass slab of a desk. On it were stacks of architectural drawings bearing the distinctive Atelier logo. She rifled through them until she found what she was looking for.

"Yesterday, this came in the mail. Marc says it's nothing... but now with the fire...Evie, I'm worried sick."

Her fingers shook as she handed me a small stiff envelope. Inside was a small card, like a wedding invitation, embossed with six little words

STOP BEFORE IT IS TOO LATE

"Stop what?" I flipped the card over. The other side was blank.

She sank into Marc's chair on the opposite side of the desk, her tone shifted from frightened to irate.

"Those NEO imbeciles. They want to kill the Ballet House." Angry, she pushed a pile of papers to one side and a spiral bound set of drawings slid off the desk and flopped open on the floor. She picked it up and set it in front of me. "Look at this, Evie. It is perfect. No one should be allowed to destroy such beauty. It's criminal."

The Ballet House, light and airy, splashed across the watercoloured page. Despite Marc's promises of porous paving and bioswales, the activists refused to believe the river would not be harmed by its presence, especially during construction. As an environmental lawyer I understood their concerns, all the promises in the world are just words on a page when the unthinkable happens.

"What does Marc say? About the STOP IT card, I mean."

The envelope in my hand bore no stamp. It would have been hand delivered. *They came to her house.*

Outside, the sound of tires crunching across the snow-slick driveway.

"He says to ignore it, it's just a kook." She blinked rapidly, her eyes brimming with tears.

The keypad beeped and the front door clicked open.

"Sabine?" Marc was home.

She leapt out of the chair and rushed out inro the foyer to greet him. He cupped her face in his hands and kissed her wet eyelids and she snuggled closer, pressing her face into his neck. He murmured that he was all right. Everything would be fine. He gave me a gentle smile and the three of us went into the kitchen.

"How bad was it?" I asked.

He flung his slim brief case onto the marble countertop. Despite the lack of sleep, his eyes were alert, ready for battle. "The delivery bay is destroyed, but the sprinklers kicked in and smothered the flames before the fire got out of control. Still, smoke entered the HVAC system and circulated throughout the building. The businesses on the lower levels took the brunt of the damage." He gave a dry chuckle. "Unfortunate for them, fortunate for us."

"Marc," I said as I passed him the STOP IT card, "given what just happened, this is a death threat. You must take it seriously. Is this the only one you've received, here or at the office? Are there more?"

Carelessly, he flipped the card onto the counter and turned his gaze back to Sabine. "My silly darling, I told you, the card is nothing. This sort of thing happens all the time in business. The stakes are high. Everyone is emotional. They lash out. It's best to ignore them."

"Marc," my tone caught his attention, "bombastic

threats on social media are one thing but sending anonymous threats to your home and firebombing your office, that's taking it to an entirely new level. You told the police about the card, right?"

A look of frustration flashed in his eyes.

I crossed my arms. "Right?"

"As I've already told Sabine, many, many times, there is no need to bring the police into this. It's nothing." He shot me a hard look as if to say: drop it.

In desperation I turned to Sabine. "This card, the firebombing, the pressure is escalating. You must tell the police before someone gets hurt."

Sabine glanced at Marc as if she were asking for permission. He took her hands in his and gently kissed her fingertips and I knew it was over. The minute I left he'd destroy the card.

CHAPTER FOURTEEN

Traffic crawled along Fourth Street and the sidewalks were packed. It was lunch time and everyone was racing around trying to beat the rush. My stomach was growling when I spotted AJ heading into Seb's. I tootled the horn—the Mini beeps like clown car—and he turned and scowled at the road, then recognized me and smiled.

I pantomimed: *you, me, Seb's*. He nodded and I sped through the light and around the corner into the office parking lot.

A chinook had melted the snow on Seb's patio. A few hardy souls sat outside, basking in the radiant heat of the propane heaters. Thankfully, AJ was not one of them. I found him inside sitting at a small table opposite the large chalky blackboard and the hissing coffee machines.

"I got you your usual," he said as I draped my jacket over the back of the chair and sat down.

"That's nice. What's my usual?"

"Grilled cheese," he said through a mouthful of BLT on sourdough. "According to the menu it's 'epic.'"

My sandwich was hot and very gooey. AJ was right, from now on this was going to be my usual.

He passed me my coffee and said he'd been calling Marc's number all morning but hadn't been able to reach him.

Wiping my greasy fingers on the paper napkin, I said, "That's because he was with Sabine and me." And explained that someone had left a threatening note in their mailbox but Marc refused to take it seriously. "I'm worried about them, AJ. Who knows what those NEO nutbars are going to do next."

AJ took a sip of coffee and jiggled around in his chair trying to get the sun out of his eyes. "This is completely out of character for NEO; however, I do agree it's not worth taking the risk"—suddenly he snapped his fingers—"unless Marc's afraid a police investigation will slow down the construction schedule." He squinted in the brightness of the noon sun. "They're a month behind already."

"Really. Why?"

"Supply chain problems. GCL, the construction company, can't get its hands on copper piping and other building materials. The delay has a cascading effect, slowing down everything else, inside and outside the building." He glanced around the café and lowered his voice. "I'll take you through it when we get back in the office."

———•———

No sooner had we set foot in the parking lot than a crow divebombed AJ's head. "Bloody hell!" he yelped as it pulled up at the last minute and sailed off into the trees along the riverbank, allowing us to make it inside unmolested.

"It's your fault, AJ. They ever forget a face. Obviously they hate you."

"Yeah, well I never forget a face either," he muttered,

sounding very much like the old man who shakes his fist at the clouds.

The master construction schedule was pinned to AJ's wall. We leaned against his desk, our arms crossed, and stared at the vertical and horizontal lines. There were about forty of them.

"The emoji stickers are a nice touch," I said, pointing at the red angry face emojis stuck on two horizontal lines.

"Bridget's idea. She says it's easier to see what's going on."

"She got that right." One angry face emoji showed the site sustainability work was behind schedule. The other indicated a drop in fundraising dollars.

"What's this line?" I pointed to a vertical line that intersected all the other lines.

AJ bent down and picked up an emoji that had fallen to the floor, the party-popper emoji, and stuck it at the end of the vertical line. It held for a second, then peeled off and drifted back down to the floor.

"That's election day for the new City Council, mid October. Bridget, ever the optimist, is assuming it will be a happy party-popper day. But based on the rumours I've heard; the old Council will be turfed and replaced by new guys who've pledged to cut the budget for the Ballet House. Drastically reducing its scope and scale."

"But the Ballet House will be finished by then. It won't matter who's on council."

"Not if they can't make up for lost time, they're all ready four weeks behind, it's going to be really tight."

There was a soft tap at the door and Madeline popped her head into AJ's office. "Have you two seen the latest news on the firebombing? They're interviewing a NEO spokesman. Some guy called Paul Adams."

"Good," AJ said. "Paul will set everyone straight. NEO is not an eco-terrorist organization. They're not violent. They wouldn't do this."

"Yeah," I said, "tell that to the guy who got a brick in the face."

"That was a fluke, not a premediated attack."

There it was again. AJ's staunch defence of NEO. It was unsettling, like blind loyalty. "AJ, how can you be so sure? Do you know these people?"

He moved closer to the window, looking through the glass at the snow covered river beyond. Madeline glanced at me, then announced she had work to do. As she left, she closed the door softly behind her.

I sat down in his visitor's chair. "AJ, what's going on? Do you know these guys?"

Finally he returned to his desk and sat down, staring hard at a spot on the wall over my left shoulder. "To say I *know* NEO would be an overstatement. I did however meet some of them at Dalhousie back when I was an undergrad in environmental science. That was years ago. We lost touch after I went to law school. You know how it is."

"That burly bearded guy who almost broke your windscreen; he seemed to know you pretty well."

"Paul Adams? Yeah, well, we were roommates. Let's just say we didn't part on the best of terms. So tell me, why are you so interested in NEO?"

"Because they want to stop the Ballet House and someone firebombed Marc's office and sent a death threat to his home. Marc can downplay this all he wants, but I won't let him endanger Sabine. My mom would never forgive me if I let something happen to her."

"If Marc refuses to go to the police there's nothing you can do."

That's when I realized AJ was wrong. There was something I could do, but AJ wouldn't like it.

CHAPTER FIFTEEN

I told AJ there were two ways to make the death threats stop. I'd tried to force Marc to report it to the police and failed. Now it was time for Plan B. "You have a contact at NEO, Paul Adams, We could call him—"

"Absolutely not." AJ was adamant. "We're lawyers, not mediators. Marc—you remember Marc, he's our client—has not instructed us to make contact with NEO. So let's not make a bad situation worse."

"Why would we make it worse? We're calm. We're rational. Adams sounded pretty rational in his interview"—Madeline had shown us the video clip, NEO denied any responsibility for the firebombing—"let's go talk to him, broker a meeting between him and Marc. Set some ground rules. De-escalate the tension before it gets any worse."

It took me thirty minutes to wear AJ down and another hour for us to locate NEO's base of operations: Unit 201 at the EconoLodge in Motel Village just off the TransCanada highway. We left the office around four o'clock; traffic was light and we arrived at the EconoLodge in record time.

AJ shook his head at me one last time to indicate just how much he hated this idea, then rapped on the door to Unit 201. The ice machine down the hall groaned and clunked while we waited. AJ leaned close to the cheap plywood door and knocked again, this time more loudly.

"Keep your shirt on." Heavy footsteps shook the floor, even out here in the hall. Then the door swung open and we came face to face with a grizzly bear. This was the man with the wild hair and red beard who hammered the hood of AJ's car.

There was a tense moment while AJ and Paul eyed each other up and down. I stepped forward and introduced myself. I knew I wouldn't have to introduce AJ; it was obvious those two knew each other only too well.

The bear-man shook my hand with a massive paw. He could have driven his fist through AJ's windshield if he wanted to without even breaking a sweat.

"It's been a while, Paul," AJ said. "Can we talk?"

Paul shrugged and stepped to one side to let us squeeze by. The motel room was small and equipped with a kitchenette that was so close to the bed that Paul could reach out and turn on the coffee maker in his sleep.

He dropped his ample frame into a small chair tucked under the pint-sized desk which was built into the kitchenette. There were no other chairs in the room.

"Take a seat." Paul gestured at the unmade bed piled high with pamphlets and placards. Despite the clutter, the room was relatively clean.

AJ and I sat down on the edge of the bed, it sagged and we leaned into each other.

Paul stared at AJ for a moment then said, "What do you want?"

I hadn't expected a warm welcome but he was downright hostile.

"We're working on the Ballet House; we represent the architect—"

"Yeah, Sam said you'd changed sides. So tell me, what's the going rate for a sell out these days? A hundred thousand, a hundred and fifty?"

It went straight downhill from there; not surprising when you start the conversation by telling someone they're an immoral, unprincipled bastard.

———•———

Ten minutes later we were back in the car and AJ was darting in and out of traffic, driving like a maniac. I asked him to slow down, but he didn't appear to hear me.

"Who's Sam?" I asked as AJ gunned the engine. We were approaching a flashing LRT crossing. "AJ, slow down." The horrified C-train conductor blasted his horn as the MGB raced across the tracks. The barrier came down and bounced across the trunk and we made it through with just seconds to spare.

By then I was braced against the dashboard and clutching the door handle. "Have you lost your frigging mind? Slow down or let me out of this frigging car!"

He loosened his hands on the steering wheel and lifted his foot off the gas pedal allowing the car to slow to a more reasonable speed.

"I knew this would be a colossal waste of time," he grumbled. "These NEO guys live in their own little world, untainted by reality."

"Yes, I gathered that. What's the deal with you and Paul Adams? Clearly you two have history."

As he took the turn onto Fourth Street he opened up about Paul, also known as Grizzly because he resembled the lead in a seventies TV show. They'd met in university, two young idealists studying environmental science. Kindred spirits who wanted to save the world. Organizing demonstrations and being dragged away by aggressive cops.

"I can't remember how many cold wet miserable nights we spent under a tarp in the Great Bear Rainforest," a wry smile crossed AJ's face, "then it all went to shit. Grizzly became convinced we had to up our game to make meaningful change. He started talking about the environmental imperative and how the time had come for direct action—what a wonderfully vague word that is, direct action."

"Grizzly became an eco-terrorist?"

AJ's brow furrowed. "It's hard to say, he and some of the others..." His words trailed off as he cruised up to a stop light.

"Something happened. What was it, AJ?"

He gazed steadily out the windshield, his hands gripping the steering wheel, waiting for the light to change. Finally, he told me about the protest that went too far, the one where a logger had been killed. His chainsaw hit a tree spike, bucked and—AJ didn't finish the story—he didn't have to.

"But Grizzly told the press NEO wasn't an eco-terrorist group."

"Yeah, well. There are degrees of direct action. Back then it was tree spiking and dumping sugar in gas tanks. Pretty tame stuff compared to what eco-terrorists get up to nowadays." AJ flicked his eyes at me, then back to the road. "The only reason I let you talk me into this meeting was so I could see for myself whether they're more radical now than they were back then."

We still didn't know. Grizzly threw us out before we could get into their modus operandi.

"AJ," I said as he pulled into his usual space in the parking lot, "what aren't you telling me?"

AJ turned off the engine and unclipped his seat belt, then rolled down his window. A hard cold breeze invaded the car. Sharp with no scent at all.

"A bunch of us were arrested after the tree spiking incident. My granddad"—this would be the fertilizer tycoon—"pulled some strings and the RCMP dropped the charges. I couldn't believe how lucky we were, but the hardcore guys were livid. If you believed in the cause you fought for it in every forum, including the courts. And if that meant going to jail, then so be it."

"But you didn't support using tree spikes... did you?"

"I didn't know they were using them. But they never forgave me for involving my granddad. They said I sold out."

When he looked at me his eyes were troubled. What wasn't he telling me?

"AJ—"

"I'll be damned," AJ said, glancing over my shoulder with a bemused look on his face. Madeline was approaching the car. It was dark and the wind whipped her flaming red hair around her face. Her long, dark coat thrashed against her body and behind her hopped three silent magpies. "She's like a witch, and I mean that in the nicest possible way, with her familiars."

I rolled down my window and she peered in. Green eyes gleaming, she said, "If you two stay out here much longer the office is going to talk."

I shook my head. AJ may have a secret, but it wasn't an office romance.

CHAPTER SIXTEEN

Louisa tapped her foot on the black tiled floor, eyes boring into me as she licked her ice cream cone with exaggerated care.

"Stop that," I said. "You're throwing off my concentration."

"How hard can it be?" she retorted. "Just pick one."

It's these little decisions that trip me up. I'd wasted fifteen minutes sampling flavours at Village Ice Cream and still couldn't make up my mind. I blame my mother who believed eating ice cream in the dead of winter would lead to a nasty sore throat and or something more lethal. It took me years to figure out ice cream was safe (and delicious) any time of year, although I'll say this for Mom, she was right about fish, it *is* full of bones that can stick in your throat and kill you.

The kind young man behind the counter handed me another small wooden spoon, this one loaded with brown butter snickerdoodle. I dithered some more and in the end went with what Louisa was having: chocolate ice cream in a waffle cone.

I told the clerk we'd take a small bucket of Crème Brûlée

too. That was for Sabine. It was Saturday afternoon and Louisa said we were long overdue for a visit.

A few minutes later we were stuck in the thick of traffic and Louisa was haranguing me to drive faster or 'this one'—she waved the sticky brown cone that was dripping down her fingers—would be mine.

"No way, you already licked it," I said. We continued to bicker like kids in the backseat of Dad's car until I swerved into Sabine's driveway. The Mini is a rough riding vehicle at the best of times and Louisa swayed in her seatbelt while Sabine's Crème Brûlée rolled from one side of the back seat to the other.

When Sabine opened the front door she hustled Louisa, who was a sticky mess, down the hall to the bathroom and I wandered into the kitchen and set her ice cream down on the marble countertop.

"Robert," Sabine called out over her shoulder. "Go help Evie in the kitchen."

I hadn't noticed him in the living room and didn't recognize him at first. He was casually dressed in jeans and a soft wool shirt that was buttoned right up to his chin. He reminded me of the boys in chess club who stayed inside to avoid the thick-necked bullies patrolling the school yard. A little bit of a nerd, but more muscular.

He smiled as he ambled by me; that's when I recognized him. Robert, my dinner companion from the Silent Auction. The percussionist with the Calgary Philharmonic.

"Louisa," I said when she reappeared, "this is Robert, the musician responsible for that magnificent boom on the kettle drum at the Marsalis concert."

Louisa smiled in a polite distracted way, she had no idea what I was talking about.

Sabine and Robert shooed us out of the kitchen and we

settled on the sofa, a sleek camel affair perfectly suited to Sabine's monochromatic living room. I noticed that Louisa had something in her hand.

"Sabine," she called out, "I found a cool photo in your study, I hope you don't mind."

"You are such a snoop, Louisa," I whispered at her.

"Shhhh." She scootched over next to me and passed me a large gold framed photograph.

Sabine returned to the living room with two small glass bowls heaped with ice cream and a cloth napkin for me. Louisa's cone was gone and I was down to the tip of mine, it's the best and messiest part. Robert trailed after Sabine carrying a coffee carafe and four porcelain cups on a tray.

Sabine brightened when she saw the photo in my hands. "Oh my," she said, "that was a lifetime ago."

Robert set the tray down on the coffee table and circled around behind the sofa, hanging over us as Sabine settled back in her chair and explained that the photo had been taken in 1975, right after the judges announced the winner of the Prix de Lyon.

The photo glowed like a pastoral painting with fresh faced boys in white open-necked shirts and coloured tights and girls in soft bell-shaped tutus with their feet turned out. The backdrop was a luminous sky blue and gold confetti drifted down from the rafters like exotic snowflakes. Everyone was smiling, everyone was holding a single red rose.

A young and slim Sabine stood slightly to one side, her chin up, her raven hair pulled back in a tight bun at the nape of her neck. She couldn't have been more than sixteen but looked calm and self assured even then.

Sabine took the photo from me and pointed to the other dancers, rattling off names I didn't recognize, saying this one was artistic director with the Royal Ballet in London and that one had just retired after a brilliant career with the Stuttgart Ballet company.

"That was a magical day," she said, a faraway look in her eye. "I remember it like it was yesterday." The Prix de Lyon drew contestants from all over the world. Thousands submitted video clips, desperate to be chosen to be one of the eighty who would compete in the semi-finals. The eighty was winnowed down to twenty and the top four would go home with scholarships and placements with the world's best ballet schools and dance corps. One of the top four would win the Grand Prix.

In 1975 the winner was Sabine.

She stared at her youthful image for a long time. "Being the Grand Prix winner changed my life. I was sixteen when I joined the Paris Opera Ballet School. Can you imagine a young girl from Toulouse moving to Paris to study with France's premiere dance company."

At eighteen she joined the corps du ballet. By twenty-one she was a principal dancer and by twenty-two she was named *danseuse étoile*, star dancer.

"And then she met Marc." Robert made no effort to hide his disapproval. "And destroyed her magnificent career."

Sabine pressed her lips together, her eyes on Robert as he circled the couch and returned to the caramel slipper chair. "Robert, you silly goose, you know that isn't true. When one is named *danseuse étoile* one is *danseuse étoile* for life."

He held his bowl of ice cream close to his face and lifted his spoon slowly to his lips. "Sabine, I'm talking about reputation, not titles." He grimaced as if the ice cream was too cold. "Karen Kain danced for twenty years; she became Canada's darling, a big fish in a small pond. But you, if you'd stuck with it, you would have been as famous as Anna Pavlova or Margot Fonteyn." His glass bowl clattered on the tray when he set it down. "You'd have been the world's darling, Sabine."

"Robert, how you exaggerate." Her ice cream was melting, untouched in its crystal bowl. "As it happens, at the moment I'm working with the Prix de Lyon people on a very special project. It will be glorious." She sat back in her chair and gave him a triumphant *so there* look.

"This is the first I've heard of it," he said with a frown.

"I don't tell you everything, Robert."

Louisa gave a small cough and I said, "Sabine, how old were you when you met Marc?"

Her face softened. "Twenty-five. He was nineteen. Such a beautiful man."

The image of Marc and Sabine on Halloween came to mind. Antony, strong and distractingly virile to my sixteen year old eyes, and Cleopatra, serenely beautiful with a filigreed gold headpiece tangled in her hair.

That reminded me of the cat. "Where's Jasmine?"

Sabine pursed her lips in disapproval. "Jasmine is in the basement. She's been a naughty girl. She won't leave Bijoux alone."

Who's Bijoux? I glanced at Louis. She shrugged, no idea.

There was a light tap on the French doors leading out to the terrace.

"Lola, there you are." Sabine hurried off to the kitchen where we could hear her rummaging in the pantry before reappearing with a large bowl of nuts and seeds. On the other side of the glass stood a small grey squirrel, its fat, fluffy tail curled on its back.

"Sabine, you've got rodents!" I said, trying to sound calmer than I felt.

Louisa lay a hand on my shoulder. "Relax, it's just a squirrel."

"Exactly," I said with a shudder. I detest squirrels, they're erratic and unpredictable, nothing more than cute rats.

Then the damn thing made two little fists and thumped on the glass.

I yelped. "For God's sake Sabine, don't let it in."

Sabine laughed and opened the French doors clicking her tongue and waving the bowl over the squirrel's tiny head. She took a couple of steps across the heated flagstones and placed the bowl next to a large metal planter. When she stood up a huge crow swooped out of the sky and settled at her feet with a soft rustle of glossy black feathers.

"Bijoux, you can strut about showing me your fine feathers all you want, but you must be a gentleman and wait your turn."

I glanced at Louisa, Lola? Bijoux? Has Sabine named all the creatures that visit her garden?

As Sabine reached into the bowl to scatter sunflower seeds across the flagstones, the squirrel darted after the crow, which arched its neck and pecked the squirrel's head and shoulders.

"No, Bijoux, stop!" Sabine reached down to shield Lola. The crow raked its razor sharp beak across her hand and she cried out, clutching her thumb.

Bijoux cocked a bright black eye at Sabine, then spread its wings wide and soared up into the towering mountain ash. The squirrel became even more manic, running around in circles until it stumbled into the bowl, flipping it over and sending nuts and seeds flying across the terrace.

Louisa was on her feet and out the terrace doors before I could move. She grabbed Sabine by the wrist and dragged her back into the house and down the hall to the bathroom to clean the gash.

Robert heaved a dramatic sigh. "Evie, I'm with you and Jasmine on this one, squirrels are rodents, crows aren't much better. They should all be exterminated."

"Exterminated? That's a little extreme, Robert," I said as I stepped outside to retrieve Sabine's bowl. Overhead Bijoux fluttered in the treetops making an awful ruckus. Out of the corner of my eye I saw a squirrel, maybe Lola, galloping across the roof of the McMansion next door. The orange tarp was gone and the house was nothing more than an ugly, stained plywood box, naked and defenceless against the elements.

"Shouldn't that house be gone by now?" I asked Robert as I passed through the living room on my way to the kitchen where I set the bowl in the sink. Robert was pouring himself another cup of coffee when I returned. He eased back into his chair and told me the saga of the house.

"That Sidney Foster fellow missed the last installment payment. It's an expensive build and Marc's worried Foster might back out."

"Surely that would be a good thing. A new buyer might build a house that's more sympathetic to the rhythm of the street."

"No, you misunderstand me. Marc's not worried about the McMansion per se. He's concerned that if Foster is experiencing cash flow problems with the McMansion, he may renege on his pledge to make a sizable donation to the Ballet House. He's their biggest donor by far."

"That thing is an eyesore," Sabine grumbled as she swept back into the room. Louisa had wrapped Sabine's hand in gauze right down to her fingertips. "If Foster hadn't contributed to the Ballet House, we wouldn't be stuck with that place." She sighed. "Never mind, Marc says it will all be over soon. Everything will move quickly once the demolition crew gets here."

In the car on the way home Louisa said the gash on Sabine's hand was surprisingly deep. "What do they call a flock of crows? An unkindness?"

"I don't know, Louisa, but Bijoux is wild and nasty. Unkindness doesn't begin to describe it."

CHAPTER SEVENTEEN

Madeline's office feels like a yoga studio, calm and uncluttered, all that's missing is the Tibetan bowl music and the whale sounds. Unlike the lawyers, Madeline has moved fully into the digital age. There isn't a file folder or a piece of paper anywhere to be seen; just stretches of empty space dotted here and there with huge vases of flowers (magnificent white lilies today) that lift the eye past the parking lot to the leafy woods beyond.

"Are you going to come in or just stand there admiring me from the hall?" she asked.

I stepped inside and joined her at the small round table next to the window. "I've got a question, but first let me preface it: I am not gossiping."

Her green eyes flashed; she was amused. "Gossiping, Evie Valentine? Never!"

"Gossiping, Madeline Moreau? Always," I retorted. She made a little face but didn't dispute it. If anyone knows anything about anyone in this town, it's Madeline.

"Go ahead, what do you want to know?"

After Robert accused Marc of destroying Sabine's career, I couldn't stop thinking about Marc and the small blonde woman I'd seen him with at the Marsalis concert. Sabine had given up her career for him, the least he could was remain faithful.

When I told Madeline about the pretty young woman with the pixie cut, she said the same thing Louisa had said. "It could be perfectly innocent, a business associate, a donor, a potential client."

"Sabine gave us their tickets because she had a headache and Marc was supposedly at the office working late."

"That tired old excuse?" Her eyes narrowed. "You're sure his little friend was blond, not an exotic looking woman, tall, with thick black hair?"

"No. Who's this dark-haired woman?"

"His mistress, this one is a thirty-eight year old architect from Beirut. Long black hair, tawny complexion. Absolutely stunning. She's been around for a year; maybe he's tired of her and ready to move on."

"Hold on, 'this one'? Are you saying Marc has had a string of affairs?"

She caught the look of disapproval on my face and smiled. "Oh please, Marc's French. What do you think?"

"I think that's a cliché, that's what I think." I struggled to keep the irritation out of my voice. Madeline and I agree on most things, but the sanctity of marriage is not one of them.

She eyed me for a moment before continuing. "François Hollande, the former French president, lived with—but didn't marry—three different women. He had four kids with the first one, left her for the second one, then left her for a third one, and guess what, these *unions libre* had zero impact on his political career. They do things differently there."

Perhaps, but Sabine and Marc lived here, in Canada. "I wonder if Sabine knows," I said quietly.

"Oh, Evie," she said, sadly shaking her head, "the man is attractive, he's charming, and he's famous. He travels constantly to the most cosmopolitan cities in the world, what do you think?"

"I think this is a depressing conversation and I'm going to go back to work."

———

When AJ knocked on my open door, I was still fretting about Marc betraying Sabine with a blonde who'd replaced a statuesque brunette, who'd replaced God knows how many other women.

"Guess who just called me," AJ asked as he dropped into a chair. He carries himself with the easy grace of an athlete, the kind that plays soccer, not football. When he first joined the firm he'd barge into my office, blue eyes blazing, with tidbits of information, what this client said or that lawyer did, excited as an overgrown puppy. Over the years he's settled down but sometimes I miss the easy camaraderie of it all.

"I have no idea, AJ. Who just called: Genghis Kahn? Taylor Swift? Who?"

"Grizzly Adams. He wants to talk."

"The NEO guy? I thought he hated you."

AJ shrugged as if what Grizzly thought of him was neither here nor there. "We're meeting tonight at the National. The pub with the bowling alley. Want to come along?"

"Bowling with a grizzly bear? I wouldn't miss it for the world."

CHAPTER EIGHTEEN

You're going bowling? When was the last time you went bowling?" Louisa asked from her perch at the kitchen island. She was shredding cheese for an omelette and flicking cheese curls off the counter at the dog.

"This is why he's fat," I said. "And for the record, we're not going bowling. We're going to the pub with a bowling alley to meet an eco-terrorist." I clapped my hand over my mouth. "Forget I said that. We don't know if he's an eco-terrorist."

A migraine folded the light around the edges of the room like a prism. Louisa forced me to down two Tylenol tablets and suggested we change the venue from a noisy bowling alley to a quiet café somewhere, but it was too late for that.

"At least have something to eat before AJ gets here," she said. Migraines upset my stomach as well as give me a blinding headache. It occurred to me that I was going to be utterly useless at this meeting.

I was stuffing a peanut butter sandwich in my mouth when AJ texted to say he was in the driveway. As we drove into Beltline I asked if he thought I looked like a bowler. He replied I looked like a ghost. "I never seen you so pale."

"It's my superpower. I may look frail and insubstantial but I'll be mentally recording everything Grizzly says." With a migraine and an upset stomach.

Grizzly warned AJ that his credibility would be shot if he was caught consorting with the enemy but he was willing to risk it because there were things we needed to know. But there was one condition. This meeting was strictly off the record. Against our better judgment we agreed.

The wall of noise, music blaring, people shouting, bowling pins crashing, hit me hard when AJ pulled open the door at the National. If the Tylenol didn't kick in soon, I wouldn't survive.

"We're not bowling, right?" I turned to AJ. "Please tell me we're not bowling."

"We're not bowling."

We made our way past the bowling lanes and into the dining hall which was slightly quieter and more dimly lit. Thank God for small mercies. We stopped at the edge of the room, straining to find Grizzly in the crowd.

A movement in a booth at the back of the restaurant. The big bear of a man lumbered to his feet, waving one giant hand to attract our attention while at the same time trying not to look too obvious. *Good luck with that, Grizzly.* AJ plowed ahead, then stopped so suddenly I plowed into the back of him.

"AJ," Grizzly said with a sly smile, "you remember Samantha Berman." A small, self-possessed woman gazed cooly at us. She had big brown eyes and a mass of curly chin length hair. She didn't bother getting up, not that she could get past Grizzly who'd wedged her in the corner of the booth against the wall.

AJ's face became an impersonal mask. He made perfunctory introductions. "Evie, meet Sam, she was a year behind us at Dalhousie. Sam, this is Evie, my law partner." Sam and I nodded at each other as I slid into the bench across from her.

AJ sat down next to me and busied himself with the menu. Grizzly snatched it our of his hands. "We don't have time to dick around. Sam ordered for us. By the way, you're picking up the tab."

"Fine by me," AJ replied. His eyes bounced around the room, looking everywhere except at Sam. Her large brown eyes never left his face. Soon the server appeared carrying a heavy tray on her thin shoulder. Before she could ask who was having what, Sam grabbed the pizza and passed the dry ribs to Grizzly. That left the two burgers for us.

I glanced at AJ, flicking my eyes in Grizzly's direction. *He's your university buddy, go for it.* AJ took a long swig of beer and asked Grizzly how the protest was going.

Grizzly mumbled through a greasy rib. "This is Sam's meeting. If it was up to me, we wouldn't be here." He nodded at Sam. "You're up, babe." A thin stream of red marinade stained his mustache, he picked up a serviette and rubbed it hard across his mouth.

AJ set his beer down on the table and looked at Sam. "We're all ears, *babe.*"

Unfazed by AJ's tone, Sam flashed a bright but insincere smile and said, "Right, here's the bottom line. Marc Hubert's remediation and sustainability measures are a joke. He's going to destroy the river and its ecosystem, assuming he hasn't done so all ready."

"You're not on site." AJ sounded derisive. "How the hell would you know?"

"Believe it or not, the workers talk to us. They have to

because the GCL"—that was the construction company—"isn't listening to them. You guys represent Marc on the environmental side, aren't you supposed to be monitoring this stuff?"

"So now NEO is the worker's friend." AJ hadn't touched his burger. "Tell that to the poor schmuck who got hit in the face with a brick."

"Watch it, Braxton." Grizzly set a gnawed rib down on the stack of bones he'd sucked clean.

Sam touched Grizzly's arm as if to stop him from interrupting. Her eyes never left AJ's face. "That wasn't intentional, AJ. You of all people should know that."

You of all people? Babe? What was with these two?

I tried to bring the meeting back on course, not that I knew what the course was anymore. "The contracts set out the reporting requirements. GCL receives updates every day. If there's a problem, we'd have heard about it."

"In a perfect world, sure," Sam replied. "No one is reporting half the shit that's happening at the site. Omission is another form of misrepresentation, isn't that right, AJ. If they're lying to the regulators, what makes you think they're not lying to you?"

"Because if Marc misses his targets, he loses his donors and the City funding. The Ballet House will never be finished," I said firmly.

She sat back with a smug look on her face. "Precisely!"

AJ stared at her, shaking his head slowly. "You guys don't trust anyone do you?"

The smug look on Sam's face changed to concern. "Look, all we're asking is this: please consider the possibility that we might be right. They're on a tight schedule, you know that. They're going so fast they're degrading the environment more and more each day. Pretty soon they'll reach the point of no return. And while we're on the topic, their safety practices onsite are so slipshod it's only a matter of time before someone gets killed. Your partner here"—Sam flashed her eyes at me—"may be fine with that but honestly, AJ, I expected better of you."

"That's it." AJ's face hardened. In one smooth motion he stood up and yanked his coat off the back of his chair. "Let's go."

"What?" I didn't think I'd heard him right.

Grizzly glared at AJ, then turned to Sam. "I told you this was a waste of time."

AJ was winding his way past the crowded tables when Grizzly shouted after him, "Hey, it's your tab, buddy." The sound of bowling pins crashing on hardwood masked the bang of the front door. AJ was gone.

I grabbed my coat and pulled my wallet out of my pocket. "I've got it," I said, flinging my business card down on the table. "Just in case..."

Just in case of what? In case they were right?

AJ was fuming when I caught up to him beside his car. "Did you pay?" he asked.

"Yeah, I paid." I held the receipt between my fingers, wondering whether this was a legitimate business expense. He unlocked the doors and I eased into the passenger seat, slowly adjusting my seat belt, trying to gather my thoughts. "Do you want to tell me what that was about?"

"Not particularly," he said, flinging one arm across the back of my seat and backing out of the parking stall in a whir of icy tires.

If I hadn't had such a wicked migraine I would have pressed him for an explanation. Looking back I wish I had.

CHAPTER NINETEEN

The naked trees along the riverbank behind the office looked fragile, as if they wouldn't last until spring. The recent chinook had melted the middle of the river and the water sparkled like diamonds on velvet. It was very early, I was wandering around in my dark office, trying to muster the energy to go down the hall and make some coffee.

Someone hit the switch behind me and room was ablaze with light, making my migraine throb even harder in my temples.

"Christ! Turn it off," I said as I slumped lower in my chair. The barometer was falling, snow was coming, and my head was ready to explode.

AJ flicked the switch and entered quietly. "No offence," he said, "but you look like a vampire. White and glassy eyed. Shouldn't you be at home in bed?"

I gave him a weak smile. "Give me a couple of hours and I'll be fine. Listen, we have to talk about last night. Sam made some serious allegations; what's with you two, anyway? The tension between you was palpable. Much worse than with you and Grizzly. God, I'd love a coffee." I stared at the Seb's cup in AJ's hand.

"All yours," he slid his cup across my desk. "Not that it's going to do you any good. You look like you need a blood transfusion."

Despite the headache, I laughed. "So what's with you and Sam?"

He deflected my question. "If Marc is in breach of his contract we can't turn a blind eye."

"Who's in breach of their contract?" Keith froze in my doorway. "What are you two doing here?" It's a rare day when we beat him into the office. "Evie, you look awful. Why aren't you at home in bed?"

Migraines muddle my brain and I flailed around trying to string some words into a coherent sentence. We'd promised Grizzly and Sam that everything they told us would be off the record. What could I say? Desperate, I glanced at AJ. *Over to you.*

AJ explained we'd heard rumours that the Ballet House was not being built in accordance with its permits and contracts. "Marc may be in breach."

Keith strolled into my office. He looked less stressed than usual, maybe the baby goat was healthy and gamboling about in the barn. "Well," he said, "Marc could be running a little behind. He's got a lot on his mind, with the protesters and the firebomb."

"That's no excuse for breach." It sounded harsher than I intended when I said it.

He nodded. "Yeah, you're right. But even if what you say is true, you can't go to the regulator. Can you talk to the construction company, GCL?"

I stopped massaging my temples and looked at him, too surprised to speak. Usually Keith has a coronary when I want to dig into a file that's gone—oh, how to put this—off the rails, but this was a good idea. GCL's crew was building the Ballet House to Marc's design. It was bound by Marc's environmental covenants.

"Characterize it as a follow up meeting," he continued. "For feedback: Your business is import to us, how can we serve you better, that kind of thing."

I laughed. "Keith, you're bloody brilliant!"

He shot us a self-deprecating grin and wandered down the hall to his office. By the time he reached his door he was humming something neither of us recognized. Keith is a nice guy, but he can't carry a tune to save his soul.

We gave Bridget five minutes to settle at her desk before we swooped down on her like two vultures waiting for their prey to die.

"May I help you?" Bridget asked as her fingers flew across her keyboard. "I'm assuming whatever it is, it's urgent, right?"

Bridget is smart, one of the best admin assistants I've ever had. Her superpower is her looks. With her round blue eyes and peaches and cream complexion people underestimate her. It works to her advantage every single time.

"As a matter of fact, it is." I explained we wanted a meeting with the head of GCL but we didn't want him to think it was urgent because we didn't want him to invite Marc along. It was too soon for that.

"I see," she said, "it's an ambush."

"In a manner of speaking."

Thirty minutes later she sent me a text: You're meeting with Dave Dudik at 5:30, his office, tonight. Be nice.

———

By five o'clock the sky was thick with dull grey clouds. I

checked my weather app as AJ turned right on Elbow Drive heading north to GCL's corporate headquarters.

"A blizzard is coming," I said, holding up my phone. He glanced at it, unconcerned. Unlike AJ, I hate being on the roads after a fresh snowfall. Calgarians pride themselves on being good—no, great—winter drivers. Hah! The number of cars straddling medians and nose down in ditches proves otherwise. We parked in GCL's warm dry underground parkade and rode silently up to the top of the building.

Dave Dudik's employees glanced up from their busy desks as his assistant led us down to his corner office. GCL's annual report boasted the company was committed to environmental sustainability and reducing the impact of climate change. Soon we'd find out if that was true.

Dudik was around fifty with a high forehead, a ruddy complexion and very white teeth. I didn't know him well but by all accounts, he was a decent guy.

"Pardon the mess," he said, nodding at the stacks of plastic binders and engineering drawings spread across the long table by the window wall. Big, fat snowflakes swirled on the other side of the glass. "We've got an investor conference next week. There's a lot of work to do to get it right. Well, you guys are lawyers, I don't need to tell you that." He indicated the two visitor's chairs facing him. "So what can I do for you fine folks?"

"We just wanted to touch base," I said, "now that you're going full bore on the Ballet House." I hoped he wouldn't ask why it took a personal visit from two lawyers to 'touch base' when a simple phone call would do. "Specifically with respect to the contractual obligations relating to health, safety and environment. Are you finding them workable on the ground?"

He frowned and glanced out his door into the hall. "You're talking about incident reports, that kind of thing?"

AJ interjected, "More or less. We're trying to ascertain the ease of adhering to the contractual obligations calling for environmentally sustainable construction." It sounded like bafflegab when AJ said it, but we couldn't flat out ask Dudik if he was in breach of the contract. At least not without proof.

"That's Brianna's department. I can pull her in here if you like." Dudik shot another troubled glance down the hall.

"No need," I said, "can you ask her to send us what you've got on environmental compliance? That should do it."

Outside the snow was bucketing out of the dark sky. Dudik turned to me with a puzzled look on his face. His antennae were up. "Are you concerned about anything in particular? As far as I know there haven't been any breaches. Am I missing something?"

We rushed to reassure him that we were simply looking for feedback to ensure the contract had been clearly drafted and no one was hung up on the legalese. After five more minutes of babble about the importance of feedback, we shook hands and left.

———

In the elevator on our way down to the car park I turned to AJ and said, "I don't think he bought it, do you?"

"An out of the blue meeting because we want some face-to-face feedback? I don't think he bought it at all. He's probably on the phone to Marc right now, trying to figure out what we're up to."

"When you put it like that, it wasn't one of our better ideas," I said.

"It wasn't our idea, it was Keith's. Let's blame him."

CHAPTER TWENTY

The MGB's wet tires squealed as AJ zipped through the GCL parkade to the exit. The underground parkade was clean and bathed in soft yellow light. It's one of the few in town that doesn't give me the heebie-jeebies. AJ crept up the exit ramp and the garage doors slowly clanged open.

Outside there was nothing. Just a wall of swirling grey snow.

He leaned forward, peering into the blankness, then eased out onto the sidewalk. To our right was a wall of disembodied headlights and to our left taillights flickered as drivers braked and skidded through the intersection.

My phone wailed with a warning alarm. "AJ, weather alert. It's a blizzard warning, we have to get off the road."

"Tell that to these guys, they won't let me in."

After ten minutes of AJ trying to nudge his way into traffic, I rolled down my window and waved my arms, pointing at the cars that blocked our way. Finally a driver flashed her lights indicating she wouldn't ram us if we budged in front of her. I gave her a thumbs up and we inched into the left turn lane.

"We're never going to make it back to the office, not in this traffic," I said.

"What an idiot!" AJ said through gritted teeth. He was talking about the driver of the red Toyota in the next lane. Toyota guy had sped up to beat the red light but the car ahead of him decided at the last minute to stop. Toyota guy slammed on his brakes and his car began to spin. It rammed the car ahead, shoving it into the intersection; its back end slewed into the next lane and both cars shuddered to a stop. Seconds later both drivers were out of their cars screaming at each other.

"Brilliant," AJ said, "now no one's going anywhere."

"Except us. Stay in this lane, squeeze by them, then go down to Twelfth to my place. You can stay with Louisa and me until this blows over."

It took us an hour to make our painstaking way back to the house. I held my breath as AJ navigated the last few meters down our street. Snowdrifts the size of ponies lay across the road. I texted Louisa to say we'd arrived and she opened the garage door so AJ could ease his MGB into the spot reserved for my Mini which was back at the office being buried in the parking lot.

We staggered out of the car like two zombies, our knees stiff and our muscles tight from white knuckling it the fifteen blocks from City Centre to Mission.

Quincy went berserk when AJ and I came up the basement stairs, greeting me with a broadside lunge and springing up to plant a doggy kiss on AJ. He laughed and knuckle-rubbed Quincy's head. "Give me a second to get my shoes off, you silly mutt." AJ is one of the few men Quincy doesn't try to dismember the minute they cross the threshold.

By the time I'd changed into warm fleece pants and

woolly socks they were in the TV room in front of the fire. Louisa was curled up under a heavy throw and AJ had pulled an armchair closer to the fire. stockinged feet propped up on the hearth. When Louisa said dinner would be up in ten minutes, I suggested a drink.

"I'll pass," AJ said. "Got to keep my wits about me for the drive home."

"Are you nuts?" I went to the front window and peered through the darkness into the silent, snow-covered street. The shrubs gleamed in the streetlight, looking like giant melted marshmallows. "You won't make it to the end of the driveway let alone to the end of the block. You're spending the night here, my friend."

After we polished off Louisa's chicken divan—she's on a retro cooking kick, we were lucky she wasn't serving tomato aspic—and topped up our wine we returned to the TV room where AJ took up his position by the fire and Louisa and I claimed the opposite ends of the sofa. The fire wheezed and popped sending tiny sparks into the air, some kind of Euro Lounge music was playing in the background and the wine was making me sleepy.

"I always wanted to be a ballerina," Louisa said, a dreamy look in her eye.

I gave a strangled cough. "You did not. Mom put us into dance when you were in kindergarten and I was in grade one, you lasted until Christmas before you bailed."

"Yes, but I cried—"

"Pitifully."

"—at your year-end showcase. I wanted it so much."

I turned to AJ and said, "We were wearing popcorn costumes and Louisa wanted to be a popcorn kernel."

"That's true," she said with a sad sigh.

AJ grinned at me. "I'd give my left arm to see you and your spindly little legs in a popcorn costume."

"Spindly legs?"

He laughed and started talking about the Ballet House.

For years the idea of a purpose-built venue for the ballet, opera and the symphony floated around the city like a dream. Committee after committee had been struck and disbanded after failing to line up the necessary funding. Then Sabine, the Parisienne *danseuse étoile*, stepped in. Suddenly *tout le monde* was clamouring for the Ballet House. Sabine said it was exactly what Calgary needed to shake off its redneck cowboy reputation. We would no longer be known as Houston North. Her charming French accent muted the disparaging sting.

Louisa snuggled deeper into her throw. "Evie, remember Sabine's news conference? The one where someone dismissed the Ballet House as an elitist vanity project? She said they were uncultured rubes who'd order Coke for breakfast at a Paris patisserie."

AJ set his wine glass down on the end table and said, "Speaking of uncultured rubes, have you got any milk? It's my bedtime beverage of choice." Louisa hopped off the couch to fetch him a glass and he turned to me. "Back to the Ballet House, I agree that Sabine did a lot, but it would still be a pipe dream if the City didn't cough up forty percent of the funding."

"That's true," I said, "Sabine is nothing if not shrewd." When the City agreed to pay more than half the cost of the new hockey arena—total cost around a billion dollars—she pointed out we could certainly throw a few million into the Ballet House. "What's good for the goose, and all that."

"The gander," AJ said. "For that maxim to work, the

arena is the gander, for the men who love sports, and the Ballet House is the goose, for the women who love ballet."

I almost choked on what was left of my wine. "AJ," I said, "it's not just women who love the ballet. I swear, sometimes you're such a neanderthal."

He gave me his farm boy grin, accepted a cold glass of milk from Louisa and announced he was ready for bed.

When he took his empty glass out to the kitchen and put it in the dishwasher Louisa whispered, "He's made himself right at home, hasn't he?"

"His momma trained him well," I replied.

Louisa directed AJ upstairs to the guest room, telling him she'd set out clean towels in the bathroom and had even found him a toothbrush. He stifled a yawn and said good night.

After checking the fire to ensure it was dying down, I went to the front window. It was so white and still out there. In the dark came the muffled sound of a car stuck somewhere, it's tires whirring, desperately trying to break free.

The Ballet House would be beautiful in winter as well as summer, glistening like a diamond in the snowy landscape. Sabine was convinced it would launch Marc into the architectural stratosphere. His reputation would exceed that of Gehry and Pei.

CHAPTER TWENTY-ONE

Madeline hovered at my office door, a wicked grin on her face. Her only concession to the snow still pelting down was a hat. A furry Doctor Zhivago hat that would look silly on anyone but Madeline who could wear a bucket on her head and look stylish. "So, what's the deal with you two?" she asked.

"That's not real fur, is it?" I pointed to the silvery blue pillbox pulled low on her brow.

"Have you ever seen an animal this colour? It's faux fur. Don't try to change the subject, I saw you and AJ come in together this morning. In his car. He dropped you off and sped out of the parking lot like he was fleeing a crime scene. That's the second time this month."

"Yeah, well he's gone home to change." *Damn, that came out all wrong. Maybe she wouldn't notice.*

Her eyes widened. And she marched in and sat down in front of me. "So how long has this been going on?"

Nip it in the bud. Right now. I sat back in my chair and tried to stare her down. "Really Madeline, that's not at all what I meant. We got caught in the blizzard on our way back from GCL. AJ couldn't make it home, so he spent the night with Louisa and me. In the guest room, I might add."

She narrowed her eyes at me. My face felt hot, which was annoying. Keith and AJ say it's my 'tell.' *You go red when you're angry.* But I wasn't angry now, just embarrassed. Lord knows why. I gave a little cough and in a brisk, no-nonsense tone said, "Now that we've got that out of the way—"

Bridget swept into my office, glanced at Madeline, then back at me and asked, "What's going on?"

"Nothing." Now I sounded huffy. Madeline laughed and took her sweet time sashaying out of my office.

"This just came in for you by courier." Bridget placed a stack of paper on my desk. The loopy handwriting on the sticky note said: Environmental reports—Brianna. It included a summary sheet and highlighted a number of pages that merited extra scrutiny.

When I called Brianna to double check that I'd interpreted her stats correctly, there was a long pause on the line. She'd taken a risk leaving a trail of breadcrumbs for us in the first place, now I was asking her to confirm my suspicions. Finally, she admitted I was right and in a tiny voice added that both Dudik, her boss, and Marc, my client, were fully aware of the breaches.

"Marc is aware he's in breach?" I asked in disbelief.

Brianna gave a heavy sigh. "Evie, no one here is happy about this, but Dudik says the schedule is the schedule and the budget is locked. End of story."

"This is insanity." With that I hung up.

A half an hour latter AJ strolled into my office and sat down. "What's with Madeline?" He'd changed into fresh clothes. His blue button-down shirt matched his eyes, making them look even bluer. "She's acting weird."

"She's always acting weird. Ignore her. Look at this." I showed him Brianna's reports. "I'm amazed Dudik let her send this to us, knowing what it contained."

"Either he didn't understand the extent of it or he knew it would have looked strange if he didn't deliver the reports after he said he would. He probably figured we'd be too busy to go through them carefully."

"We're lawyers, AJ. That's our job. Besides with Brianna's annotations you'd have to be blind not to see how bad it was."

He flipped through the pages. Then looked up at me shaking his head in dismay. "Christ, the site is an environmental time bomb."

Ten minutes later we were hanging over Bridget's desk again. She lifted her fingers off her keyboard and said, "Let me guess, you want another ambush meeting, this time with Marc." Clever girl, our Bridget.

"Yes to the meeting with Marc, no to the ambush," I said. "Let Marc know we've reviewed the incident reports and have some concerns. I don't want him to fob us off by professing ignorance and promising he'll look into it and get back to us later, because he won't." It never ceases to amaze me how high powered (and ridiculously overpaid) executives think if they kick the can down the road, it will magically disappear.

Turning to AJ I said, "This isn't an ambush, but I swear if we don't get some decent answers, it's no more Mr. Nice Guy."

AJ smiled. "Or Ms. Nice Guy, with an 'S'?

"Or an 'X.' All of the above."

An hour later Bridget sent me a text: You're on at 6:30. Do NOT skin him alive.

CHAPTER TWENTY-TWO

The sun, a hard red ball in a hazy grey sky, had set an hour ago and the pale light seeping out of the windows from the surrounding office buildings did little to chase the shadows away. The road outside of the Atelier was under repair and the block looked like a bombed-out battle zone.

"Oof!!" I snagged my heel on the uneven pavement and AJ caught my arm.

"If you don't watch yourself, you'll be dead like that poor woman who cracked her head open on the sidewalk." Last month there had been a tragic accident. A young salesclerk hustling off to her job at Holts slipped on the ice. The first and only call she made while she lay bleeding on the pavement was to her best friend. 'I think I did something really stupid,' she said just before she died. I couldn't get the thought out of my head: Did she know at that precise moment her life was over?

AJ pulled my arm into the crook of his elbow and patted my hand, making me feel like I was ninety. We continued to pick our way down the sidewalk, past heaps of broken concrete, haphazard signs and barriers poking out of the snow until we reached Marc's building.

The lobby was a high airy space, deserted except for a security guard who gazed at us with disinterest as we headed to the glass enclosed elevators. We floated up to the fifth floor with the city sparkling in the ice fog all around us. It was eerie and I couldn't stop thinking about the elevator's hydraulics and whether they'd crack in the extreme cold.

That's the trouble with being a lawyer, you learn that literally everything is a death trap. Way back in law school I'd dated an architecture student who'd shown me his design for a hotel lobby. As he extolled the esthetics of the mezzanine suspended by thin wire cables I quizzed him on their composition—would they snap one day flinging dozens of people to their deaths on the hard marble floors below? — he said I was a killjoy and dumped me two days later.

Marcie, Marc's assistant, met us in the Atelier's reception area and led us to Marc's office. Other than the black and beige African carpet lying on the polished concrete floor and a small bronze sculpture sitting on the corner of his desk, the space was a riot of colour, blues, greens and reds.

"What a vibrant room," I said, gesturing at the cobalt blue sofa and bright yellow armchairs. "So different from Marc and Sabine's house."

Marcie smiled. "Marc works best in a high-octane environment. He'd fall asleep if he had to work in the muted palette he has at home. But you'll note the room has its own internal dynamic. Rules, if you will. There's a place for everything and everything is in its place which keeps the colour scheme from being jarring." I had no idea what she was talking about.

Down the hall we could hear Marc talking to one of

the architects toiling at her computer. Finally he swept into the room. He directed us to the blue sofa and he and Marcie took their places in the buttercup yellow armchairs across from us.

When I asked if the police had had any luck tracking down the arsonist who'd firebombed the building he frowned.

"Not yet. But in the grand scheme of things they have better things to do than chase after a vagrant trying to keep warm."

"Vagrant? Marc, this was more than a vagrant."

He waved my concerns away and turned to AJ who pulled Brianna's file out of his bag and set it on the burl wood table between us. Marc sat back, crossing his arms. Waiting.

"Marc," I said, "it appears that the Ballet House is having some difficulty meeting its environmental commitments." I was using vague, nonjudgmental language. That's how it's done in business. We interact through carefully choreographed language, like a minuet, to allow the other party to save face when they're cornered.

Except it didn't work this time.

A small muscle twitched in Marc's jaw but his smile held. "I don't see—"

"Please, Marc, let me finish. There are too many violations on the site. You don't need me to tell you you're in breach of the funding agreements. In the worst case scenario you could lose the City's support... and kiss the Ballet House goodbye." I'd stopped dancing.

He rose and moved to his desk, resting his hand on the small bronze sculpture as if it were a talisman. Then he launched into a lecture about broken supply chains and tight construction windows. All blah, blah, blah. Like a poker player bluffing with a pair of twos

I held up a hand to stop him. "Totally irrelevant, Marc, if you can't meet your commitments you need to revise your numbers and submit them to the City. It wouldn't hurt to include a detailed plan showing how you'll meet your commitments in the future."

His eyes flashed. "A detailed plan? Just what do you propose? This is a GCL problem, not an Atelier problem. Dudik underbid the project. If he can't find the equipment and the skilled labour he needs, that's on him. Regardless of what those idealists at NEO think."

Marcie shifted uncomfortably as Marc's voice rose in volume. She hadn't said a word during the meeting and I'd almost forgotten she was here.

"Look Marc," AJ said, reasonably. "We get where you're coming from but the Ballet House is a Marc Hubert project. It's synonymous with your name. If, heaven forbid, it damages the river ecosystem—particularly after you agreed to stringent environmental conditions to prevent that—that's on you. Your reputation will be toast. NEO is just waiting for you to slip up. Have you considered talking to them to bring them onside?"

Marc snorted. "NEO? Why do you think I agreed to those asinine conditions in the first place? Those head-in-the-clouds activists will never be satisfied."

Irritation flooded through me, preventing the analytical part of my brain from fully grasping what he'd said. I had to make him understand how precarious his position was.

"Marc, this is about more than reputational damage." I pulled out my litigation argument. "This situation is ripe for a lawsuit. Failing to do what you promised to do leaves you defenceless. Who do you think the public will blame if the Ballet House pollutes the Elbow or the Bow and their reputation for world class fishing goes belly-up—"

"Ah, so that's it." Marc stopped pacing. "That's what this is really about. You're pushing NEO's agenda. Isn't that a conflict of interest?"

"Oh for the love of God." I stood up to face him. "Listen to yourself. You sound like a wacko conspiracy theorist. As your lawyers we're simply advising you to honour your contract so you don't get sued from here to kingdom come."

Then a strange thing happened. The man who looked like he was ready to throw us out the window took a deep breath, smiled and thanked us for stopping by. He'd take care of everything. Marcie on the sofa looked as confused as I felt when Marc asked her to show us out.

Something had shifted in Marc, but for the life of me I didn't know what it was.

CHAPTER TWENTY-THREE

The next day I was rushing into the photocopy room when Bridget stopped me. "Sabine called, she wanted to know if you're free tonight. I checked your calendar and you've got nothing on. Looks like you're going to a dinner party. Won't that be grand?"

I groaned. I love this girl, she's perfect... but she has a habit of meddling in my social life. "Bridget, we've talked about this." Ever since she met her husband Theo on a dating app she's been trying to find me a soulmate. Any social occasion, including dinner with a client, would do.

She lowered her eyes and for a moment I thought she was going to apologize, then I realized she was looking at a flashing button on her phone. She picked up the receiver and said, "Yes, Sabine, she's right here." Turning to me she said she'd put the call through to my office, then with an innocent smile shooed me away.

Sabine's voice was filled with concern, the kind you express when someone is suffering from a bad cold. "Evie, I understand you and Marc had a tiny misunderstanding the other day. He feels terrible about it and we'd like you and AJ to join us tonight for a small dinner party. Nothing fancy, just the Dudiks and another couple. What's AJ's number... oh, never mind, I've got it."

"You're inviting AJ?"

"Of course I'm inviting AJ. You two are a couple, yes? He can talk business with the men while we women discuss life and love and what really matters."

I sagged in my chair. "No, Sabine, AJ and I are not a couple, but more importantly, lawyers and clients disagree all the time, there's no need to include us in your dinner party to make amends."

She tut tutted that it was no problem at all and hung up.

I raced over to AJ's office, frantically signalling him not to pick up his phone, but he already had the receiver to his ear and had said hello. He nodded a few times and hung up. If he'd said ten words, I'd be amazed.

"Judging from the look on your face, I'm too late." I wondered if Sabine had AJ on speed dial.

"We're going to Marc and Sabine's for a dinner party? Together? Socially, I mean?" He was stammering.

"Look, it wasn't my idea. They're French. They view workplace relationships differently than we do." My Hungarian mom was the same way. If you couldn't date someone from the office then who could you date. No one went to church anymore; the bars were full of lowlifes and those dating apps were a serial killer's hunting ground.

That evening when I told Louisa about our dinner invitation, she thought the Evie-and-AJ thing was sweet. From the foot of my bed she offered silly comments while I agonized over what to wear.

"Absolutely not. You can't wear that." She stared at a pair of black slacks and the long black cashmere sweater I'd arranged on the bed. "You need to show off your décolletage."

"My décolletage? What century are you living in?"

When she told Quincy I was going to *ze dinner avec ze boyfriend*, I swore I'd never speak to her again, ever.

———

"You're alone?" Sabine said as she shot an anxious look over my shoulder and out into the cold black night.

"No, AJ's here. We came in separate cars." Behind me I could hear the whine of AJ's tires as his MGB bucked in and out of the icy ruts carved into the snow by the construction workers next door.

"Separate vehicles? Did you have a fight?"

Jasmine tore through the foyer, like a convict making a break for freedom. I scooped her up on the threshold and passed her back to Sabine. She looked into the cat's eyes and chirped, "We will give AJ some wine and all will be forgiven, isn't that right, Jasmine." The cat, like me, had no idea what she was talking about.

AJ soon joined me in the foyer. Sabine hung our coats in the closet and we followed her into the living room to meet the other dinner guests. Marc reintroduced us to Dave Dudik, the head of GCL, and his wife, a tall, athletic-looking woman with short, no-nonsense hair. The other guests were an investment banker and his very young wife. Sabine noted that they were patrons of the arts; no doubt they'd donated piles of money to the Ballet House.

Soon we were seated in the dining room, listening to Rosemary Clooney's greatest hits while the candles in an ancient silver candelabra flickered over the sparkling silverware. Endless bottles of wine and plates of savory appetizers followed by steelhead salmon put everyone in a mellow mood. Sabine's an excellent cook; she could give any chef a run for his money.

By the time the cheese plate arrived we were deep in a wine-infused political debate.

"You Canadians like your politics simple." Mark was pontificating now. "The French see the world as it is. A complex place easily misunderstood by the unsophisticated mind."

The banker snorted as he set down his wine glass. "Marc, you're an elitist." The words rolled slowly off his tongue; he'd consumed more alcohol than the rest of us put together. His young wife laughed and sat back in her chair, awaiting Marc's response.

"No my friend, you're confusing elitism with education," Marc replied. "I am not an elitist, but I am well educated. Sadly, it is difficult to get a decent education in this country. Look at your politicians"—Marc and Sabine were Canadian citizens; 'our' politicians were 'their' politicians as well—"they are real estate salesmen and farmer's sons. It is no surprise they fill their days passing silly laws to hamstring business. They simply don't know any better."

"Surely you're not suggesting it's better in France," the banker said. "There the rich and the government are like this." He raised his hand, two fingers entwined.

Marc took a sip of wine. "In France if the government passes a stupid law, the people simply ignore it. The French have the gift of common sense. This is something only a few Canadians would understand." He tipped his half-empty wine glass at Dave Dudik as if he'd just delivered a toast and Dave touched his glass to Marc's—a meeting of the mutual admiration society was in progress.

Marc took a leisurely sip of wine and continued. "The French police understand this. They don't enforce stupid laws. For example, they never fine people for smoking in a non-smoking area if they're outdoors."

AJ coughed gently and said, "This is Canada, not France. Here people and companies are not allowed to ignore laws they don't like."

Dudik topped up Marc's glass, then his own. "What Marc means is the French work closely with government to ensure their laws are practical; he's not saying they flat out ignore laws they don't like."

I smiled. "Dave, I get the feeling you said that for the benefit of the two lawyers in the room."

"Speaking of the lawyers," Marc cut in, "why did you ask Dave for the Sin List when you could have asked me?"

"What Sin List?" AJ shot a puzzled glance at Dudik.

"AJ," I said, "I think Marc is referring to the list of environmental infractions Brianna sent over." I was stalling for time, trying to dream up an excuse because Marc was right, we could have asked him for the list, but didn't, for the simple reason that we didn't trust him to give it to us.

"No, no, no," Sabine scolded as she returned from the kitchen with a carafe of coffee. "If we're going to talk about sin, let's talk about sin, not the law, it's so boring." She set the carafe on the table and returned to the kitchen to fetch the apricot mouse.

Marc called out after her. "Sabine, my darling, what sins would you like to talk about?"

When she returned, she said, "Canadians don't know how to enjoy life. For them it's all work, work, work. What about love?"

At first, I wondered whether Sabine was intentionally goading Marc. Not only did he work all the time, but everyone at this table knew about his extramarital affairs.

Marc, of all people, had no trouble making time for work and love.

But her face was sincere. "The work life here is so dull. In France men and women are sexual beings even at work, especially at work. A little flirtation makes the day go faster. It doesn't hurt. But here it's against the law."

The banker's wife tittered and I didn't know where to look. Sabine was right of course; most companies had No Fraternization rules in their HR policies. Not that it mattered to men like Marc. They 'fraternized' with whoever they liked.

Louisa was still awake when I got home. She bounced onto to my bed and asked how it went. "Are you and AJ engaged yet?"

"Ha ha, very funny." I stripped off my long black sweater and tossed it in a chair. "It was a very pleasant evening. Sabine is a terrific cook. Marc is an entertaining host and it was like we'd never argued with him in the first place. But I've got to tell you, Louisa, the French are nothing like us."

CHAPTER TWENTY-FOUR

In the earlier hours of Monday morning the snow stopped. The air was crisp and thick with the buzz of snow blowers—something I've never understood, they don't remove the snow, they just blow it around—Louisa was outside, head down, hunched over a snow shovel, pushing the heavy wet snow to the edge of the driveway. It was six a.m. and Quincy and I were shivering in the doorway. The breeze caught the hem of my bathrobe, sending an icy blast right through me.

"Louisa!" I hollered again; she hadn't heard me the first time. And tightened my grip on Quincy's collar, he was quivering with excitement, determined to dash out into the front yard and fling himself into a snowbank. "Louisa, for the love of God, leave it for the snow removal guys. You're going to give yourself a heart attack."

She pulled off her toque and shook her hair loose, then tapped her shovel on its side to dislodge a clump of wet snow. "They sent an email," she yelled back. "They can't get here until after lunch." She lifted her hair off the nape of her neck and shoved her toque into her parka pocket. The air was cold but her face was red from exertion.

"Let it melt, then."

"It will flood the basement."

She had a point. The driveway slopes down to the attached garage. We'd had to tear the basement apart after The Great Flood. The prospect of ripping it out again didn't bear considering. "Wait, I'll get dressed and be right there."

"No need," Louisa said as she carved a path up the driveway. "I'm almost done."

I told Quincy we were going to make Louisa a hearty breakfast as a reward and we went back inside. "She deserves it, right?" I said to the dog who started bouncing around like a rubber ball when I lay the bacon strips into the frying pan.

Louisa is one of those strange people who, at the first sign of snow, grabs a shovel and rushes outside, tearing up and down the driveway like the Energizer bunny. You'd think she'd have had her fill of it last night after Sabine called to say her snow removal guys had come and gone, but the snow continued to fall all day and her driveway was impassable.

"Marc won't be back until nine or ten. Evie, I'm trapped in the house. It's horrible."

So we went to rescue her. It was dark when we pulled up in front of Sabine's place. Four inches of snow had settled lightly on the driveway.

"Pfff," Louisa said, "this is nothing, we'll be done in twenty minutes."

It took ten. As we sat around the kitchen table sipping *chocolat chaud* I asked Sabine what was going on with the McMansion. "It doesn't look like there's been any progress over there for weeks."

"Well." She leaned forward as if she was going to share a state secret. "Sidney Foster's money problems are finally resolved and the demolition men will be here tomorrow to knock the house down... unless it's too cold."

"Sabine, this is Calgary, it's never too cold to flatten a beautiful house and replace it with an ugly glass box."

An angry moan emanated from under the table. Sabine scooped up the cat and began to stroke its silky head and it began to purr; it sounded like a tiny engine revving.

"Let's not talk about that horrible house anymore," Sabine said with a pout. "I have wonderful news; the Ballet House will host the Prix de Lyon competition this fall."

"The competition you won back in 1975?" Louisa asked. "Sabine, that's fantastic."

"Shh." Sabine put a finger to her lips. "Don't jinx it. We are finalizing the details now. That horrible woman at the National Ballet wants the Prix for herself. Don't they have enough prizes and enough prestige? Everyone knows the National Ballet. Now it is our turn to be in the spotlight."

Sabine paused as if she'd had a flicker of doubt, then continued in a determined tone. "No, the Prix *will* come to us. They will dance on the stage at the Ballet House. The Prix committee loves Marc's design. Yes, they will definitely come."

I remembered Robert's words: Sabine would have been a world class dancer, as famous as Anna Pavlova or Margot Fonteyn, had she not left the Paris Opera Ballet to dedicate her life to Marc. Convincing the Prix to come to Calgary would be a tremendous boost to her reputation and her self esteem.

The spatter of frying bacon brought me back to reality, I was making breakfast for Louisa and the stove top was smeared with bacon grease. I resolved to stop daydreaming and focus on my task lest we have a repeat of the flaming toaster incident.

Louisa clattered into the foyer, sniffed the air and said, "Don't tell me you're making breakfast. You'll burn the house down."

Hands on hips I turned to face her and said, "Louisa, that was six years ago, drop it already."

The toast and eggs came out fine but the bacon was napalmed. Luckily Louisa likes it that way. She was crunching on a bacon strip when my phone pinged with a text. It was Marc asking me to check on Sabine over the next three days, he was going to Washington, DC on a business trip.

"Since when did you become Sabine's babysitter?" Louisa asked.

"Good question," I said and sent him a quick reply: Sure. She'll be fine.

And she was, but not for long.

CHAPTER TWENTY-FIVE

The next morning when I came downstairs, I found Louisa in the kitchen, humming as she pulled the egg carton out of the fridge. She cocked her head at the Scrabble game on the kitchen table and raised an eyebrow. A challenge.

"You're damn right we're playing again," I said. "Enjoy your day off, kiddo, because tonight I'm going to clobber you."

"You, my dear, are delusional." She laughed as she pulled the score sheet out of the box and made a show of studying it. "Let's see, last night you had a respectable 239 and I had, hmmm, what does it say here, 362. I shellacked you." She was chortling now. "For a lawyer you don't know many words."

"I know lots of words, I just don't know every conceivable combination of Q words, including those without a U." I glanced down at Quincy. "She's ridiculing me again. Are you going to let her get away with this?" He was unmoved. Clearly, I was on my own.

A graceful winner Louisa is not. That being said, neither am I. We've always been competitive. We played 'I'm the winna and still champ' with such intensity in elementary school that Mom threatened to ground us for life.

"Stop gloating," I said, reaching for my iPad to check the morning news. She was fiddling with a tin of dog food when my phone rang.

"Evie?" the voice was faint. "Evie?" In the background, the sound of crows and magpies. Harsh and raucous. They must be right on top of her.

"Sabine?"

Then a man's voice, rich, with an accent I couldn't place. "Hello?" He was panting.

"Who is this?" I demanded. Louisa heard the fear in my voice and set the dog food tin aside.

"Vincent," he said, "Vincent Bonnard. The asbestos guy from next door."

I shot a worried glance at Louisa. She whispered, "Is everything all right?"

Vincent spoke quickly, his accent making him hard to understand, but one thing was clear. Everything was not all right. Far from it.

"I'm coming," I said. "I'll be right there." And hung up.

"Evie, what's happening?"

"Sabine's been hurt." I slipped my phone in my pocket and hurried out to the hall closet, pulling my jacket off a hanger and fishing around in a jumble of boots for my Doc Martins. "Vincent's there—look, I can't talk now, I'll call you when I get there."

"No." She slipped into her jacket and grabbed her car keys from the green bowl on the table in the foyer. "I'm coming with you. I'll drive."

It's pointless arguing with Louisa once she's made up her mind. I grabbed my wallet, patted my pockets to ensure I had my phone and followed her downstairs to the car.

The engine coughed a couple of times when she gunned it up the driveway, then settled into a steady purr as we raced through the chill dark morning to Sabine's place.

The moon was still up, full and bright in the morning sky. It would have made a splendid photo on any day but today. Louisa was wearing her 'nurse' face, ready to deal with this emergency without becoming so emotionally involved that she couldn't function. She turned up Sabine's street and we skidded to a bumpy stop in front of her house.

"Why aren't the streetlights on?" she grumbled. In the predawn light the gutted Georgian manor next door loomed large but insubstantial like a shadow.

A blue van, likely Vincent's, was parked out front but there was no sign of the man. We'd barely mounted the short front steps when we heard the music, a blast of opera, something Italian, pulsating on the other side of the front door.

"What the hell is going on?" Louisa asked as I pressed the doorbell which pealed unanswered. "She'll never hear us over that racket."

Louisa thumped on the door with her fist while I studied the keypad. Sabine was furious when Marc installed it, refusing to memorize yet another *stupide* passcode. What code would she have chosen? Something simple and easy to remember. I glanced at the house number and punched four digits into the keypad. The door clicked open, we were in.

"Alexa, turn off music," Louisa yelled. Alexa said she didn't understand, and Louisa moved deeper into the kitchen, repeating her command. Finally the racket stopped. I looked around. Where were they?

Louisa ran down the hall to check the bedrooms and I took the stairs two at a time down to the basement. Nothing.

Louisa was in the kitchen when I returned.

"I found the cat," she said, "Jasmine's locked up in the study. But there's no one here."

Something creaked in the living room. We found the French doors ajar and ran outside, tearing across the terrace and into the garden frantically shouting Sabine's name.

"Here!" A deep voice. Vincent. He was in the shadow of the giant mountain ash. His coat was off, draped over Sabine who was lying motionless on the cold hard ground. "I didn't know if I should move her." He looked frightened and helpless.

Sabine mumbled and tossed her head from side to side. She was very pale and her hair was loose and matted with blood and snow. Overhead the crows shrieked and swooped.

"Jesus," Louisa said as she touched Sabine's throat and ran her hands down Sabine's arms and legs. "Looks like nothing is broken. What the hell happened?"

"I don't know." Vincent looked up at the crows. "I found her in the alley, covered in blood, crying." His breath shuddered in his chest. "I don't know."

"Evie," Louisa's tone was firm, "we have to get her to the hospital."

"I'll call an ambulance."

"No, it'll take too long." This was true, people have been stranded, some almost died, waiting for an ambulance to arrive. It would be faster if we took her in ourselves.

Effortlessly, Vincent scooped Sabine into his arms, she was so light and frail, and strode back into the house, through the living room and out the front door.

"Vincent." Louisa ran past him in the driveway. "We're taking my car." She unlocked the doors. Vincent slipped into the backseat, cradling Sabine in his arms. Her head flopped as he jostled her trying to tuck his jacket around her body to keep her warm.

———

We got lucky. We reached the Foothills Hospital just before seven o'clock and while the ER was busy, it wasn't insanely busy, and they bundled Sabine into a wheelchair and rolled her down the hall to an examining room.

"I'm a nurse," Louisa barked, in full nurse-mode now. "I'm going in with her." The ER nurse nodded, who was she to argue.

As they disappeared down a wide corridor, the noise level in the waiting room increased. All it took was ten minutes before it turned into Grand Central Station. People flooded through the doors, dishevelled, hacking and coughing, wearily passing their health care cards to the intake clerk, then turning around and trudging back to the chairs where they would wait listlessly until someone called them into the back, where they'd wait some more.

I motioned to Vincent that there were chairs at the far end of the room and we parked ourselves in the corner. His dark brown eyes were bloodshot and his face was ashy gray.

"Vincent? What happened?"

He rubbed his eyes with thick calloused fingers. "I don't know. I knocked, but she didn't answer the door. The music was so loud I thought she couldn't hear me and I went around to the back." He stopped, his eyes crinkling with a memory. "She's such a kind woman. She used to come over when we were working next door. She'd bring us little sandwiches and hot chocolate at teatime."

I nodded; knowing Sabine she'd be pumping them for information about the McMansion.

"The crows were screaming and the back gate was wide open." He paused, running one hand through his closely cropped grey hair. "She was in the alley, the birds were swirling around her, diving at her head, clawing at her hair." His voice trailed off. "I've never seen anything like it."

"Why would they attack her? She likes them. She feeds them. Christ, she's even given them names. Vincent, are you certain? It was early, still dark—"

"There was the moon. A big, white moon." Vincent glanced up as if expecting to find the moon hanging in the corner of the room like a lamp. "She was carrying a dead crow in her arms. The others were mobbing her, like they wanted it back."

I recoiled. "She'd never hurt them. I don't understand."

Vincent sagged in his seat, the rough fingers of one hand massaging the top of the other. Overhead the sound system called out a doctor's name. The wait time displayed on the monitor was three hours and thirteen minutes. A few years ago that would have been unacceptable, but now it was commonplace. *No.* My mother's voice rang in my ear. *Don't get used to it. Demand better.*

Ninety minutes later Louisa strode back into the waiting area, glancing around until she found us huddled in the far corner under the harsh neon lights.

"How is she?" I asked.

"They think she'll be okay, but they want to run some tests." Louisa was talking a little louder than normal as if we were elderly or hard of hearing, still in nurse mode. "She's in shock. She's not making much sense; it doesn't help that she's babbling in French." Louisa touched Vincent's arm. "Can you come back with me? My French is good, but not when it comes to medical terms."

He jumped up and followed Louisa back to the

examination room. A ripple of irritation ran through the crowd. *Why are they going back? We're sick too.*

My head buzzed. I wanted to go home. Quincy would be starving, we'd raced out the door without feeding him, but I couldn't leave. And that's when it occurred to me that no one had told Marc his wife was in hospital.

It was ten a.m. here, that's noon in Washington, DC. With any luck I'd catch him having lunch with a client or something. My call went to voice mail. I tried his cell again. Same thing. I'd been calm all morning, but suddenly I was frantic. Marc had to be told. I called the hotel and asked to be put through to his room.

The hotel phone rang once, twice, three times. Then clattered against the nightstand as it was picked up.

"Hello?" A silky voice answered.

Not Marc.

CHAPTER TWENTY-SIX

My first thought was the front desk had connected me to the wrong room. "I'm so sorry, I'm trying to reach Marc, Marc Hubert, I must have—"

The velvety voice faded as she turned away from the receiver. "Marc, it's for you." There was soft rustling in the background as the phone changed hands. I could picture the room in my mind's eye. Opulent, with tall windows, the drapes tightly drawn against the bright DC sky, a king-sized bed covered with plump, white pillows, the fine Egyptian sheets in wild disarray. Christ, how many mistresses does this man have?

"Hello?" Marc's tone was light, unconcerned.

"It's Evie. Sabine's in the hospital. We're here in ER waiting for test results."

"*What?*" Marc fired off a barrage of questions giving me no time to respond. "It's the demolition, the noise and the trucks, they've upset her. I should never have left her there to face it alone."

"Demolition? No, the McMansion is still standing."

In the background music played softly. The woman asked what was going on.

"Quiet." Marc's tone was harsh. She didn't say another word.

It took five minutes to explain what had happened—not that any of us really knew—and Marc said he'd catch the next flight out of DC. "Keep me posted. Text or call my cell anytime."

He hung up, leaving me staring at my phone, who was that woman? Gradually I became aware of the young man sitting in the plastic chair beside me. A young woman was hovering over him, her arms folded across her chest, her eyes darting anxiously around the waiting room. The young man was hunched over, cradling his arm in his lap. His right hand was so swollen it looked like a football with fingers. He caught my gaze and said with a goofy smile, "I fell off the roof."

The young woman glanced at me, shaking her head. "This idiot was shovelling snow off the roof, don't ask me why, and fell off and landed on his hand." She sounded furious but I knew her anger masked her fear. He shrugged with a helpless puppy dog look on his face. Her eyes softened and she said, "Won't be long now, hon."

"Here, take my seat," I said to her. She protested at first, then bobbed her head, thanks, and sat down beside her partner, sliding her arm across his shoulders and giving him a quick side-hug.

I moved across the room to the opposite wall and stared at the public health posters. It was flu season, were all my vaccinations up to date?

Was there a vaccine for Sabine to protect her from a broken heart? To inoculate her from the pain caused by her philandering husband? *Damn it, Marc. How could you?*

By the time Louisa and Vincent returned from the examining room I was so angry I could barely speak. The doctors decided to keep Sabine in for a couple of days, just to be on the safe side. She'd suffered multiple lacerations in the bird attack.

"She's lucky she didn't lose an eye," Louisa said. "The scratches are treatable, but she was outside in the cold for a while and at her age"—my mind recoiled at the thought of the Black Swan being labelled anything but strong and vibrant—"she's not a resilient as she used to be. They want to make sure she doesn't catch pneumonia."

We walked back to the car in silence, each lost in our own thoughts. I resolved to keep the fact Marc had a lover in DC to myself.

As Louisa backed the car out of the parking stall she caught Vincent's eye in her rearview mirror. "Vincent, we can give you a lift home if you'd prefer not to drive." He looked pretty rattled to me too. He'd found Sabine around six-thirty, it was now well past noon, but he brushed off Louisa's concerns.

We swung onto Crowchild and headed into Marda Loop. I shifted around in the front seat to see Vincent better. Curious, I asked him what he'd been doing at Sabine's place so early in the morning.

He glanced out the window not meeting my eye. "I wanted to talk to her about Luke."

I nodded, AJ and I had met Vincent's nephew the night we'd taken Sabine to the town hall meeting. Taller and leaner than his uncle, with grey-green eyes and a lighter complexion.

"Luke used to work for Marc," Vincent explained, "then he got himself fired. I thought maybe Sabine could put in a good word and get Marc to give Luke his job back."

"At six-thirty in the morning?" I sounded skeptical and Vincent shifted awkwardly in his seat.

"I was heading out to another job," he replied. "It was on the way and I had a few minutes to spare. But then the ruckus with the crows started..."

There was a long silence. The image of Sabine limp on the ground was still sharp in my mind.

Louisa had entered Mount Royal and was winding her way deeper into the Estate District. "Is Luke an architect?" she asked.

Vincent brightened as he talked about his nephew. Luke was a junior architect. He'd been with Marc for two years. "He's put in his time in the back room designing fiddly details. Those big firms never let the young guys work directly with the clients. Not at the beginning at any rate. Luke was so excited to be put on the Ballet House project."

Here he paused, staring out the window at the houses hidden behind great stone walls and tall hedges. "The promotion made him cocky. Luke's a smart kid, too smart for his own good sometimes. My sister—she's in Martinique—says take care of my boy, tone him down." Vincent chuckled softly. "He's like his mother; they don't have a tone-it-down button."

He cleared his throat. "The boy is still young. He has to learn how to play the game. There's a time to speak up and a time to hold your tongue. He yapped off to the project manager and his big mouth got him fired."

I stopped fiddling with the heater button—on our way to the hospital the car had been an ice box, now it was an oven—and turned my full attention to Vincent. "Really? What did Luke say that got him fired? Specifically."

Immediately Vincent became guarded. "You're asking the wrong guy. I'm just a labourer, half the things Luke said flew right over my head. You'd have to ask him."

"That's a good idea, where can I reach him?"

Vincent spotted his decrepit blue van. "Louisa, thanks, you can put me out here."

She pulled up behind his vehicle, he clicked open his seatbelt and was out the door before Louisa rolled to a full stop. He popped his head back inside and said, "I'll let Luke know you're looking for him."

As he made his way across the icy road and slid behind the wheel of the van, Louisa glanced at me and said, "Get the feeling you'll never hear from Vincent or Luke again?"

CHAPTER TWENTY-SEVEN

Louisa shivered behind me while I punched Sabine's house number into the keypad. I'd barely gotten the door open when we heard an ungodly howl. Poor Jasmine was still trapped in the study. When I opened the door the cat shot out and wrapped herself around my ankle, purring and growling at the same time.

"You are one weird cat; do you know that?" I peeled her off my pantleg and passed her dangling body over to Louisa. "Feed her, will you? I'll get Sabine's things." I'd agreed to run back to the hospital with some fresh clothes and toiletries.

While Louisa talked to the cat asking her what she preferred for breakfast, chicken or tuna, I went down the hall to the master bedroom and rifled through the long dresser opposite the bed. "Don't forget her meds," I yelled over my shoulder as I flung silky underwear and an ivory nightgown and matching robe onto the king-sized bed.

"Who's? Sabine's or the cat's?"

"The cat's; I've got Sabine's meds here." I was in the master bathroom now. A large, marble enclosed space as big as my office with an elegant white spoon-shaped bathtub and one of those modern shower heads that stick out of the wall with no glass enclosure or anything to keep the water from spraying all over the bathroom. Hence the white Carrara marble running from floor to ceiling.

It wasn't until I was pawing through the drawers under the softly illuminated bathroom mirror in search of Sabine's hairbrush that I realized something was missing. There was no trace of Marc. No medications, no luxury masculine scents, nothing, not even a toothbrush. Had he taken the whole kit and kaboodle with him to DC?

I returned to the giant closet in the master bedroom. Sabine's designer suits, beautifully tailored blouses and elegant gowns hung from padded wooden hangers; her shoes and purses were neatly arranged in a custom designed storage rack and her sweaters and scarfs were carefully folded on open wooden shelves. Again, no sign of Marc.

In the second, smaller bedroom at the front of the house, I found him. Everything Marc owned was on display in its own special place. Sabine and Marc may share a house, but they no longer shared a bedroom.

"So what," Louisa said, on our way home. "Lots of people have separate bedrooms. Kings and queens don't just have separate bedrooms, they have separate wings in the palace. Maybe Marc snores and Sabine booted him out so she wouldn't smother him with a pillow."

"Or maybe Marc doesn't want to wake her when he's sneaking back home after a tryst. That man is worse than a common alley cat."

"Evie, it's none of our business and don't you dare raise this with Sabine."

"Jeez, Louise, I'm not an idiot. It's not as if I'm going to sail into her hospital room and say, what's up with you and Marc having separate bedrooms."

"Promise?" Louisa said.

I promised, not because I wanted to spare Sabine's feelings but because if anyone had any explaining to do it was Marc, not Sabine.

———

A cheery woman in a wine-coloured smock carried a plastic tray into Sabine's hospital room and announced that since Sabine had missed breakfast *and* lunch, she could have a small snack before dinner. Sabine shot her a grateful smile and waited while the woman adjusted Sabine's tray table. I was on my hands and knees poking around beside Sabine's bed trying to find a socket for her phone charger. "Enjoy!" the woman said over her shoulder as she disappeared into the corridor.

"We will, thank you!" Sabine chirped back.

A patient was lurking just outside Sabine's room. He stopped the nurse who'd delivered the food, demanding to know where his snack was. She laughed and said, "Three more hours, Mr. Wilkinson, three more hours." I felt sorry for the poor man, other than code blues (crash cart) or code whites (violent person on the loose) mealtimes were the highlight of the hospital experience.

"Evie. Look at this." Like a queen who'd been served a bowl of gruel, Sabine poked her spoon at the beige mixture in a small bowl. "What do you think it is?" I plugged in her phone and set it on the tray table, it pinged as it loaded her texts.

"Hardy oatmeal," I said, reading from the slip of paper half covered by a small plate of cold toast. "Here, start with coffee."

Sabine always takes her coffee black; she lifted the cup

to her nose, sniffed and reached for the creamer pods. She stared out the window as her spoon went round and round, turning her coffee a strange beige-grey colour. The steri-strips above her right eye tugged on the alabaster skin at her temple. Her forehead was a mottled purply blue. I couldn't see the damage to her forearm which was swathed in gauze bandages.

"Sabine, I don't want to push you, but can you tell me what happened?"

She set her mug down and started to pick at her toast, tearing off small pieces and popping them into her mouth. Her lips were dry and I made a mental note to bring some lip balm on my next visit.

"The doctors asked me the same thing," she said with a soft sigh. "I wish I knew, but I can't remember."

"Do you remember talking to Vincent?"

For a moment she looked puzzled, then she nodded. "Oh, that's right. He was there, wasn't he. How strange."

I was debating whether to ask her about the dead crow when her phone pinged with a text. She glanced at it and her face fell. "Oh dear. Marc can't get a flight until tomorrow morning."

It was uncharitable of me, but my first thought was he wanted to squeeze in one last hedonistic night with his lady friend in his lavish hotel room.

"Who will feed Jasmine? Is she all right?"

"Louisa and I fed her this morning. She won't starve."

"She's very fat, I know. Evie, would you stop by the house tomorrow and feed her breakfast. Marc says he's going to come straight to the hospital after he lands."

"Of course," I said.

And that's how I discovered why the crows attacked Sabine.

CHAPTER TWENTY-EIGHT

The next morning the Mini picked its way past the heavy trucks rumbling into position on Sabine's street. A guy wearing wraparound sunglasses and a ball cap was talking to a man leaning out the window of a truck which was hauling a large yellow excavator. The truck driver watched me pull into Sabine's driveway and said something to the guy wearing sunglasses as I got out of the car.

Sunglasses Guy turned around, he had a short stubble beard and was younger than I expected. He extended his hand and said his name was Levi, was there anything he could help me with. I explained I'd be in the house for a little while and didn't want them to trap me in the driveway.

"No problem." Levi glanced back up at the man in the truck. "We can't start till the boss gets here." He stared at the wreck of the Georgian manor and mumbled something about permits.

"Out of curiosity." I asked, "how long will it take to demolish the house?" With any luck it would be gone before Sabine got home.

The guy in the cab pulled a pack of cigarettes out of his shirt pocket. "Two to three hours, give or take." He narrowed his eyes as he flicked his lighter, a thin trail of smoke curled out of the window.

"Are you doing the honours?" I asked.

He laughed. "You bet."

"Three hours isn't long. How can you get it down so fast?"

"Nothing to it." The cab door creaked open and he climbed out and pointed at the stained wreck of a house. "I start with the roof, then move down to the walls. Rip them up and punch them into the middle of the house. The basement acts like a big bowl. You gotta tamp it down real good, mulch the big pieces till they're nothing but matchsticks. That way you're not transporting air to the dump. Saves you money. It's the clean up that takes time, you gotta break up the foundation, chop down the trees and cart it all away."

Levi said, "Kenny's a pro. After he's done mopping up a house, you'd never even know it was there."

I bit my lip, what was once a splendid house would soon be nothing but scraps of wood rotting in the municipal dump.

—◆—

Jasmine curled around my legs, whining pitifully as I read the labels in Sabine's gigantic refrigerator. Glass containers with pink and blue plastic lids filled the shelves, packed with the remnants of pork ragù and nasi goreng. Sabine, like Louisa, liked to cook. However, unlike Louisa, or me for that matter, Sabine does not like to eat, consequently half the stuff she cooks ends up in the cat dish or the compost bin.

"I don't know, Jasmine, this is pretty ritzy food for a cat."

Jasmine disagreed. Everything in the fridge was cat food as far as she was concerned. After I nudged her out of the way with my foot, she disappeared into the living room and I continued rummaging in the pantry until I found a tin with a fat white cat on the label. I was rooting around in a drawer for a can opener when I heard an eerie moan that raised the hairs on the back of my neck.

I found Jasmine dancing in front of the French doors overlooking the terrace. Her back was arched and her puffy tail was twice its size. She hissed and yowled in a way that sent shivers down my spine.

"Jasmine, what is it?"

The cat glared at me. Her eyes were round and black, her teeth were bared. That fat tail swished from side to side. I peered through the French windows. It was just after seven a.m. and the vapid sun barely illuminated the gloomy corners of the garden. Cupping my hands against the glass I searched the shadows. "I don't—"

Whap! The window shuddered in its frame.

I leapt backwards. Jasmine rose on her hind legs, pawing at the glass. Something dark lay still on the flagstones.

Then the backyard erupted. Dozens of crows flew up out of the mountain ash, flying directly at us before pulling up at the last minute to alight on the eaves trough or circle back to the mountain ash. They shrieked, wheeling and swooping, trying to drive us away from the glass. A huge crow fluttered down to the flagstones, standing guard over the dazed bird lying motionless on the stone. Mobbing. It's how crows drive away predators.

Jasmine turned and like an undignified puffball, retreated to the kitchen.

"Good idea," I said, following behind her, "You'd be nuts to go out there."

I plopped four heaping spoonfuls of chicken and liver into her bowl. The tag on her collar made a delicate ringing sound as it struck the metal rim. Outside the crows nattered and clicked, as if they were plotting to kill us both.

While Jasmine picked at her breakfast I returned to the living room. The dazed bird had disappeared. As I peered through the window I heard a rhythmic thumping sound. I cracked open the French doors, straining to hear. The back gate was open. It banged softly in the breeze. I hesitated. Dare I run out and close it? I couldn't very well leave it open. This is an expensive neighbourhood, the last thing Sabine needed was to be vandalized.

"Jasmine, stay here." *Why was I talking to the cat?*

The mountain ash was packed with huge black crows, maybe twenty of them, fluttering around, making the tree heave as if it were alive. They shrieked a warning when I stepped out onto the terrace.

"It's okay," I said, with faltering confidence. "Nothing to see here, just a lady going for a walk in her garden."

When I was in high school, a guy working on his Ph.D hired me to count the number of eggs the Cinnabar moth lays on the underside of a ragwort leaf. It wasn't a bad job, it got me outside in the fresh air, I was unsupervised and had plenty of time to daydream. There was just one snag, the moths shared their fields with a herd of cows.

One day I was crossing a pasture and the cows went crazy. They formed a ring around me, circling closer and closer. I was terrified and yelled and cursed and shook my butterfly net at them to keep them at bay. I'd just thrown myself over the fence on the other side when the Ph.D student appeared and said Holsteins were a docile breed and I'd been perfectly safe the whole time. "Perhaps," I replied, "but better safe than sorry."

Better safe than sorry. Sabine's face and hands were scratched and gouged. The crows knew her and mobbed her anyway. They never forget a face, but I'd never harmed them. They won't hurt me.

"Hey crows." My voice wavered a bit. "Nice morning, eh?" The excavator out front rumbled to life. "Hey crows, they're demolishing the house next door. Isn't that cool?"

The crows fluttered, restless in the treetops. Two sailed down to the ground, mincing about in front of me before letting me pass.

I made it all the way to the back gate before I heard a harsh caw. It was a signal. They rose up, high out of the treetops, then plummeted down, fast and hard. One flew so close to my face the tip of its wing brushed my cheek.

That's when I lost it.

Screaming, I charged through the gate and collided with a someone hunched over Sabine's trash bin. The air whooshed out of him as he staggered backwards, his crumpled overcoat snagging on his rickety shopping cart, almost dragging it over. Small and slight, his oversized boots were tied with twine. The glass bottles in his hands clattered into his cart. He whipped a tattered black umbrella off his arm, flapping furiously. The crows squawked and pulled up. Soaring up to the telephone wires, enraged.

I released the man's jacket; I didn't recall grabbing it and pulled myself up straight. Despite my tailored navy suit and stylish leather boots, I must have looked as wild-eyed as he did.

He hooked his umbrella back over his arm and said, "From now on wear a mask. Balaclavas are good. They never forget the face of someone who mistreats them."

He turned back to Sabine's bin and continued rooting

around, pushing aside stuff he didn't want. "What did you do to them?"

"Nothing. I don't even live here."

He looked unconvinced. Puffing out his cheeks he said, "Well, you did something. They won't go after someone without provocation. Not outside of nesting season at any rate... and what do we have here?"

Poking out from under an old take-out box was a broken black wing. With an angry sniff he slipped the tip of the umbrella under the bird until we could see it, or what was left of it. Twisted wings and a crushed head, dark with dried blood.

"What did I tell you? There's a killer loose in the neighbourhood."

By the time I returned to my car, the excavator was chewing a path across the McMansion's snowy lawn. My hands shook on the steering wheel. Overhead, the crows wheeled in great black circles against the blank white sky. The bucket at the end of the boom jerked up, then crashed through the roof, tearing into the attic and down through the living room wall like a dinosaur chewing through cardboard. The house would be obliterated by lunch.

CHAPTER TWENTY-NINE

Crazy images filled my head on the drive back to the office. Crows attacking Sabine like a scene from a Hitchcock movie. Marc in bed with his DC paramour. The Ballet House poisoning the river ecosystem. And there was something off with AJ. It felt like the world had gone mad.

I needed to talk to someone. I needed Keith.

Bridget took one look at me and declared I looked like I'd been dragged through a hedge backwards.

"Yeah, well, being attacked by crows and colliding with a bottle picker will do that to you," I said, patting my hair into place. Which made it even more flyaway.

Horrified, she rushed out from behind her desk. "I've warned her and warned her," she scolded, plucking a small twig out of my hair. "The more she feeds them the more aggressive they become."

It took me a moment to realize she was referring to Madeline, not Sabine.

"It wasn't Madeline," I said.

"What wasn't Madeline?" Madeline asked as she strolled down the hall. "Christ, what happened to you?"

They hustled me into the bathroom arguing about what

to do next. Bridget thought a trip to the ER was warranted, just to be on the safe side, and Madeline wanted to call Animal Control, or better yet the police, so they could interrogate everyone on the block until this crow killing monster was apprehended.

"I'm fine," I said, irritably. "Would everyone just stand down?" I marched back to my office and hid behind my monitor.

"You okay?" Keith stopped at my door.

"Just the man I wanted to see." I waved him in. He sat quietly as I poured out my worries about Sabine, the Ballet House and AJ. Most importantly AJ. "Does he seem distracted to you?"

"No," Keith replied. "Not particularly."

"You never notice anything around here." That was petty of me, but I was cranky.

"I've been a little preoccupied."

"Oh, is the baby goat sick again?"

"What? No. It's Wendy." That was Keith's artist wife. "She's got a show at The Painted Moose in two weeks"—that was a small gallery in Bragg Creek—"there are paintings all over the house. 'One last push,' she says. Until then Claire and I are on our own." He shot me a lopsided grin. "Hockey practice and Brownies. That kid's got way too much on the go."

As he described the latest snafu—Claire had misplaced her goalie mask—I was struck by the contrast between Keith and Marc. Keith was willing to turn his life upside down to accommodate Wendy's dreams, while Marc sacrificed Sabine's future in service of his own.

There was a cough in my doorway. "So," Madeline said, "what's in Sabine's closet." Keith hopped up with that 'oh-oh girl talk' look on his face and with a grand sweep of his hand indicated Madeline should make herself comfortable in his chair.

"It's all designer clothes straight from the runways of Paris and New York, right?" Madeline is a clothes horse (and a snoop) so her question wasn't a surprise.

"I can tell you what's not in Sabine's closet," I replied. "Marc's stuff. It's all in the guest room, neatly hung in the closet or folded in a big walnut dresser. And his fancy soaps and little black bottles of Creed, they're tucked away in the guest bathroom."

With a dismissive wave of her hand she said that apart from a few hours here and there, sharing your bed, let alone your closet, with a man was barbaric. "You know my rule, they can visit but they can't stay."

Madeline is a harsh mistress in every sense of the word.

CHAPTER THIRTY

Is it an unwritten rule that hospital elevators must move at a snail's pace and at least one must be out of service at all times? Ten of us civilians and a couple of staffers in wine-coloured smocks milled about in the main lobby, staring at the lights blinking over each elevator and shuffling left or right trying to second guess which one would reach the ground first. Mine got stuck on the third floor and I edged over to join the others who'd bet on car number four.

Visiting hours were almost over but I wanted to check on Sabine. Marc was supposed to get in today but had texted to say he'd missed the flight and couldn't get back until tomorrow. Again I cursed his lady friend. They were probably up to their eyebrows in a scented bath guzzling champagne and oysters at this very moment.

At last, the elevator arrived and we surged in, practically trampling the poor sods trying to exit.

On the sixth floor the elevator doors clanged open and that peculiar hospital smell intensified. I stopped to get my bearings. Every floor looked the same to me, green walls, speckled white rolled linoleum floors and unhelpful signs pointing every which way.

I heard Sabine's laughter echoing down the corridor long before I found her room. She was chatting with Robert, the percussionist. He glanced up when I said hello, eyes sparkling behind his Harry Potter glasses.

Sabine's hair was pulled back in a tight bun, exposing the steri-strips on her temple. Her arm was still tightly wrapped in gauze. Even without makeup, the Black Swan was beautiful, perhaps more so now because nothing detracted from her luminous eyes and her magnificent cheek bones.

"Evie." She greeted me with a radiant smile and waved me into the room. "You must hear this. Robert, tell it again." It occurred to me that I hadn't seen her look this joyful in months.

A nurse popped her head in the door as I took a seat on the other side of the bed. "Sabine," she scolded, "I've told you before, you must keep it down."

Robert looked sheepish and Sabine offered the nurse a piece of chocolate. "It's good for your health." The nurse raised an eyebrow. "It's true, I have a square every night, but it must be of the highest quality."

The nurse shook her head at us and left. Playfully, Sabine slapped Robert's arm. "You're going to get me thrown out!" The look of contrition on his face was comically insincere.

For thirty minutes Robert entertained us with tales worthy of Scheherazade; there was the time they were performing Mahler and a fellow timpanist, a big roly-poly guy—"Jocko, Sabine, you remember him"—left the stage to set off the cannons. He tripped over a cable and fell flat on his face, right there in full view of the audience. Then he tripped over the same cable coming back. The audience could barely contain itself. "They gave us a terrific round of applause at the end, it was only later I realized they were clapping for Jocko for having survived his pratfalls.

"Sabine, remember last year when the dress code changed? The busybodies flooded administration with complaints"—Robert raised his voice to a falsetto—"'I come to the Philharmonic to hear the music not to see the violinists flash their ankles.'"

Laughing, Sabine passed him a plastic cup. He reached into his bag and pulled out a bottle of sparkling water—none of this hospital tap water for Sabine—and topped her up.

Robert slipped the bottle back into his bag and reminisced about life before he joined the Symphony full time. "One of the best gigs I ever had was with an oompah band over Octoberfest. I made more money in one week than I did in six months waiting tables."

When the nurse returned to shoo us out. Robert gave Sabine a delicate peck on the cheek and held her hands, promising to return tomorrow. I hugged her frail shoulders and caught up with Robert by the elevators.

He let out a long breath and stared bleakly into space. The neon lights overhead carved great hollows under his eyes. We waited in silence as an old man shuffled past pushing an IV pole, his slippers slapping the hard lino floor as he tottered around the corner.

Finally I couldn't take the silence. "Have you known Sabine long?" I asked.

When he glanced at me, his eyes were damp as if he was on the verge of tears.

Taken aback I said, "I'm sure she'll be fine. They're just keeping her in for observation. She was in pretty rough shape when we brought her in. You know, dehydration and exposure, and the scratches where the birds..." The crow attack was too horrible to think about.

He made a face, more of disgust than concern, and said, "Of course she'll be fine. No thanks to her damned husband. If Marc gave a fig for Sabine, he'd be here with her, not galivanting around the world with some floozy."

Good Lord, does everyone know? The elevator bell dinged and a small mob of people emerged, chattering past us as if we weren't even there.

"A floozy?" I kept my voice light as I punched the elevator button to the main floor.

He flicked his eyes at me and said, "Come on, everyone knows the score. Marc has women all over the place. A woman in every port, right? He considers it a perk of the job."

"And she knows?" Why did I ask that?

He shook his head at me as if I were a simpleton. "Of course she knows, but she pretends not to know." He stared at the flashing lights over the door. "She can't stay with him. He's killing her."

The elevator lurched to a stop on the main floor, the doors took an interminably long time to open. It wasn't until I was in the Mini heading home that I realized Sabine had not mentioned Marc. Not once.

CHAPTER THIRTY-ONE

"Has he fixed any of the outstanding items on the Sin List; or at least made a start?" I asked.

"Who, Marc?" AJ was lolling in my visitor's chair. He's used to my non sequiturs. Which become more frequent as the day winds down.

"Who else? He assured us he'd take care of it, but I haven't seen any updated reports, have you?"

"No, but—"

"We have to do something. He's driving me crazy." Although if I were completely honest, I was just as upset about Marc's shoddy treatment of Sabine as I was about his failure to rectify the Sin List.

AJ crossed his arms. "Look, I want to protect the river ecosystem as much as you do but I'm afraid we're running out of options. There's nothing more we can do."

I sat back and looked at him. "Don't tell me you're giving up. Weren't you an eco-warrior in your day?" The minute I said it, I regretted it.

His face tightened. "If you're going to smear my character, I suggest you get in line behind Grizzly and Sam."

I mumbled an apology. He was right, it was an unfair

jibe. Lawyers can't violate their obligation to keep a client's affairs confidential just because they don't like what the client is doing. There had to be another way. If we could just get more information...

"He can run but he can't hide."

"Marc?" AJ asked.

"No, Luke. Vincent said he'd get Luke to contact me. Luke works at the Atelier, or he did until Marc fired him off the Ballet House job."

"Ah, the disgruntled employee angle. How do we find him?"

"Leave it with me."

They can run but they can't hide... not from me because I have Bridget. That woman is a bloodhound. I caught her in the lobby slipping on her boots. She was heading home.

"Consider it done," she said after I explained what I wanted. Bridget's network of admin assistants and PAs was legendary so it came as no surprise that she was good friends with Barbara Major.

The Major (as she's called behind her back, never to her face) was the last person you'd expect to find working for an artsy type like Marc Hubert. Unlike the other pretty young things scattered about the Atelier, the Major was a starchy, old-school secretary, a throwback to the 1950s. She kept Marc's calendar with military precision and knew exactly where he was and what he was doing at any time of the day or night. Which meant the Major was very discrete.

Normally she wouldn't give out any information about one of Marc's former employees, privacy and confidentiality concerns and all that, but the Major owed Bridget a favour.

Ten minutes later Bridget stood in my doorway, her face was as pale as the white hand knit scarf wrapped around her neck. "Well, um, that was interesting."

"What did Barbara Major say?"

"A lot." Bridget made herself comfortable across from me and handed me a slip of paper. Luke's contact information. "More than a lot."

I raised my eyebrows.

"Marc fired Luke…" Two spots of colour appeared on Bridget's cheeks. She's so capable sometimes I forget she's still a small-town girl at heart. Whatever Barbara had told her was making her very uncomfortable. "So Marc fired Luke…"

"Yes, Bridget, I got that. Did she say why?" Vincent characterized Luke as bright and competent but prone to shooting off his mouth. What had he said to get himself fired? "Was he complaining about the Ballet House?"

"He was." Bridget fiddled with the button of her winter coat. "But that's not the only reason why Luke was fired." Bridget glanced at me and it all came out in a rush. "Barbara said Marc discovered Luke was dating his daughter and told him to end it. When Luke refused to dump her Marc terminated his employment."

"*Daughter?* What daughter, Marc and Sabine don't have any kids."

That's when Madeline sailed through my door. That woman has an uncanny sense of timing. Toss out a piece of salacious gossip and Madeline on it like a ravenous beast.

She sat down beside Bridget and said, "You're talking about Alice, right? Marc's daughter by Diana Barros."

I pressed my fingertips to my temples and began to move them in a small circular motion. "Who on earth are Diana Barros and Alice? Madeline, why didn't you tell me about them before?"

Madeline shot me a cool glance, then casually crossed

one leg over the other. She wasn't happy with my tone. I gave her a small apologetic smile and waited.

"Well," she said, her eyes shining, "twenty or so years ago"—that would be around the time my mother met Sabine—"Marc fell madly in love with a young female architect working at his firm, a stunning petite blonde."

"She sounds like the polar opposite to Sabine."

Madeline nodded. "Oh, the scandal when Marc got one of his employees pregnant. It rocked the city. Back then we were such a parochial little town, we still are to some degree. Then to make matters worse, Diana insisted on keeping the baby. I have to hand it to Marc, he may be a cad, but he did the right thing."

I glanced at Bridget whose eyes were huge and round.

"He promised to care for Diana and the baby until the child became an adult. Diana left the firm, obviously, and had the baby. Eventually she started her own firm, specializing in restaurant design. Much to everyone's surprise, Marc adored baby Alice and maintains a close relationship with her to this day."

My mind went back to the Marsalis concert. "Alice is a petite blonde with a pixie cut, right? "

Madeline nodded.

"Why didn't you tell me this when I told you Louisa and I had seen Marc with another woman at the Symphony?"

Madeline raised an eyebrow and said, "You asked about Marc's *mistresses*. As in does he have any that fit that description and he doesn't, at least not in this town. If you'd asked me whether Marc had a daughter that would have been an entirely different conversation. Really Evie, you're a lawyer, you of all people know the importance of being specific."

"Oh my goodness." Bridget tugged at her wool scarf,

pulling it away from her neck as if she were overheating. "Marc has an illegitimate daughter. Does Sabine know?"

"Bridget," I said, "that's not how we talk about these relationships anymore."

"Of course she knows," Madeline replied. "They're French. It's all good as long as everyone is discrete and Sabine is not forced to publicly acknowledge Alice."

———————

Later that evening as Louisa and I walked Quincy, I asked her about Sabine. "She looked good last night, why won't they let her come home? Surely her GP can monitor the scratches on her face and hands."

"Evie, I can't tell you anything specific, you know that, but in cases like this they worry about respiratory infection. Bird bites and scratches can cause bronchitis, pneumonia, or septicemia. It can be very serious."

Louisa tugged on Quincy's leash urging him to move along. He pulled his head out of a bush and stared at her, *one moment please.* The temperature was dropping and the cold air seeped into my puffer jacket. Quincy wasn't even my dog, yet here I was whipping a small green compostable bag out of my pocket while trying not to lose sight of my target in the dark.

The dog let out a sharp yip. He'd spotted something moving at the end of the street. Louisa hauled him back to the house and we scrambled through the front door with Quincy bouncing around like a wind-up toy until she unclipped his harness.

"The doctors could also be worried about hypothermia," Louisa continued. "No one knows how long she was outside in nothing but her nightgown. They'll keep her in hospital until they're confident she won't wander off again."

Wander off again? This was Sabine we were talking about. The Black Swan. A fierce, independent woman, not a pathetic little creature who can't be left unattended lest she wander into traffic.

"Louisa, something awful happened to her that day. It triggered the crows and drove her half-dressed out into the garden. Whatever it was, it's clouding her mind and causing her great distress—"

"Stop right there." Louisa was halfway to the kitchen when she spun around to face me. "Don't even think about it. Do not go poking your nose into this. Sabine needs medical attention and she's getting it. What she does not need is your well-intentioned but misguided interference."

With that she gruffly called Quincy and marched straight up to bed.

"Okay," I hollered after her. "No need to get your knickers in a knot. I get it."

And I did. For fourteen straight hours, until Sabine called.

CHAPTER THIRTY-TWO

Church bells chimed. Had I dreamt it? Outside my bedroom window, there was nothing but an icy black sky. The bells chimed again. My ringtone. Sabine. It was 6:03 in the morning.

With a small moan I rolled out of bed, picked up my phone and wandered out into the hall. Quincy raised his head; he was sprawled at the foot of Louisa's bed and watched me shuffle across the landing and downstairs to the kitchen. On the other side of the kitchen window the moon was suspended like a Christmas ornament, a shining silver crescent low on the horizon.

"Sabine, hi. Are they letting you out today?" I stifled a yawn. "The demo crew flattened the house next door. It might be completely gone by the time you get home. Won't that be nice?" Why was I talking to her in this silly sing song tone?

"Did they fence the mountain ash and the burning bushes next to the stone wall?" she asked in a small thin voice.

"Trust me," I said, pulling a coffee filter out of the cupboard and trying to pry the lid off the top of the coffee tin with one hand. "The crows won't let the demo guys come within two meters of your mountain ash. They almost took my head off the last time I was there." God, what a stupid thing to say.

"Last night I dreamed of crows. Something bad happened to Bijoux."

Bijoux? The broken black wing sticking up out of Sabine's trash bin? Was that Bijoux?

"Bijoux is fine. They're all just fine. They miss you, Sabine. They don't like strangers wandering around in your garden. When are you coming home?" Her response was lost when a loud, cheery voice said it was time for Mrs. Ariti's blood pressure reading. Sabine had a new roommate. The nurses were doing their rounds.

"Hold on." Sabine sounded hoarse. There was the sound of shuffling, then the loud squeak of a door hinge in need of oiling. "Evie, can you do something for me?" Her words echoed strangely; she must have locked herself in the bathroom.

My heart sank when she set out my task. Louisa warned me not to meddle.

"Sabine, shouldn't you be discussing your concerns with your doctors?"

She dismissed the suggestion out of hand. Morning rounds were over, the doctors had come and gone. She might see the hospitalist at the end of the day—if she was lucky. But her doctor wanted her to stay another day, maybe two. More tests and more bed rest.

The longer she talked, the more agitated she became, her voice ringing hollow in the cramped, tiled space. In her dream the night wind came and tore the Georgian manor apart. The roof flew up and turned into hundreds of screaming crows. A bird appeared in her arms, laying limp like a child. She fought to save its life but it was too late. When she awoke, her pillow was soaked with tears.

"Sabine, it was just a bad dream."

"Where's Marc?" she said. "I need Marc."

"His flight was delayed, remember. He's coming home today, this evening, and will drive straight to the hospital from the airport. He's dying to see you, Sabine. He'll be there by dinner time." *Assuming he's not spending another day with his velvety-voiced girlfriend.*

"Did I hurt them? I can't remember. Why would they attack me?"

"Oh Sabine." I imagined her curled up on the cold bathroom floor with her phone pressed against her ear. "Please listen to me. You would never hurt them. You know that."

In a voice so tight she could barely speak she begged me to go to the house, to check the basement and the garage.

I bit back my frustration. "Sabine, I don't even know what I'm looking for."

"Rat poison, vermin poison, anything like that."

I almost said we don't have rats in Alberta—supposedly the Rat Patrol turns them away at the border—it was as absurd as the suggestion that Sabine could hurt a living creature, but in the end I agreed. Louisa is going to kill me for playing along with Sabine's fantasy.

"Thank you." She said in a grateful whisper. The bathroom door squealed on its hinges once more and a gentle voice called Sabine back to her bed. The last thing I heard before her phone went dead was the clang of bedrails being raised.

It was noon by the time I made it over to Sabine's place. The sun was high and the musty smell of dust and decay hung heavy in the air. Next door, everything was quiet. The workers were gone, off to lunch likely, and the excavator, its boom curled like a scorpion's tail, hunched over the rubble. All that was left of the Georgian manor were broken bricks, splintered wood and jagged chunks of concrete heaped into a pile in the basement. It was a sobering sight. Even the crows were subdued, muttering to themselves in the bare branches of the mountain ash.

Feeling like an intruder, I tapped Sabine's code into the keypad and crept inside. Is it a break-in if one homeowner knows you're in their house but the other one doesn't?

"Hello?" I called out, Lord knows why, there was no one here. In the kitchen there was a thump as Jasmine dropped heavily down to the tiled floor and sashayed out to greet me. "You're not supposed to be on the counters, you silly cat." She purred loudly and tried to crawl into the cupboard under the kitchen sink while I peered inside. There was nothing there but cleaning supplies.

Jasmine followed me down to the basement, meowing as if we were playing a new game. Sabine's basement was very European. Empty but for a washer, dryer, and a very large drying rack on which she'd draped two fine knit sweaters. Jasmine flew past me, leapt high into the air and yanked the black one down to the floor pawing at it as if she were making a nest. "Jasmine! You're in so much trouble," I scolded as I pried her claws, one by one, out of the fabric and lugged her back upstairs.

We were standing at French doors looking out onto the terrace when three things happened at once. Something black fell out of the mountain ash and landed in the middle of the garden; I opened the door a crack to see what it was, and Jasmine shot outside.

The crows rose in a hysterical mass out of the tree and were on top of her in a flash. They swooped down from the treetops, bashing her with their wings and screeching with wide open beaks. There were so many I couldn't see her anymore.

"Shit!" The glass door crashed against the outside wall as I hurtled into the garden, waving my arms and screaming at the crows to leave Jasmine alone. The cat's eyes were huge, her ears flattened against her head. "Gotcha!" I scooped her into my arms, ignoring the prick of her claws and the screaming of the birds and raced back inside.

The crows chased us right up to the terrace. I flung Jasmine inside and flew in after her banging the door shut behind me. She crashed to the floor, landing on her side, then stalked down the hall to Sabine's bedroom.

In the garden, the crows rose, wheeling and swooping before finally settling in the top of the mountain ash. The twisted black lump in the middle of the garden looked like it was moving, but it was only the breeze ruffling its feathers. Eventually the crows stopped crying.

"Please. Just go away," I begged. "Sabine's been through enough. The last thing she needs to see when she comes home is a dead crow on her lawn." As if they'd heard me, the crows rose up out of the tree and flew away.

After a brief reconnoiter of Sabine's pantry, I returned to the garden armed with a large tinfoil pie plate and a wooden spoon. I nudged the dead crow onto the pie plate and carried it through the back gate into the alley. That's two, I thought as I dumped it and the pie plate and wooden spoon into the bin.

The demolition crew returned from lunch just as I was backing out of Sabine's driveway. Rolling down my window I called over to Levi and his excavator friend. "You pulled it down in record time."

He laughed. "It's Kenny's forte. All his life all he's ever wanted to do is wreck things."

Kenny beamed when I complimented him on a job well done and said it would take them another week to clear away the rubble pilled in the basement.

As it turned out, he was wrong.

CHAPTER THIRTY-THREE

A chinook wind had melted the snow creating deep piles of slush that would freeze overnight into rutted tire traps. Pedestrians trekked down the sidewalks trying to avoid being sprayed with globs of grey mush. Buses were the worst, roaring by, drenching anyone in the splatter zone. You'd think it was a contest: whoever soaks the most pedestrians wins.

AJ surveyed my car. The Mini was covered in road spray right up to the windows. "When was the last time you took your car to the carwash?" he asked.

"I know." I set off in the direction of his car. "I can't see through my windshield. You're driving."

It was mid afternoon and we were on our way to ambush Luke. He still hadn't called and I'd run out of patience—you can run but you can't hide.

Traffic was light and soon we were pulling up in front of Luke's place, a tiny house built in the 1940s under the war-time housing plan. Single file we marched up the narrow path to the front door. I've always liked these strawberry box houses with their steeply pitched roofs—this one was one and a half stories—and simple clapboard facades.

Architects probably think they're boringly pedestrian, but there's a lot to be said for forking out three hundred dollars for a house and having it delivered to your lot and finished a week later.

The net curtain in the front window twitched and heavy footsteps came down the hall when I pressed the doorbell. When the aluminum screen door creaked open, we came face to face with Vincent.

Confused, I apologised for the intrusion and said we were looking for Luke. Vincent stepped to one side. "You're in the right place." Luke was staying with him until he'd saved enough to get a place of his own. "He doesn't have a job... well, you know that... so he'll be here a while." Vincent showed us into the doll-sized living room and hollered Luke's name up the miniature staircase that led up to the bedrooms.

AJ and I settled on the nubby green couch which dominated the blue and yellow room. The place felt like a beach cottage. When Vincent offered us something to drink, we demurred, but he insisted. "It's never too early for a beer." By the time Luke trundled down the stairs—he made so much noise I thought he'd crash through—four bottles of beer were waiting on the long narrow coffee table in front of us.

Luke sat in a small orange armchair and Vincent carried his beer into the parlour on the other side of the staircase. The living room and the parlour were so close together we could see Vincent reach for the pipe resting on the small wooden table next to his oversized leather chair The air was filled with the sweet, spicy smell of pipe tobacco as Vincent drew long, contented puffs. All that was missing was the crackle of a fireplace and a red setter dozing at his feet.

Luke took a slow swig of beer. "So you tracked me

down." His grey-green eyes shifted from me to AJ. "I was going to get back to you, but well, you know how it is."

We did. Marc fired him and he had better things to do than waste time talking to Marc's lawyers.

"How can I help you?" Luke sat back in his chair, holding his beer bottle in his lap.

I rattled through our concerns with the Ballet House project. There seemed to be an inordinately high number of violations on the site. Were the measures we'd written into the contracts unclear?

"You're joking, right? For a company that says safety is its number one priority, they've had more than their share of accidents and near misses." He picked at the label on his beer bottle. "And I'm not talking about workers getting hit in the face by bricks."

"By 'company' are you referring to Marc's company or GCL?" I asked.

"Both. In the beginning GCL pushed Marc to ease up on the schedule, but Marc wouldn't budge. Consequently the trades are rushed. They're exhausted and they're getting sloppy."

"How do you mean?" I asked.

"Not cleaning up at the end of the day, forgetting to turn the heaters off before they leave, right there you've got a fire hazard." This reminded me of the firebomb at Marc's office, they still hadn't caught the arsonist.

Luke leaned forward, eyes bright. There was no stopping him now. "It's just a matter of time before someone gets seriously hurt or killed."

In the parlour, Vincent's newspaper snapped, like the wind catching a sail. He folded it in half and in half again, then set down his pipe and picked up a pen. Doing the crossword.

"Luke," I said, "is the construction activity having an adverse impact on the environment?"

He snorted. "I'm not an expert, but I can tell you this, his water sustainability plan is shit"—I raised my eyebrows and he added—"it's the rainwater collection system for the toilets and irrigation systems. He's digging temporary holding ponds all over the place. They're not in the original plans so they're not covered in the original permits. There's overland flow running all over the place."

Luke shook his head. "Those NEO guys are right. He's going to kill the river if someone doesn't stop him."

Stop before it is too late. The words on the small white card that terrified Sabine. Stop risking your workers' lives? Stop destroying the ecosystem? Stop all of it?

In the next room, Vincent's cell phone rang, a twangy country tune. He pressed the phone to his ear and said hello.

Slowly he rose to his feet and the crossword puzzle slid out of his lap onto the floor. "Merde!" It's the one French word all Canadians understand.

CHAPTER THIRTY-FOUR

Luke hurried into the parlour and we followed him but Vincent was already heading to the kitchen. He's a big man, much too big for this tiny house, his thigh grazed the small Formica table as he lumbered past and circled through the living room and back into the parlour. Where he slumped in the puffy leather chair and set the phone down on the small table. His hand was trembling as he reached for his pipe. It slipped out of his grasp and fell to the floor.

"Vince, what's wrong?" Luke picked up the pipe and passed it back to his uncle.

Vincent shook his head like a bewildered bear and said, "There's been an accident at the site, Carlos"—that must have been the guy on the phone—"doesn't have the details. Just that someone is dead. It was brutal. The police shut it down."

"Didn't I tell you." Luke was staring at AJ. "It was just a matter of time."

Vincent's phone pinged with a text. No caption, just a photo.

"Sweet Jesus," Vincent said. His face was grey as he

handed his phone to Luke. AJ and I crowded around him to see the image on the tiny screen.

"But this..." Luke shot a confused glance at Vincent, "this isn't the Ballet House." It was hard to see at first, too many police cars blocked the view, but there at the edge of the shot stood a majestic mountain ash.

"AJ"—my lips struggled to form the words—"it's the McMansion next to Sabine's place."

I remembered the chatty young guy, Levi, who wore sunglasses all the time and Kenny, the excavator operator, all he'd ever wanted to do was demolish buildings. And the others, running around the site, salvaging the copper piping before Kenny scooped the rubble into the back of a gigantic dump truck for one last journey to the nearest landfill.

Which one had died?

—————

By evening, social media was clogged with photo after photo of the excavator, its bucket high in the air, jaws gaping, surrounded by people in hard hats and safety vests, and police cars parked willy nilly on the snow hardened grass.

Louisa perched at the kitchen island searching for an official account of what had happened amid the amateur reporting and speculation.

"You'll want to read this." She glanced at me. I was at the kitchen sink, up to my elbows in soap suds. "Never mind, listen."

In a hushed voice she read the story. "At approximately 4:45 p.m. today police officers were called to the 1100 block of Marquis Avenue S.W. for reports of an unknown body that had been found at an empty residence. The house was in the process of being demolished. An autopsy is pending. Officers believe the death is suspicious and are asking to speak with anyone who may have been in the area within the last two days."

"Poor, poor Sabine." I set a gleaming frying pan down on the other side of the double sink and dried my hands. "It could have been a squatter. That place was vacant for so long she was worried they'd move in and accidently burn it to the ground. This is just what she needs, if a dead crow is enough to push her over the edge, God knows what she going to do when she hears about the random dead guy next door."

Dryly, Louisa said, "I'm sure the random dead guy isn't too happy about it either."

CHAPTER THIRTY-FIVE

The next morning everyone in the break room was buzzing about the body in the rubble. Bridget said since we represented Marc there was just one degree of separation between us and the dead guy, which meant there were two degrees of separation between us and his murderer. Madeline retorted that the Kevin Bacon six degrees of separation rule applied to people, not plots of land, and since we didn't know the identity of the dead guy, this entire discussion was moot.

"The body was crushed," Madeline added, "identification will take a while."

"How can you possibly know that?" Bridget asked.

I suspected one of Madeline's sources told her, but it stood to reason given that the body had been buried under tonnes of wood, brick and concrete.

AJ was leaning against the kitchen counter waiting for the coffee to brew. He looked at me and said, "If half of what Luke said about the Ballet House is true, Marc has one hell of a mess on his hands."

The coffee burbled; it was ready. Madeline pulled out

the carafe and poured coffees all around. "On the bright side, Sabine's problems are over."

"Why would you say that?" AJ asked.

"No one is going to build an expensive mansion on the spot where someone's been brutally murdered?"

"It's classified as a suspicious death at this point," I said, "not a murder." Although it was hard to see what else it could be.

"I'll bet you a thousand bucks the owner will fill in the hole and put the property back on the market," Madeline continued. "What's the land value, two million? He'll have to drop the price at least five hundred thousand if he wants a quick sale."

AJ cocked an eyebrow. "Since when did you become a real estate expert?"

"Since the Murder Mansion case in Vancouver." She caught my blank stare. "You know, where a high-ranking member of a Chinese gang—the Tong, maybe—was murdered on his property."

"The Triad," AJ corrected her.

"That's right. His wife put the house on the market without disclosing the murder. When the buyer found out, they refused to close the deal. Everyone sued everyone else and in the end the wife lost. The first deal collapsed and she was forced to drop the price by a half a million to unload it."

Down the hall my phone started to burr like an insect calling its mate. I left Madeline and AJ debating whether it was fair to make someone disclose their house had been a crime scene and returned to my office.

Caller ID said it was Sargeant Pritchard, Calgary Police. I hadn't talked to Pritchard in months. We have a peculiar relationship, not friends per se, more like acquaintances who've bonded over a nasty experience like a train wreck or being lost at sea. Every few months he buys me coffee at his favourite café. I do all the talking for the first ten minutes to give him time to warm up, then he tells me what's on his mind. Lately it's been police misconduct. He listens and nods, never letting on where he stands, then disappears until the next time.

"Pritchard, how are you?" I could picture him sitting in his tidy office staring out his narrow window at the railroad tracks at the far end of a large scruffy field. He has unusual eyes, one blue and one green. Or was it one blue and one brown? When we first met, it took me weeks to realize it was his eyes that made his gaze so unnerving.

Pritchard came straight to the point. "I'd like to talk with you about Marc and Sabine Hubert."

"Why me?"

"His office says you're working with him on the Ballet House and with his wife on the property next to their place." Technically Sabine was not a client, but I let it go. "You've heard about the body found in the demo on Marquis Avenue, right?"

"The McMansion? Yes, hold on a sec, I'm going to get AJ."

AJ had his back to the door when I entered his office. His feet were propped up on the low windowsill and he was reading something in his lap. I called his name and he almost jumped out of his skin. I covered the receiver, whispering, "It's Pritchard. He's got some questions about the McMansion."

We put Pritchard on speaker and walked him through Sabine's futile attempt to block the destruction of the Georgian manor. "The new house looks like a second-rate dentist's office. Even with the support of the community, she couldn't stop it," I said.

Pritchard made a sound, to indicate he was listening I supposed, but said nothing. We waited, staring at the cell resting on a file in the middle of AJ's desk. This is what Pritchard does. He goes quiet, the silence makes everyone uncomfortable, then he broaches what's really on his mind.

Pritchard cleared his throat. "Let's talk about the Ballet House." And there it was.

I nodded at AJ to indicate I would take the lead. "We're one of several firms involved with the project. But you should be talking directly to Marc, not us, we're his lawyers—"

"I know, solicitor-client privilege. His office says he's out of town."

"That's right, he's flying home from DC tonight. He should be back around seven-thirty or eight."

Pritchard continued as if he hadn't heard me. "I'm sure you've noticed there's been a lot of controversy over Marc's projects. Demonstrations and blockades at the Ballet House site, the arson attempt at his office, and now a body buried in the basement at Marquis Avenue next door to his house. It's like someone is tightening the screws."

"Then there's the death threat," AJ added.

"What death threat?" Pritchard spoke more slowly.

"Well, it's not an explicit death threat." As the words left my mouth, I wondered what else one could call it.

"Tell me about it," Pritchard said.

"It was delivered to their house." I described the shiny black words embossed on the small white card: Stop Before It Is Too Late.

"It looked like one of those fancy cards you use to RSVP to a wedding. It frightened Sabine, but Marc just laughed it off. He says the Ballet House is bringing all the kooks out of the woodwork."

"She should have reported it," Pritchard said. His tone was sad, but that's how he sounds when he's annoyed.

"Maybe Marc stopped her," AJ cut in. "The Ballet House is on a very tight schedule; the last thing he needs right now is a police investigation gumming up the works."

I nodded, remembering just then something my mom had said. Despite Sabine's fierce reputation as the Black Swan, at the end of the day she always deferred to her husband.

CHAPTER THIRTY-SIX

Later that afternoon I received a frantic call from Louisa. "Can you get up here? Sabine's had a serious setback." Louisa explained she'd popped in on Sabine before starting her shift and was shocked to discover her heavily sedated with Robert pacing the floor in a rage.

After circling the Foothills Hospital parking lot for twenty minutes I finally squeezed the Mini into a tiny space next to a stairwell. By the time I found Louisa, who was waiting for me when the elevator doors creaked open, I was beside myself.

"How is she?" I asked.

"Not good."

Louisa hustled me into a cubby hole of a room crammed with computers on wheels—she'd once told me they're called cows—they looked like they'd accidently wandered into the wrong room and got stuck there.

Louisa's eyes blazed with anger. "Apparently the cops came by to interview her this afternoon. I don't know how they broached the topic of the dead body next door, it's not as if Sabine's been following the news or anything, but something they said triggered her. She became so agitated they had to sedate her, and now she's making no sense.

"Evie, she's right back to where she was the day we brought her in. She's been asking for Marc"—I glanced at my watch, his plane wouldn't land for another two hours—"and Robert, and Mom."

"Mom? Our mom? She's been dead for six years."

"I know that," Louisa snapped. "She's blurring the past and the present. Look I have to get back to work. Just act normal and try to keep her calm, okay?" Louisa's face hardened. "I swear I'm going to report Pritchard for this."

When I entered her room Sabine was propped up against three pillows. Her face was slack and her eyes were closed. The sunlight streaming through the dust specked window made her look sallow. Robert hovered by her side, speaking softly and stroking her hair. His face suffused with love. He lifted his eyes when I called his name, then gently placed Sabine's thin hand on the light blue blanket pulled tight across her chest.

"Still asleep?" I whispered.

He nodded and I indicated he should follow me outside. "Do you know what happened?" I asked when we were a few steps down the hall.

"Those fucking idiots," he said. Then repeated what the nurses had told him. Two police officers showed up around noon to talk to Sabine. "Christ only knows what they said to her because she pitched her tray to the floor and started screaming. You could hear her all the way down to the nursing station. They sedated her and she's been drifting in and out of consciousness ever since. Evie, she's convinced she killed Vincent."

"Vincent? We don't know who the body is, but it's definitely not Vincent."

"Robert?" Sabine's voice floated into the hallway, thin and reedy. "Robert?"

We hurried back to her room. When she saw me she reached out. I took her trembling hands in mine and whispered in her ear that she looked well. She gave me a weak smile, then shut her eyes and was asleep again. By the time Robert and I left her room she was snoring softly.

Robert gave a small shuddering sigh as we waited for the elevator.

"When did you last eat?" I asked as the doors opened. "Come on, there's a café downstairs. You look like you could use a coffee, perhaps a scone."

"Or a whiskey," he said with a grim smile.

"Why on earth would she think she killed Vincent?" It was bizarre. Vincent finished stripping the asbestos out of the Georgian manor before Christmas. It was now late January and there had been no activity on the site until the demolition crew arrived a few days ago. They put in one day's work and thanks to the body in basement were forced to stop because the site was now a crime scene.

Lost in thought, Robert stared at the floor saying nothing.

The Good Earth Café isn't far from the elevators and soon we were through the line and sitting on a cracked vinyl bench next to the windows. Robert gazed outside at a scrawny woman in pink pyjamas, beat up hiking boots and a short green jacket. She was in a wheelchair and smoking a cigarette with the grim intensity of someone facing a firing squad.

"How long have you known Sabine?" I'd asked Robert this question before but I couldn't think of anything else to say. It was like turning on a spigot. He couldn't get the words out fast enough.

"We met in 2000 shortly after she moved here, I was on the board of a non-profit arts group, we'd just spent a bundle on that crazy Y2K stuff and our coffers were dry. Enter Sabine, fund raiser extraordinaire. Honestly, I didn't think she'd stay. She's too sophisticated for this rinky dink town. Then Marc announced he was moving his practice to Chicago." A look as dark as thunder passed over his face, then he smiled. "Sabine, our feisty girl, flat out refused to leave."

Robert waved his hands as he recounted the story. "She'd set up the Calgary Ballet School by then and had a stellar reputation as one hell of a fundraiser. She told Marc she wasn't giving all that up to start over from scratch in Chicago. Let me tell you Marc didn't like it one bit, but what choice did he have? She made it clear: If he was going, he'd be going alone."

Outside, the woman in pink pyjamas tossed her cigarette into a spindly shrub where it landed on a small pyramid of cigarette butts, she shot us an indifferent glance before maneuvering her wheelchair through the front door.

Robert sat back in his chair, assessing me. There was something else he wanted to say. Carefully, he brushed some crumbs off his fingertips. "I know Marc is your client, but there are a few things you should know."

Here we go again.

"He's a despicable man. No woman should have to endure what that man has put her through."

"You mean his affairs?"

"He has no shame. He doesn't know the meaning of the word. And his mistresses are no better. None of them has an ounce of decorum. This last one..." Robert's face flushed as he struggled to find the words. "We were at Masters—"

"The art gallery?"

He nodded. "For a fundraiser. It was Sabine's big night. She was going to announce she was bringing the Prix de Lyon to Calgary when one of Marc's harlots appeared outside.

"Marc spotted her through the glass doors, standing right there next to the Van Gogh sculpture whose eyes follow you around. He was in the middle of introducing Sabine and started stammering like someone having a seizure. So it fell to me to prevent this woman from entering.

"Oh she was a cheeky little thing, smiling at me with her big brown eyes, what did she think, that she could enchant me the way she'd bewitched Marc? I had to protect Sabine. This was her special moment and no one was going to spoil it."

"So you sent her away?"

"Not before she told me to tell Marc this was far from over."

"The affair?"

"I said she could tell him herself; I'm not their go-between." With a glint in his eye, Robert reached for his paper cup. It was empty and he set it down again. "If Marc can't keep his harlots in line, I'll do it for him."

He stared out the window watching a young woman cross the pavement. She had a small child on her hip. He turned to me and said, "Sabine always wanted a family but agreed to wait because Marc's career came first. Then when Marc finally decided he was ready it was too late. She lost two babies before she gave up trying."

"Oh, I didn't know."

Robert jammed his napkin into his paper cup and stood up. "No problem for Marc. He just went off and got that Barros woman pregnant. He's got a child, Alice. Who does Sabine have? Nobody."

By the time we returned to Sabine's room Robert had calmed down, ready to entertain Sabine with more beguiling stories but there was no need, she was still asleep. We chatted quietly until Robert had to leave for The Jack—the Jack Singer Concert Hall—he was performing with a Grammy award-winning violinist. "I need to be there by seven."

That was when Marc would be arriving back from DC. Assuming he showed up.

Robert kissed Sabine's forehead. Her eyelids fluttered, but she didn't awaken.

—••—

In the cold, damp parkade, I rested my head against the steering wheel, whipsawed by emotions; pity for Sabine who'd sacrificed everything for Marc, anger at Marc for ruining her life, and fury at Pritchard's incompetent officers who'd undermined Sabine's recovery.

I couldn't do anything about Marc and Sabine, but I could do something about Pritchard. I dialed his number and waited while the call rang through to the front desk. Pritchard had left for the day; would I care to leave a message?

Damned right I would. My message was five minutes long and every second word was an obscenity.

CHAPTER THIRTY-SEVEN

Early the next morning Pritchard called me back. It was bitterly cold and Quincy and I were taking a very short jog through Mission. Our progress was slow because the dog slowed down at every bakery and coffee shop, lifting his nose to catch the aromas floating out onto the street.

"I understand you want to file an official complaint." Pritchard's tone was bland.

I couldn't recall what I'd said so I went for it. "Jesus, Pritchard, what the hell are you guys playing at?"

His calm voice bounced back at me. "You'll have to be a bit more specific."

By now Quincy and I were on the move again, loping briskly towards the intersection. "You know exactly what I mean, Sabine's had a relapse, thanks to your Keystone Kops. She's in a fugue state or something." Whether this was medically accurate didn't concern me. I was making a point.

He let my accusations wash over him, then said, "I'm sorry to hear that, but this is a murder investigation. I can assure you my officers are well trained; they know how to talk to people who've been hospitalized."

Murder investigation? It's official then.

The wind stung my cheeks as we turned the corner and began our ascent up the hill. The cold air was thin and I was gasping for breath. Pritchard asked I was feeling all right.

Before I could reply he said, "Given Sabine's state of mind, I may need your help."

"What are you going to do, fire a cannon through her window?" Despite the cold I was overheating. I unzipped my waterproof jacket, jogging in place until the stoplight changed.

"No. but we may need her help in identifying the victim."

"You have got to be fucking kidding me."

"No," he said mildly, "I'm not. She may have seen something. The crew working at the McMansion say she was over there every day and nothing escaped her attention."

He had a point.

—·—

I'd barely made it into the lobby when AJ intercepted me. He was wearing his long black overcoat and looked like something out of *The Matrix*. "Good, you're finally here," he said as he spun me around to face the parking lot. "Let's go for a walk."

"Walk? No way. It's minus 28°C out there."

"Won't take long. Evie, we need to talk... privately."

Privately? I shot a confused glance at Bridget who was talking on the phone. She hung up and said, "Be back by nine, you've both got meetings." I told her she was no help whatsoever and she told me to go already and dismissed me with a flick of her wrist.

A breeze as sharp as a scalpel blew up off the river as

we crossed the little bridge into Rideau Roxboro. It froze the tips of my ears and made my eyes water. I should have worn a hat. AJ, bless his heart, unwound his scarf, a scratchy red wool thing, it was his Secret-Santa gift from Bridget, and draped it across my shoulders. I considered wrapping it around my head like a babushka.

We passed the steps leading down to the river and entered an exclusive residential enclave. The large well-maintained homes on either side of the boulevard deadened the rumble of morning traffic. Soft warm light spilled from generous windows, illuminating state-of-the-art kitchens where families readied themselves for work and school.

"So what's up?" I asked, the wind whipping my words away.

He kept his eyes on the road ahead. "I need to tell you about Sam and me."

"Sam and you?" I stopped dead on the pavement. "There's a Sam and you?"

"It's complicated."

I raised my eyebrows, which isn't easy when you're squinting against the wind. "Well, hurry up and uncomplicate it before we freeze to death." The wind was howling and I stepped closer to him to use his body as a windbreak. With our long coats and earnest expressions we looked like the bronze sculpture of two businessmen in front of the Bay. All we needed were matching fedoras.

"Listen," AJ said, leaning close, "I haven't been entirely honest with you about my relationship with Sam... or NEO. The truth is back in university Sam and I were more than protest buddies, we were...involved."

I should have been surprised, but I wasn't. Sam struck me as an intelligent, passionate woman. Sixteen years ago she would have been irresistible to someone like AJ. *Perhaps she still is.*

"She believed we could save the world. And so did I. Back then I would have followed her through a mine field."

A black Mercedes backed out of an attached garage and we edged to one side to let it pass. Inside a middle-aged woman was lecturing a teenaged girl in a private school uniform.

"What happened?" I asked.

"Reality happened." He squinted after the car speeding down the road towards downtown. "Despite all our protests and sit ins and lie ins, despite all the fine speeches and lofty promises made at international climate conferences, nothing changed. The industry promised to go greener even as it pumped more emissions into the air. Governments passed regulations, but corporate lobbyists made sure they had no teeth. The world was going to hell in the proverbial handbasket."

"AJ that's a little bleak. We've made some progress since then, look at the uptick in solar and wind energy. And companies that screw up are fined."

"The fines are nothing, simply the cost of doing business for these guys."

We were getting side tracked and I was freezing to death out here. "Back to Sam..."

He gazed past me to the end of the street where a small, yellow school bus was idling, belching exhaust fumes into the air. "Over time Sam became desperate, more open to the idea of grand gestures, even if they harmed innocent people. As far as she was concerned, they were collateral damage in the battle for the greater good."

"Oh God." My voice caught in my throat. "Don't tell me. You thought you were converting Sam, but in the end she converted you. You joined NEO and they really are a gang of dangerous eco-terrorists." I was practically yelling; no wonder AJ didn't want to have this conversation back at the office.

Across the street two small children charged out of a house, their coats unzipped and flapping behind them as they sprinted for the bus. Its door rattled open, they hopped on, and it accelerated to the end of the block to pick up the next batch of privileged youngsters.

"No," AJ said, watching the bus trundle around the corner. "I attended a few meetings, enough to figure out these guys were too extreme for my liking. I quit and she made it clear she wanted nothing more to do with me. We haven't spoken since."

AJ paused, staring at me with those icy blue eyes. "Sometimes I wonder whether she was right, whether trying to fix the system from the inside is a waste of time."

"AJ, how can you say that? We're facilitators, helping those with brains and money offer alternative energy to the world. What Sam is advocating gets people killed. You made the right decision, never doubt yourself."

His smile lasted five seconds before it slipped. "Um, I need to clarify something. The last time we spoke wasn't sixteen years ago, it was last week."

"Last week? We met them at the National three weeks ago."

His cheeks redden, but not from the wind. He glanced over my shoulder and said, "Yeah, well, she called. She wants to meet. She's got something on Marc and says we need to see it."

"*What?* That's absolutely out of the question. Marc is already paranoid because we got the Sin List from Dudek.

If she has something on Marc she has to take it to her own lawyer because we can't help her."

"Evie, she says what she's got will shut Marc down, permanently."

I shook my head. "Marc's our client. Are you sure your feelings for Sam aren't clouding your judgment? We're not activists, we're lawyers who put words on a page. Enforcement is someone else's job. We can't act against our client's interests." And that's when the penny dropped. "You're going to meet her regardless of what I say."

He looked sheepish and shrugged.

"Right, then I'm coming with you." Not because I wanted to hear what Sam had to say, but because I didn't trust AJ to meet her alone. Try as he might to deny it, AJ still had feelings for her.

"Come on," I said. "Let's get back to the office before we die out here."

"Wait." AJ touched my arm. "What do we tell Keith?"

Keith? He'd have a heart attack if he found AJ had been a member of NEO once, even if it had been a long time ago, let alone that we were going to meet with NEO without informing our client.

I shuffled from one foot to the other, the cold was seeping through the soles of my boots. "Nothing. We tell Keith nothing until we have some concrete information. For all we know Sam's just messing with you."

"That's entirely possible," he said.

We turned into the wind and started walking back to the main road. And suddenly I laughed.

"What?"

"You're a bad influence on me AJ."

He smiled. "I wasn't this reckless until I met you."

"Yeah, sure."

At the end of the day AJ appeared in my doorway, bundled up in his coat, his red scarf tight around his neck, his gloves clutched in his hand.

"No thank you," I said. "I've already had my freezing cold walk for the day."

"Hah," he said, pulling on his gloves. "Sam won't return my calls. So if the mountain won't come to Muhammad, then Muhammad will go to the mountain."

"Which one are you, the mountain or Muhammad?"

"I figure a surprise visit to the EconoLodge is in order."

"We've been making a lot of surprise visits lately. How do you know they'll be there?"

"I don't, but it's too cold and too dark to be out on the picket line, they're either holed up in that fleabag hotel room or drinking themselves silly at a nearby bar."

And that's how we almost ended up in jail.

CHAPTER THIRTY-EIGHT

The EconoLodge was one of those places that looks sad in the daylight but is quite lovely at night. It was dark, almost seven o'clock, when we parked the car and trudged across the gravel towards the warmth of the lobby. If you half-closed your eyes you might be fooled into thinking it didn't deserve its two-star rating.

AJ had said little on the drive over and I amused myself by reading the motel's on-line ratings: Bob didn't like the ants in the bathroom and said the continental breakfast was pitiful but gave it an eight out of ten. I wondered what it would take for Bob to give it a two, an axe murderer stalking the halls?

We went straight through the lobby and into the elevator. There was no point in checking the restaurant because there wasn't one. If Sam wasn't home, we'd scour the bars nearby.

AJ rapped on the door to Unit 201. The TV went silent inside. Then the clatter of someone fiddling with the chain lock. Grizzly Adams loomed before us. His hair was wild and flattened on one side as if he'd been sleeping. He adjusted his jeans around his beer belly and glared at us. "You again."

Grizzly puffed up even bigger when AJ attempted to cross the threshold. "Listen," AJ said, "we just want to talk to Sam."

"Yeah, well she doesn't want to talk to you."

"That's not my understanding," AJ said as he craned his neck to peer around the hulk in the doorway. This infuriated Grizzly. His elbow came up and he nailed AJ in the chest. It was a small shove but it caught AJ by surprise. He stumbled backwards, cracked his head on the door frame and backed into me, knocking me into the hall.

Just then the elevator doors opened and a young couple stepped out.

AJ surged through the door, driving his head into Grizzly's belly. They careened off the bed and crashed to the floor. A grunting, tangled heap. Behind them the TV ran a silent commercial touting a cruise to the Bahamas. I charged into the room just as the couple down the hall jumped back into the elevator.

"Will you two cut it out!" I could have been talking to the wall for all the difference it made.

Grizzly was on top of AJ now, smashing his fist into AJ's face. "She doesn't want to see you!" Each word was punctuated by a blow.

I grabbed Grizzly's matted hair and yanked his head back. Furious, he reared up, flinging me into the dresser. For some reason this woke up the TV and the hockey game blared into the room. The noise caught Grizzly by surprise and AJ's fist shot up into the big man's face. A crunch of cartilage and a spurt of blood. Grizzly squeezed his eyes shut, roaring in pain.

Then bam, bam, bam, fists thumping on the hotel room door. Christ, were there more of them?

"Police. Open up!"

We froze. Grizzly eyed the window, we were on the second floor, surely he wasn't going to jump. The room looked like a slasher movie, blood everywhere, on the floor, the bed, even the TV. AJ shoved Grizzly off and yelled, "Okay, okay, we hear you. I'm coming to the door. We're unarmed."

Unarmed? For the first time I was afraid. Innocent people have been killed in situations like this. Smoothing my coat which gaped open where a button had been ripped off, I pulled a Kleenex out of my pocket and swiped at AJ's face as he passed me on the way to the door. This smeared the blood on his cheek, making him look even more maniacal.

Gingerly, he opened the door and a few minutes later two grim faced police officers frog marched us across the lobby and into the parking lot. They packed AJ and me into one patrol car and Grizzly into the other. The police radio squawked and the red and blue lights raked across the lobby making the motel look unworthy of even its two-star rating.

"Do you know a good criminal lawyer?" I whispered to AJ. The cop up front told us to shut up and we rode in silence to the police station where we were surprised to learn that being a member in good standing of the Law Society of Alberta was of absolutely no use whatsoever.

———•———

Three a.m. and police finally decided to let us go. It was hard to explain how the fight started or what it was about. The cops didn't buy AJ's he-just-hauled-off-and-hit-me story until Grizzly started raging in the next room about corrupt lawyers and abusive cops, thereby confirming that yes, he did have a hair-trigger temper. Eventually they decided it wasn't worth the paperwork to charge us and released us with a stern warning: no more punch-ups.

AJ and I shared a cab to my place—he had gotten it into his head that in my frazzled state I would not make it home in one piece—and he waited until I was safely inside (again, not necessary), then returned to the cab and proceeded back to the EconoLodge to pick up his car.

Just before I got out of the cab AJ said, "Can you imagine the headlines if we'd been charged? *Ballet House lawyers assault NEO protester.*" It was a horrible scenario, but that was exactly how Keith would see it. Maybe we could not mention it to him. No, with our luck one of his criminal lawyer buddies would have seen us.

"I think you should tell him, AJ. You're the one who got into the fight with Grizzly."

"Yeah, but you've known him longer," AJ replied. "Besides, he's come to expect this kind of thing from you."

It rankled, but AJ was right.

CHAPTER THIRTY-NINE

Holy cow, what happened to you?" On a scale of one to ten, Bridget's Mother Hen instincts are a solid twelve. I tugged my toque down, trying to cover the purple bump on the right side of my forehead. All the makeup in the world couldn't camouflage it.

"You should see the other guy," I said as I sped past her.

"I did," she replied. "AJ's in the coffee room and he looks way worse than you do. That must have been one heck of a bar fight!"

Down the corridor I could hear Madeline talking to AJ in a quiet, sympathetic voice. He'd tell her everything if I didn't get in there. She could pry state secrets out of a Russian spy if she put her mind to it.

"Jesus, AJ, what happened to you?" Keith got to the coffee room just ahead of me. Madeline and AJ were sitting at the tiny table by the window. He looked up at Keith with his good eye, the other eye was almost swollen shut, then tipped his head at me. *You're up, Valentine.*

"Right, so here's what happened." Quickly I explained we'd had an unfortunate encounter with Grizzly Adams when we went to Sam's hotel room. "She wasn't there. It got loud. Some idiot called the cops, but in the end no charges were laid." *Nothing to see here folks, move along.*

"Suggestion," Keith said in a studied neutral tone, "in future if you wish to dialogue with Sam, may I suggest the telephone." His stilted syntax was a sure sign he was annoyed.

"Agreed," AJ said.

"Of course, I concur," I said, stiffly. I can't help it, when Keith gets stuffy, I get stuffy.

"Also," Keith continued as if I hadn't spoken, "why were you meeting with NEO in the first place?"

AJ watched as I tap danced through an explanation that grazed the facts just long enough to ring true.

That afternoon Madeline swept into my office carrying her laptop. "You wouldn't know it to look at him now—of course he's been beaten up, so it's not a fair comparison— but AJ was quite the young chevalier back in the day."

"Chevalier?"

"Knight in shining armor. Crusader." She settled into my visitor's chair, clicked a few keys and turned the laptop to face me. An old newspaper story appeared, under the headline was a large photograph of a dense, fern filled forest. Lying on the shade-dappled ground were two pro- testors, the caption said they were on a mission to block a logging company from harvesting old growth trees.

"Despite the beard and the bandana you can still rec- ognize him." Madeline's face glowed with the maternal pride she usually reserved for her cats, dogs, and cockatiel.

I peered at the photograph. AJ and a young woman— Sam—had chained themselves to a piece of equipment called a 'sleeping dragon.' The logging company had brought in jack hammers, chainsaws, and excavators to remove them. An excavator operator had maneuvered his bucket to within a foot of Sam's head. A supervisor was quoted as saying 'Sure, it's a challenge to remove the protestors without harming them but an operator moving slowly and gently could probably do it.'

Probably? A shudder ran through me. My lawyer's brain instantly went to who'd be liable if the excavator operator gently crushed someone's skull or chopped off their arm. "How could they put themselves in such danger?"

Madeline stared at the photo. "They believed their cause was righteous. They still do."

The article was from the early 2000s. Around the time Sam became a full-fledged member of NEO. A decision that so worried AJ that he broke up with her. Or so he said.

I borrowed Madeline's laptop and carried it into AJ's office. The blinds were closed and the lights were off. His bruised face looked black in the reflected light of his laptop screen.

"You look like hell," I said as I set the laptop on his preternaturally neat desk.

"I feel like hell," he replied.

"Here's something that will brighten your day." I spun the laptop around so he could see the photograph.

He laughed; his good eye sparkling as he explained what they'd hoped (but failed) to accomplish out there in the rainforest. Then he became solemn. "That picture was taken just before they freed her from the sleeping dragon and threw her, kicking and screaming, into a cop car."

I clicked off the laptop. "AJ, if she's got something to tell us, she'd better make it quick." I was suspicious of Sam and I was rapidly losing faith in Marc. He still hadn't sent us a plan to fix the Sin List. "Maybe she's out protesting at the site."

"Good point, do you want to go out there?" AJ asked.

"You can distract Grizzly and I'll talk to Sam."

He arched an eyebrow. "Try not to let him kill you, okay?"

"Great, I've made a note of that."

CHAPTER FORTY

It was just after lunch when we drove out to the Ballet House construction site. As we looped past Stampede Park I turned to AJ and said, "Looks like they're making good progress on your fancy-pants arena."

I shuddered and AJ shot me a curious look.

"They filmed *The Last of Us* here," I said. "I keep expecting a pack of zombies to lurch out from behind a building." Sure, it was CGI but the image of Calgary's iconic buildings crumbling and overrun with vegetation continued to haunt me.

"Zombies?" AJ laughed as he pulled onto the old bus barn site. "Ms. Valentine, you do realize zombies are not real."

"My analytic brain knows they're not real, but that doesn't change a thing. Zombies are terrifying."

"You're one of those jump-scare people who freak out at the movies, right?" He chuckled and parked the car. As we walked through the laydown area we could see the outline of the light, elegant auditorium rising out of the mess of construction materials and equipment.

"AJ, something is wrong." I'd expected to find Grizzly

and Sam hollering into bullhorns, leading the protesters in noisy chants at the perimeter fence. Instead we found a dispirited group of twenty or so, milling about on the other side of the laydown area. They were subdued, not causing any trouble, but a squad car was here, its lights flashing in the dreary afternoon light.

"There's Grizzly." AJ spotted the burly man talking to a grave faced cop. Another officer stood beside the patrol car, a crackly radio microphone in his hand.

Grizzly shook his shaggy head slowly from side to side. His arms hung limply by his sides. It looked like he was shrinking right before my eyes. We were almost on top of them when I called his name. "Grizzly." What was his name, his real name? "Paul."

He lifted his head, searching the crowd for my voice. His face was wet with tears. That's when I knew.

AJ introduced himself to the cop. "I'm a lawyer. We represent the architect, Marc Hubert. Is there a problem? Anything we can do to help?"

"Will he listen to you?" The police officer glanced at Grizzly; concern etched on her face. "He's pretty upset. And, harsh as this sounds, we will need him to help us with an identification. The woman in the demolished house. I understand they were roommates."

The colour drained from AJ's face. "Sam? Has something happened to Sam?"

Grizzly blinked a couple of times and said, "Let's go." Just before he slid into the back seat of the patrol car, he turned to AJ. "You're fucking right it's Sam. You people got her killed."

Stunned, AJ watched the patrol car speed across the snow-packed gravel. Slowly he turned to me, unable to speak and I sent him back to the car to wait while I talked to the protesters. They were in shock, their guard was down, they might tell me something useful even though we represented 'the dark side.' It didn't take long, maybe twenty minutes and I had all the information I needed.

Back in the car on our way to the office AJ kept repeating one phrase over and over again. "This isn't happening, this isn't happening."

As we drove into the office parking lot, I told him to pull himself together. We hadn't told Keith about AJ's relationship with Sam, let alone that AJ had been in contact with her while NEO was harassing our client. This was not how Keith should find out. AJ nodded. He understood.

AJ and I drifted down the hall to Keith's office.

"I don't know what to make of it," Keith said as we sat down. Bridget had spotted the headline, everyone in the office knew.

AJ stared out the window, a million miles away, and I told Keith I'd had a chance to talk to the protesters at the site. "There's something seriously wrong out there. They were in shock, naturally, and they opened up to me about all the problems they've observed at the site.

"Marc and Dudik aren't following basic health and safety rules. Yesterday an electrician ripped his scalp open on a piece of metal. He was drenched with blood. They just patched him up and sent him home. They should have sent him to ER and filed a workers comp report."

Keith raised his hands, indicating he didn't want to hear anymore but I refused to stop.

"Last week they were priming the ceiling in the change rooms and almost gassed themselves to death with an epoxy coating, a last minute substitution not specified in the contract. It wasn't fit for purpose and they dumped it down the sewer drains. It went straight into the Elbow river. Keith, these aren't isolated incidents, it's a pattern of behavior. Someone has to stop him before it's too late."

A red blotch appeared on Keith's neck and slowly spread up to his face. "Well, that 'someone' is not us. It's the government's job to enforce their laws. That's who the protesters should be talking to."

"They already tried that," AJ said. "It didn't do them any good." That was the only thing he said the entire time we were sitting with Keith.

"Evie, you know the rules." Keith gave me a hard stare as if daring me to challenge him. "Unless someone not bound by solicitor-client confidentiality exposes Marc there's nothing more we can do." He picked up his pen and flipped open a file on his desk. The meeting was over.

AJ was on his feet. I was right behind him. When I reached the door I glanced back over my shoulder, locking eyes with Keith.

"Evie, you know I'm right. We have to walk away."

I didn't trust myself to respond.

CHAPTER FORTY-ONE

The following day Major Barbara, Marc's assistant, called Bridget to tell her Marc demanded my presence at his office immediately.

"You are to come alone," Bridget said with a worried look on her face. "No Keith and definitely no AJ." Bridget bit her lip. "Barbara says she's never seen Marc this angry."

"Tell her I'll come but not without AJ."

One day wasn't much time for AJ to come to terms with Sam's death, but he seemed to be coping. The distraction might do him good. Besides, I wanted him by my side for what promised to be an ugly meeting.

Bridget pursed her lips. "But Barbara said, just you."

I gave Bridget my 'my way or the highway' look. She shot back her 'don't blame me if this goes pear-shaped' look and returned to her desk to advise Barbara to expect both of us.

When you're summoned to a meeting without being told what it's about, it's about you. What you did wrong and how you're going to be drawn and quartered unless you fix it immediately. Normally, the prospect of such a meeting would irritate me, but this time I didn't care. Neither did AJ.

Barbara Major greeted us with a stiff 'good day' and led the way down to Marc's glass walled corner office. "Coffee?" she asked, ducking out the door before we could reply.

Twenty minutes later AJ and I were still examining Marc's new décor. Gone were the brilliant wall colours and the vibrant jewel toned furnishings. The 'high-octane' environment Marcie said Marc needed to work at peak efficiency had been replaced by a muted palette similar to the neutral colour scheme Sabine preferred at home.

I made myself comfortable on the pale Scandinavian sofa while AJ paced from one end of the office to the other.

"If Marc doesn't show his face in the next two minutes, we're outta here." AJ stopped pacing and threw himself onto the sofa beside me.

"Patience," I replied. "Yes, there are hundreds of things we could be doing instead of sitting here admiring Marc's artwork, although there's not much left to admire, but we're in the service industry. We don't want him trashing our reputation."

He looked at me, incredulous. "You don't seriously expect Marc to throw us any referrals, do you?"

I didn't but we were here now, there was no point in stalking out in a huff.

Finally Marc strode in. He tried to slam the glass door behind him but was thwarted by its pneumatic hinge. As it whispered shut, he registered AJ's presence but didn't make an issue of it. Instead he marched to his desk, picked up a clear plastic folder, and sat down across from us on the white Barcelona chair.

"Would you care to explain this?" He flung the plastic folder down on the coffee table. AJ picked it up and withdrew a single sheet of paper. It was a copy of an email. He glanced at it, then passed it to me. It was the Sin List.

"What's to explain?" I said, setting the page down on the coffee table. "Dudik sent it to us weeks ago. You know that. You scolded him for it at your dinner party, remember?" Memories of Marc lecturing us about the French and their lack of respect for stupid laws came to mind.

"I know *what* it is." Marc's tone was that of someone on the verge of losing his temper. "What I want to know is *how* Sam Berman got her pretty little hands on it."

"I have no idea," I said, holding Marc's gaze to stop him from glancing at AJ. So help me God, if AJ sent a copy of the Sin List to Sam I would absolutely kill him.

"That's bullshit," Marc said, rising to his feet. "Sam was a clever girl, but not that clever. You gave her the list. That's a breach of your oath of confidentiality—"

"You sanctimonious prick." AJ shot to his feet so fast the sofa jumped back two inches. "Sam was trying to protect the river system from your trainwreck of a building, your overblown monument to your bloated ego."

Just then Major Barbara swept through Marc's glass door, a tray in her hands. "I've brought coffee."

"Get out!" Marc bellowed. The coffee tray rattled as she ducked her head and disappeared. He turned to face us again. "I will have you two disbarred for this."

Disbarred? That was the last straw.

"Based on what?" I said. "That email? Anyone could have sent it to Sam."

Beside me AJ was cursing under his breath. *AJ, please shut up.*

"Marc," I said evenly, "if you take us to a disciplinary hearing you're going to have to introduce that email into evidence. Do you really want to put the Sin List on the public record? Where it will serve as a roadmap for anyone who wants to sue you? The plaintiff won't have to prove his case, because you and Didik will have done it for him."

That stopped him cold. I turned to AJ. "We're done here."

A few minutes later we were making our way to AJ's car. As he fumbled for his key fob and unlocked the car doors, I said, "You had me worried there. For a moment I thought you were going to deck him."

"Hell no, he's an old man." Marc was fifty-nine, and a very fit fifty-nine at that, but AJ was right. He could snap Marc in two if he wanted to.

He started the engine and put the car in gear. "Wanna go for a beer?"

———————

The Joyce on Fourth is my kind of pub. I don't go drinking that often, but when I do I prefer places that are a little tatty around the edges; dark and lived-in, with well worn furniture and quiet mind-your-own-business bartenders. Louisa says I'm getting old but the frenetic buzz of those shiny new bars is a little off-putting.

The pub was packed with the pre-Friday crowd. After a few minutes, a booth opened up in a back corner. Soon we were leaning over our drinks, straining to hear each other over twangy music blasting out of the speakers.

"AJ, where do you suppose Sam got that email?" I peered up at him over the rim of my glass. "If it was you, so help me God. I've done some pretty stupid things in my time but nothing as bad as this."

"Me? Don't be ridiculous," he replied after a swallow of beer. "Brianna sent it to her."

"Brianna? Dudik's environmental person?"

"Sure, her email address was at the top. You didn't see it?"

I didn't see it. I'd made a blind assumption, the same one Marc had made, that someone from BLV had leaked it. If I'd taken the time to actually look at the email—a piece of advice I give my clients when they're getting ready to testify—I would have noticed that it had been sent by Brianna to Sam who then forwarded it to Marc.

"This is a good thing. That email works in our favour." AJ raised his hand to catch the server's eye. "Now that the Sin List is out in the open all we have to do is get an enforcement officer to look at it."

"No AJ, we can't do that. We're still bound by confidentiality. We may have powerful information but we're powerless to use it."

AJ frowned, then changed the subject. He tipped his head in the direction of the bar and said, "Sam loved country and western music." The Joyce was an Irish pub, but this was Calgary, everyone played C&W at one time or another.

As the server set down our second round of drinks, AJ listed all the things he'd loved about Sam. She was an avid hiker but terrified of bears (that made two of us), she preferred camping to a glamorous hotel (not on your life). He became more animated as he rattled off her quirks and I wondered how much she'd changed over the last sixteen years.

Finally he ran out of words. The twang of Shaina Twain filled the silence that grew between us and I asked the question I'd been putting off all day. "Are you sure you're doing okay?" This boisterous bar was hardly the place for a heart-to-heart, but it seemed cruel to pretend everything was back to normal.

"That was a long time ago." He paused, staring into the faraway corners of the room. "Evie, I just don't get it, why would anyone want to hurt her?"

My beer mat was puffy and swollen where the foam had dribbled down the side of the glass and I couldn't stop picking at it. "Maybe someone at NEO didn't like the fact she reached out to us, to you, specifically, the guy who knew their secrets and bolted."

He thought about that for a moment, then shook his head. "I don't buy it. They're not the Hells Angels. Members who step out of line don't turn up dead at the bottom of a gravel pit. Look at me, I got out unscathed."

"Yeah, well that was sixteen years ago, things may have changed since then. Even Grizzly, the man who could wrestle a mountain lion, wasn't keen on being seen with us in public."

AJ picked up his beer glass and swallowed what remained in two long gulps, then thumped it back down on the table. "You ready? I'll drop you off at the office."

"We're leaving?" I waved the menu I'd been reading in his face. "I was going to order some onion rings."

"They don't have onion rings," he said, shrugging on his coat. "Nobody does, not since that crop failure or whatever it was a few years ago." The odd look in his eye had nothing to do with onion rings.

"AJ, what are you up to?" Quickly I pulled on my jacket and grabbed my gloves out of my pockets.

He narrowed his eyes as if debating whether to tell me, then said, "I'm going to pay Paul Adams a visit."

"You're joking. He thinks we got Sam killed. You're the last person on the planet he wants to see." I pulled my knitted hat over my ears. "He'd sooner rip your arms off than look at you."

AJ left some money on the table and headed for the door. Outside the temperature had dropped another ten degrees. It felt like walking into the side of a glacier.

"I owe it to Sam," he said as we hurried to the car.

I hate it when people say that. How can you owe the dead anything? They're gone. It's not as if they're going to applaud you for being their champions or scold you if you're not. AJ was doing this, whatever it was, for no one but himself. I buckled myself in and waited until he started the car before announcing I was going with him.

"No, you're not." He didn't look at me as he pulled into traffic. "I'm dropping you off at the office. The matter closed."

"Yes, I am. The matter is open. We can debate this all the way to Motel Village if you want, but I'm not getting out of this car."

He glanced at me as he cruised through a yellow light. "You can be a real pain in the ass sometimes, do you know that?" The words were stern, but his tone had softened.

For once, I chose not to respond.

CHAPTER FORTY-TWO

By the time we pulled into the EconoLodge parking lot AJ had become more somber. It wasn't lost on either of us that the last time we were here there was blood on the walls.

We were rolling across the snow-covered gravel in search of a parking space when I noticed a van at the far end of the parking lot. Its engine was running, exhaust fumes curled out of the tailpipe into the star speckled sky.

"AJ, isn't that the NEO van? There's someone inside." A huge melon of a head lolled against the driver's side window. "Jesus!"

We jumped out of the car and sprinted across the lot. AJ yanked the door open. Grizzly caught himself just before he fell splat on the ground.

"What the fuck—" he bellowed.

AJ shot me a confused look, we'd both thought he was trying to gas himself, which upon reflection was silly given that he was outside in the fresh air not holed up in a locked garage somewhere. Obviously neither of us were thinking clearly by that point.

Grizzly shimmied his butt back into his seat and glared

at us with red, swollen eyes. One huge hand came up and he gave AJ a weak shove. "Get out of my door."

AJ pulled the door open wider still. "Paul, we need to talk."

"I'm having a smoke here. You're letting the cold in."

Well, that's an easy fix. I scrambled around to the passenger door and hopped in beside him. This startled AJ as much as it startled Grizzly. Then AJ came around the van and climbed up onto the bench seat beside me. The van stank of stale cigarettes, dirty clothes and the delicate scent of orange peels.

The door creaked shut and Grizzly cracked the window open an inch, in deference to us I supposed, and flicked a column of ash off his cigarette. Some grey flakes floated back in through the crack, the rest drifted away, tiny flecks on the night breeze. It was hot and smoky in the van and I was beginning to feel lightheaded.

AJ threw his arm across the back of the bench seat and leaned across me, peering into Grizzly's face. "Paul is there anyone at NEO who didn't support Sam's strategy for the Ballet House. Maybe someone who thought she'd gone too far... or not far enough?"

Grizzly let out a bitter laugh, then flicked his cigarette out the narrow space at the top of the window. "Jesus, you're as dense as the cops."

AJ continued to stare at Grizzly, a cross-examination tactic he'd perfected over the years. Don't repeat the question. Just wait. Eventually everyone cracks.

Grizzly's bushy beard was moving, he was chewing his bottom lip. Finally he said, "There's no one at NEO to call her on her strategy. We don't have a CEO or a board of directors, we're not a fucking corporation—although Sam came as close to being the boss as you could get."

He blinked rapidly, his face almost childlike despite the unruly beard, and reached into his anorak and pulled a packet of cigarettes out of his pocket. I touched his hand when he flicked his lighter.

"Grizzly," I said gently, "if it's all right with you, let's go for a walk."

He shrugged. For a big man, he was surprisingly agile. Out the door and firing up his lighter before AJ and I managed to slide across the cracked vinyl seat and climb out after him. Grizzly squinted in the direction of the utility road that ran perpendicular to the TransCanada Highway and walked away. Quickly we caught up, marching down the icy road on either side of him.

AJ asked, "Did you notice anything different about Sam in the last few weeks? Any changes in her mood or her behavior?"

Grizzly stopped and laughed. A rich throaty laugh. "Changes in her mood or behavior? She's changed so much since you knew her you wouldn't recognize her."

"You guys were tree spikers and sugar-in-the-gas-tank guys sixteen years ago; I shudder to think what you're into now."

"Give it a rest, AJ. She's less confrontational, more willing to negotiate now than back in your day. Mellowing with age, I guess." Grizzly still referred to Sam in the present tense as if she'd be back any minute with a pizza.

He took a long drag on his cigarette. A car approached from behind, honked and slammed on its brakes, sliding so close to me that I could see the driver's face as he cursed us from behind the wheel. We were all dressed in black, we probably materialized out of thin air.

I looked up at Grizzly. "Willing to negotiate? That

surprises me. NEO doesn't strike me as the kind of organization that's willing to meet anyone halfway."

He tossed his cigarette into the ditch and dug around in
his pocket for the cigarette packet. This man was a chain
smoker the likes of which I'd never seen before. He pulled
out another cigarette, lit it and turned to AJ.

"Sam and I have been at this game for two decades.
Grizzly, she'd say, doing the same thing over and over again
and expecting a different result is the very definition of
madness. As far as she was concerned protests were great
for drumming up publicity. Sure, you get a few days in
the headlines, but that fades to nothing in the next news
cycle. Destroying corporate property for the cause was a
mug's game. The corporations win public sympathy and
if you're caught you go to jail. It was time to try something
different."

He coughed as he inhaled, a deep phlegmy cough. If
Louisa were here, she'd rip that cigarette right out of his
mouth and hustle him off for a chest X-ray.

"Corporate social responsibility, ESG, all that shit is
just greenwashing by another name. Sam said it was time
we changed the rules, played a new game; one where we
used our leverage to negotiate a new deal."

Negotiate? That was the second time Grizzly used the
word. Negotiation only works if one party has something
the other party wants. What could Sam possibly offer a
big corporation to induce them to reverse course, to stop
drilling an oil well or opening a coal mine or building an
auditorium next to a river?

Heads down and shoulders hunched, we turned away
from the fierce wind and headed back to the motel in the
swirling darkness. AJ asked Grizzly how Sam's decision
to negotiate sat with NEO's old guard.

"How many times do I have to say this?" Grizzly was clearly irritated. "There is no 'old guard.' We're not a hierarchical organization. Just pods of people; some pods adopted Sam's negotiation strategy, others stuck with their own tried-and-true tactics, protests, social media campaigns, and yeah"—he stared at AJ as if daring AJ to judge him—"destroying corporate property. The strategy depends on the pod."

By now we were back at the motel. After an awkward goodbye—do mortal enemies shake hands?—Grizzly disappeared into the warmly lit lobby and we returned to AJ's ice box of a car to head back to the office.

AJ muttered something as we pulled out on to the highway. The car heater was droning so loudly I could hardly hear him so I turned it off.

AJ repeated his question. "What could Sam possibly offer an oil company, or any kind of company for that matter, to get them to back down? Nothing."

"What about...?" I'd had a horrible thought. It wasn't what Sam could offer, but what she could threatened: blackmail, arson, and death threats.

"What about what?"

"Nothing."

Sixteen years is an awfully long time. Back when I was in private practice I'd worked on an acquisition where the acquiring company described itself as 'GI Joes' and the target company as 'Care Bears.' Needless to say, after the merger the GI Joes shot the Care Bears in the head. The only way a Care Bear survives in a GI Joe culture is to pick up a gun and become a GI Joe.

If Sam was capable of tree spiking sixteen years ago, what was she capable of now?

CHAPTER FORTY-THREE

It was early in the morning. I was taking Louisa to the eye doctor—she's an excellent nurse but anything to do with eyes freaks her out and I didn't trust her not to cut and run before they called her into the examination room.

On the way to her ophthalmologist we decided to check in on Sabine. We were worried she was working too hard. She'd been released from hospital and the very next day was giving interviews and setting up fund raisers. Then to add to her stress, the police released the McMansion site, the noise next door would be deafening

"Are you sure we should be here after your blow up with Marc?" Louisa asked as we approached Sabine's door. "Perhaps we should have called first to see if we were still welcome."

"Of course we're welcome," I said. "Our relationship with Sabine is not dependent on my firm's relationship with Marc."

As I said it I wondered if I was right. Lately Louisa has shown more insight into Sabine's character than I have. This was disconcerting given that I'm the big sister and Mom appointed me Louisa's guardian angel at a very young age. It was a difficult undertaking because Louisa was a feisty little thing. She scrapped with her friends, my friends, everybody, and it fell to me to soothe ruffled feelings in the school yard so she wouldn't get pulverized on the walk home. It's a miracle I had any friends left by the time I started high school.

"Well, we're here now," I said, ringing the doorbell. It chimed behind the black lacquered door but there was no answer.

"Let's check the back," Louisa said.

Visions of dead crows came to mind as we crossed the snow-hardened lawn to the walkway between Sabine's house and the McMansion. We were picking our way past the prickly burning bushes when someone haled us.

A man wearing wraparound sunglasses and a battered blue ball cap waved from the McMansion site. It was Levi. His only concession to the bitterly cold weather was a heavy unzipped parka that flapped in the breeze. He appeared to be alone, the rest of the construction crew had not yet arrived.

"Looks like you're making good progress," I said, nodding in the direction of the McMansion. The hole for the foundation had been dug, it was closer to Sabine's house than I'd expected but thankfully her sandstone wall and the massive mountain ash were still standing.

Shyly, Levi bobbed his head, saying today they would start on the wooden forms for the concrete pour. Then he paused and asked if we could help him with something.

We followed Levi back to his truck and he opened the passenger door and pulled a light blue box out of the glove compartment. It was a tin Players cigarette box, big enough to hold fifty cigarettes. Other than a few rust specks marring the gold edges, it was in remarkable condition.

"Do you think this may have belonged to the Sabine?" He glanced at her empty house.

"Sabine and Marc don't smoke." Louisa interrupted.

"That box looks like its from the 1960s," I added. "They didn't move in until 2000."

He shook his head. "No, sorry, not the box." And popped the tin open. A hint of ancient tobacco cut through the crisp air. Inside was a brass cuff bracelet, its surface deeply incised with tiny lines. He placed it in my hand and quickly it warmed to my touch.

Louisa took it from me, running her thumb over the incised surface. "It's looks like a medicinal bracelet, the kind that keeps the body in balance and has magical properties." She managed to say it without a trace of skepticism. "It could be from the Himalayas or Nepal."

I stared at her. How does she know these things?

"Where'd you find it?" I asked Levi.

He glanced over his shoulder at the flattened lot. "On the perimeter of the foundation hole. With all those people tromping around it's a miracle it wasn't crushed."

Like a greedy magpie he watched the trinket pass from Louisa's hand to mine. Slipping it into my purse, I promised to show it to Sabine. It didn't look expensive like the jewelry she usually wore, but she may have picked it up on her travels. She loved trolling through exotic bazaars looking for souvenirs for her friends.

"I'll drive," I said to Louisa when we were back in her car. We were ten minutes late and she drives like an old lady in rush hour traffic. Ahead a large truck blocked the road as it attempted to turn around in a neighbour's driveway. Impatiently I drummed the steering wheel.

"Don't honk," Louisa said, unlike me she's not an

aggressive driver, "you'll just make him mad. We've got plenty of time."

"Not really," I muttered and maneuvered the Honda around the truck. "God, now what?"

The dashboard lit up. The low tire pressure light was yellow. "Great, we picked up a nail." I lifted my hands from the steering wheel and the Honda pulled to the right, determined to throw itself into the ditch.

"You don't have run-flats?" I asked her.

"No, I don't have run flats. You have run flats; I have a spare in the trunk." And I remembered that not only is Louisa a careful driver, she's cheap. Her Honda was ancient. It was a miracle we weren't paddling with our bare feet in a Flintstone car. The steering wheel bucked and fought me on the corner.

We were trundling down Fourteenth Street heading to Seventeenth Avenue when the stoplight changed to red. Louisa was quiet, unlike me she shuts up when she's stressed.

"Jesus!" She jumped when a young man in the black watch cap rapped on her window. He pointed to the back of the car and she rolled down her window.

"Your right back tire is losing air," he said, "it's a pancake."

We told him we knew and were heading to a garage. As we pulled across the intersection, the sound of flapping got louder and louder. We'd be riding the rim soon.

"You need to buy a new car," I groused.

"There." Louisa shouted, pointing to the Shell station at the end of the block. "Pull over there. Pull over there, now."

The flapping noise sounded louder and sloppier. "If you had run flats we'd be at your eye doctor by now." I said, "She's just around the corner." That is probably my most irritating trait. When stressed, I state the obvious.

Louisa pressed her lips together, one hand flailing in the direction of the Shell station, while the other fumbled in her purse. "Evie, there. Park the car."

She had Uber on the line and almost lost her phone when I turned into the gas station and clipped the curb. With a glint in her eye she looked over and said, "So help me, if you bent the rim..."

The Honda limped into a parking spot at the side of the garage. Louisa jumped out, phone in hand, and asked the gas station attendant the address, then relayed it to the Uber guy. When he arrived, we sniped at each other all the way to the eye doctor.

It wasn't until we Ubered home that I sorted out who I was angry with. It wasn't Louisa and her ancient car and it wasn't the truck that forced me onto the shoulder where I picked up a nail; it was Sabine who had us running back and forth worried sick about her, while Marc was free to do whatever he pleased.

CHAPTER FORTY-FOUR

In the beginning when Keith and I opened our firm, I'd arrive each day and linger in the lobby savouring it all. The way the morning light warmed the wood paneled walls, the clicking of Bridget's busy fingers across her keyboard, Madeline's laugh as she teased Keith in the coffee room. We were doing what we loved, life was grand.

Then green energy and renewables took off and we were swamped. We brought AJ on board to ease the burden, he would be the vent on this pressure cooker. The vent worked for three months.

What we'd failed to consider was the strength of AJ's relationship with his granddad. The fertilizer magnate wanted AJ to join the family business. AJ resisted and the old guy bided his time, referring everyone he knew to his brilliant grandson in the belief that eventually AJ would ditch us for a more lucrative career as a high flying corporate executive. Which meant we were swamped again.

Finally we made it a policy to cut back on non-paying work. Keith reminded me of this when I got into the office and I promised to cut Sabine loose right after I'd shown her the Tibetan (or whatever it was) bracelet.

I passed Madeline on my way down the hall to my office. She was in the conference room with our accountant, a fresh faced young man with a quiet sense of humour. They were devising a plan to hold CRA—the federal tax authority—at bay.

"How's it going?" I asked.

Joel, our plucky accountant (I'm not sure why we call him that but we do) chuckled. "Do you really want to know?"

I shook my head and sat down at my desk. Sabine's phone rang three times before she answered with a curt 'Sabine speaking,' her brusque tone signalling that whoever was calling had better make it snappy.

When I said I had something to show her she asked me to meet her at the Calgary Ballet School later that afternoon. She'd started the school shortly after she'd arrived in the city and now held an emeritus position which gave her a lot of clout.

After I parked in the school's miniscule parking lot, the receptionist directed me to the small dance studio in the back. There I found Sabine and Robert watching ten little girls in pink tutus, white tights and soft shoes working in front of a large, mirrored wall. Their teacher gently led them through their pliés and tendus, while Sabine clapped and offered words of encouragement in French. In her long, black sweater and grey leggings she could be mistaken for a young ballerina taking a break from rehearsal. At least from a distance.

I wasn't surprised to see Robert here. The Symphony practiced in the morning and performed in the evening and it appeared that all his free time was spent with Sabine.

We'd just settled ourselves in a small dressing room when the administrator popped her head in the door and reminded Sabine she was going to call the director of the National Ballet.

"That's fine, Charlotte, "Sabine said with a sly smile. "We spoke this morning. She says she's thrilled for us."

Charlotte looked skeptical. "She's thrilled we landed the Prix?"

"No, of course not." Sabine became more animated as she described their conversation. "The poor woman was as green as an elm tree, she's beyond envy."

Charlotte flashed a broad grin and left.

Robert shifted in his chair to face me. "Evie, just look at her face. Isn't she utterly charming?" Charming wasn't exactly the word I would have chosen as Sabine described what the loss of the Prix would mean to the National Ballet.

"Now Robert, don't exaggerate. I said I wouldn't gloat and I didn't... at least not to her face. That would have been in such poor taste."

"She gloated," Robert told me. "I was sitting right here when she made the call. She practically crowed in triumph." He turned to Sabine. "Run away with me, my darling. We'll can fly to Madagascar tonight."

She laughed. "Silly man, what would I do about Marc?"

"Ditch Marc, he doesn't deserve you, he never has."

As they bantered, I had the feeling they'd had this conversation many times before. Their laughter died down and Sabine turned to me. "You have something to show me? May I see it?"

"Of course." I retrieved my purse from the low counter, fished out the brass bracelet and passed it to her. The burnished metal gleamed in the sunlight spilling through the high windows.

Sabine peered at the inscription carved inside. "How unusual. Is it a prayer trinket?"

I explained that a worker at the McMansion had found it and didn't want to keep it if it belonged to Sabine.

She slipped it on. The cuff was small and sat nicely on her wrist.

"No," she said, gazing at it, "it's not mine." She held her wrist up to the light for one last look before sliding it off. "It is very pretty though. Where did the worker find it?"

"Near the concrete forms, they're getting ready to pour the foundation."

Immediately her face darkened. "That horrible Sidney Foster. He insists his name must be etched on a bronze plaque in the lobby. He says it's his due because he's the biggest donor to the Ballet House."

Puzzled, I asked, "Isn't that typical with big donors?" I'd seen many public buildings where entire walls were covered with the names of donors, large and small.

She shuddered as if she'd been doused with cold water. "The Ballet House is not a typical building. It's a work of art. Did Michelangelo's patrons carve their names into the statue of David?"

For all I knew they did, but I decided the prudent course would be to stay quiet and let her grumble until I left.

On the drive back to the office, I reflected on our conversation. Sabine had always been mercurial. Mom said one of the things she liked about Sabine was she was never boring. But lately her moods had an edge. I made a mental note to talk to Louisa about it.

CHAPTER FORTY-FIVE

The office was strangely quiet. Bridget was in reception talking softly on the phone to Theo, her husband. He's an IT consultant who works from home, he must be lonely or he bores easily because he calls Bridget at least three times a day. Madeline was holed up in her office doing God knows what, Keith was out at a day-long hearing and AJ was at Sam's funeral, or was it a celebration of life ceremony?

The metal cuff bracelet glinted on my windowsill. Warming in the winter sun. It was perfectly balanced in weight and design. Curiosity made me Google the markings. The incisions were a tribal leaf design, but the symbols etched inside were a mystery, unlike anything Google could identify. When I had time, I'd take it back to Levi.

"How was it?" Bridget's voice rang out in the lobby. She was talking to AJ who'd just returned from Sam's funeral.

"Awful," he replied.

I closed my laptop, knowing his next stop would be my office. Attending Sam's funeral was a mistake; I'd told him that. "You knew her sixteen years ago, but you don't know her now. You're under no obligation to go."

"We shared a past. Evie. It's important to me..." his voice

had trailed off and he swallowed hard before continuing. "Besides she has no family; she deserves more than a send-off from a bunch of NEO activists and Paul-Grizzly-Adams."

That was three hours ago. Now AJ was back, hovering outside my door. I waved him in and he dropped into one of my visitor's chairs.

"Well? How was it?"

"You were right. It was a mistake. I didn't belong there." He took a deep breath and let it out slowly. His eyes were clear. It didn't look like he'd been crying. But he never cries at funerals. A long time ago he'd told me he counts backwards from one hundred to deaden the pain; so he may have been more cut up than he appeared.

"They handed out these little cards." He flipped a pale green card onto my desk, on one side was a photo of Sam, her big, brown eyes sparkled and her chestnut hair bounced around her face in glossy curls, on the other side was a blue-green Earth floating in the velvety void of space. "The minute we sat down, Grizzly went to the podium. At first, he talked about Sam's contribution to the movement; but then he veered off course and started to lecture us like a holy roller about the Gaia hypothesis."

"Gaia, as in we're all part of a giant symbiotic system that supports life on Earth? I didn't know NEO believed in Gaia."

"I'm not sure that they do," he said with a shrug, "because this wasn't your typical Gaia, this was Gaia on steroids. As far as Grizzly is concerned, humanity is killing the planet and Mother Earth has decided if she's going down, she's taking mankind with her."

"Well at least they're focusing on the planet, not the second coming. Did you know there have been more than forty-five 'the end is nigh' prophesies that failed to materialize?"

AJ smiled. "Your font of useless information never ceases to amaze me."

He picked up Sam's card and stared at her image for a moment. "She was always more militant than I was, but she believed in science, not mumbo jumbo."

I studied him for a moment then said, "Sixteen years ago that may have been true, but we don't know what she believed now."

"She wasn't a nutcase," he said with a stubborn shake of his head. "She trusted the evidence that shows climate change is real and we're facing an existential crisis. She would never fall for Grizzly's crap that the Earth was a malevolent entity bent on destroying humanity."

I wanted to ask AJ how he could be so sure, but he was off on a rant about zealots who did as much to damage the credibility of the climate change movement as the denialists.

Suddenly he stopped in mid sentence. "Where did you get that?" He pointed to the brass cuff bracelet sitting in a pool of light on my windowsill.

I pivoted in my chair, picked it up and passed it to him. "Levi, one of the workers at the McMansion, found it when they were getting ready to pour the foundation. He wondered if it belonged to Sabine."

"It doesn't." AJ held it gently, as if it were a small bird. "It belonged to Sam."

Setting it on my desk, he unbuttoned his left sleeve to reveal a matching brass bracelet, thicker and wider, but bearing the same tribal leaf markings. "We bought them when we were backpacking in Nepal."

His face softened. "We swore we'd never take them off,

but it turned out I'm allergic to base metals. Two days later it was stashed in my backpack and I haven't worn it since. Until today. For the funeral."

He slipped his cuff off and set it down next to Sam's, then scratched the inside of his wrist. "The damn thing is giving me hives already."

The two cuffs gleamed in the sunlight bouncing off the snowy river outside. I knew the symbols inside each cuff would be identical. I didn't have to ask AJ what they meant. What I wanted to know was how a cuff Sam never took off ended up in Levi's possession.

CHAPTER FORTY-SIX

There was a time when the best restaurants in town served nothing but steak and lobster (surf & turf) in dining rooms so dark you could barely find your fork. Frank Sinatra crooned in the background about doing it his way and raucous oilmen tossed back whiskies and negotiated deals on the back of a napkin. Who needs a lawyer, they'd say, when a simple handshake would do. A man's word—and it was always a man—was his bond.

Thankfully, those days are long gone.

Now you can eat whatever you'd like in one of the many smart, trendy restaurants tucked into the bottom of office towers or next to the bead shops and bakeries that line neighbourhood streets.

So when Keith charged through the door at the end of the day and announced there was a free dinner waiting for us at Barbarella—one of the city's best restaurants—if we could get there in the next thirty minutes, we dropped everything and raced to our cars. We had Keith's client to thank for this unexpected perk. He was so grateful Keith managed to convince the regulator that wind turbines in the middle of nowhere were not a blight on the landscape that he told his brother-in-law, Barbarella's top chef, to squeeze us in.

Madeline rode with me and spent much of the drive lamenting the fact we'd had no prior notice to prepare for the gastronomic delights we were about to enjoy. "Rushing around like a chicken with its head cut off is not good for the digestion." She sounded like my mother.

I laughed but said nothing. Madeline, a patron of all the best restaurants in town, was just miffed she hadn't been the one to pull off this miracle.

Barbarella is an unusual space with a double height dining room, a mezzanine, and a tall orange fireplace like the kind you'd find at a ski chalet. From our table we could watch the see-and-be-seen crowd milling about at the bar.

Madeline murmured with approval as she pored over the menu. "Coastal Italian food. Did I ever tell you about the time poor Francis and I drove down the Amalfi coast? He finally let me drive his fancy car, a pretty red convertible"—I could picture her in oversized sunglasses and a silk headscarf, flying through hairpin turns—"then he had a panic attack and grabbed the steering wheel right out of my hands. It's a miracle we weren't killed."

AJ choked on his diavolo and I coughed into my napkin. Bridget, never one to mince words, said, "Madline you're a terrible driver, poor Francis probably saved you from driving off a cliff into the sea."

Keith was about to add a comment when my phone rang. *Caller ID, Sabine Hubert.*

Madeline shot me a look. "Let it go to voice mail." I frowned; Madeline could see I was wavering. "Fine," she said, "pick it up, but mark my words, you'll regret it."

I rose from the table and crossed the dark wooden floor looking for a private corner while Sabine whispered apologies into my ear. "Evie, I hate to bother you with such a silly thing, it's trivial, really, but I've been having nightmares"— God, Madeline was right, now we're talking about Sabine's dreams again.

"Yes, you mentioned the crow dream."

"No, not crows."

The crowd was noisy and I moved around the arc of the horseshoe-shaped bar in search of a quiet place. "Sabine you'll have to speak up, I can hardly hear you."

"It's the bracelet, it's haunting me. It... well..."

I pressed the phone closer to my ear. Sabine said something but I missed it. "I'm sorry, can you repeat that?"

More firmly, she said, "I'd like to see the bracelet again."

"Sabine, it's okay, I've found its owner."

She insisted she didn't care who it belonged to, she just had to see it again.

Over at our table Keith was telling a joke. He's notoriously bad at telling jokes but must have made it to the punch line without mangling it because everyone was laughing.

"Sure, fine." I shuffled to one side to let a man and woman press by me to claim a couple of chairs at the end of the bar. "Come down to the office whenever you'd like."

She thanked me again. AJ and Bridget were waving at me, *get back here*, I nodded and hung up.

The server and I reached the table at the same time. She smiled and said it was Aperitivo Happy Hour and if I ordered fast—"As in right now," Bridget chimed in—we could get our drinks and our pizzas at half-price. Half-price off of a free dinner. It doesn't get any better than that.

When the fragrant pizzas arrived, we devoured them so fast we scalded our tongues and in the chatter over limoncello spritzes, Nutella espresso martinis (for Bridget) and Italian beers I forgot all about Sabine.

Many hours and a few perfectly awful Keith jokes later, AJ declared it was time for us to go home. As Madeline and I made our way to the door, she nudged my arm and tipped her head in the direction of a quiet, dark corner. "Don't turn around"—of course I turned around—"it's Marc and his paramour."

A surreptitious glance confirmed Madeline was right. Marc and a lively, middle-aged woman were laughing over their menus. Marc leaned in and smiled a lot. In his charcoal blazer and slim fit slacks he blended in with this young urbane crowd. The woman laughed and tossed her long blonde hair over one shoulder, then sat back in her chair watching Marc chat with the server.

Back in the car I said to Madeline, "I thought his mistress was a sleek Brazilian woman, dark hair, dark eyes, exotic?"

"*Mais, oui,*" she said with a theatrical French accent. "That's not the mistress, that's the infamous Diana Barros, the mother of his child, Alice."

Unlike his beleaguered wife, Marc didn't have a care in the world.

CHAPTER FORTY-SEVEN

The next morning everyone except Madeline who can stay up past ten p.m. on a weeknight was hiding behind their computers radiating don't-talk-to-me vibes. None of us are getting any younger.

Bridget tapped on my door, then stepped into my office and squinted into the sunlight as if she were trying to get her bearings. "You've got a visitor, two actually."

When I first met Bridget, she reminded me of Rosie the Riveter but today she looked so pale I wondered whether she'd be safe operating a mouse, never mind a power drill. Without waiting for a reply she faded out the door, returning a minute later with Sabine and Robert.

Sabine swept into my office, her long white coat swirling behind her like a cape. It wasn't until she took off her sunglasses and perched them on top of her silvery hair that I saw how tired she was. Her dreams of crows and bracelets were taking their toll. Robert on the other hand beamed with robust good health. With a hearty hello, he sat down, gently tugging Sabine to sit down beside him and said, "Right, let's get this show on the road."

The brass bracelet snagged on a red elastic band when

I pulled it out of my desk drawer. I untangled it and set it in front of Sabine. Cautiously, she ran her fingertip along the tribal leaf markings, then spoke to Robert in rapid-fire French. He responded just as quickly in French. Outside in the hall Madeline appeared, then quietly disappeared.

"Robert," I said. His head popped up like a prairie gopher. "I didn't realize you spoke French."

He shrugged in a self-deprecating way and said, *un peu*, a little. I envied him. To my ear Robert's command of the language was more than *un peu*.

Gently, Sabine placed the cuff in the middle of my desk.

"Evie, it is beautiful, thank you. But I don't know this bracelet." She shot a quick glance at Robert and said she was sorry to have dragged him away from work for nothing.

He assured her it was no bother at all, then turned to me and said, "This poor woman, all she does is work, work, work." Smiling gently at her he said, "My dear, if you don't slow down, you'll drive yourself into an early grave." Then he slipped his hand under her elbow and guided her to the door. "Come along. I'll take you home."

I'd never seen the Black Swan look so frail. It was unnerving.

No sooner were they gone than Madeline swept in. "Oh please, spare me." She flopped into the chair just vacated by Sabine and lifted a hand melodramatically to her brow in a mock swoon. "Oh Robert," she mimicked Sabine's voice, "take me home."

"What are you going on about?"

"Sabine recognized that bracelet all right. She said as much to Robert."

"You were eavesdropping?"

"Of course I was eavesdropping," she sniffed. "And it's a good thing too. My Quebecois French may not be as refined as her Parisian French, but she lied to you. The first thing out of her mouth was, 'Oh, c'est Bijoux.' Bijoux means jewelry, did Marc give it to her?"

"Bijoux was Sabine's favourite crow; she was carrying its dead body around when Vincent found her in alley."

"Whatever. It took Robert a few minutes to catch on. She said it was Bijoux's bracelet. She found it by the trash cans. Then Robert told her to be quiet, quite rudely too I might add."

The crow's bracelet? Before I could process what Madeline was saying, AJ barged in. Like me, he looked a little worse for wear after Barbarella's and like Madeline he had no qualms about eavesdropping. "Sabine's crow found Sam's bracelet by the trash cans? And a McMansion worker—"

"Levi."

"Levi found Sam's bracelet at the McMansion when they were getting ready to pour the foundation? That's impossible. She never took it off."

"Who found it isn't the issue," I said. "The—"

Another rap at the door. Bridget announced that our next client had arrived and she'd put him in the conference room. Madeline left to get her file but AJ lingered, silently watching me gather my yellow lined pad and BIC pens.

"AJ, what is it?"

After a moment he said, "I'm going to talk to her."

"Sabine?"

The look in his eyes made my heart sink. AJ is slow to anger but when he finally loses his temper it's like a category five hurricane making landfall. From the look in his eyes, storm clouds were gathering, the winds were picking up speed.

"Please AJ, don't go haring off after her. Wait until the

end of the day and I'll go with you. She trusts me. She'll be more honest with me." Why did I think that? She'd just lied to my face, nevertheless AJ agreed to wait until after work.

Madeline was just outside the conference room when I caught up to her. As she reached for the doorknob she said, "There was a time when I admired Marc and Sabine Hubert. They were so cosmopolitan, so urbane, so *je ne sais quoi*. And now look at them. Marc is flaunting his mistresses all over town and Sabine is a liar or losing her mind. You never really know what's going on inside those glittering lives, do you?"

With that she pulled open the door and flashed her wide green eyes at Mr. Hanley. "Charlie, how lovely to see you again." The middle-aged entrepreneur grinned like a star-struck schoolboy. She gripped his hand and gave it a firm shake. Poor Mr. Hanley didn't know what hit him.

CHAPTER FORTY-EIGHT

Quincy and I were curled up on the teddy bear sofa watching a documentary about an unsolved murder in Arkansas. "Aren't you glad you don't live in Arkansas?" I asked the dog. It was a brutal murder, a young woman slaughtered, blood everywhere. He sighed deeply, he didn't care where he lived as long as it was with Louisa and me.

After AJ's insistence that we confront Sabine immediately he'd sheepishly returned to my office at the end of the day to say he'd forgotten he had a hockey game—"If I pull out now, the guys will kill me"—and we postponed our visit to Sabine until tomorrow.

It was past eleven. Louisa would be home soon and Quincy and I could barely keep our eyes open. "I work," I said to the dog, "that's why I'm tired. What's your excuse?"

He opened one small black eye and rolled over onto his side almost shoving me off the sofa. A minute later he was snoring like a buzz saw. "You can sleep all you want, you're still my thinking partner." It's a term my HR friend uses when she wants to bounce ideas off someone. Until Louisa got home, Quincy would have to do.

AJ had told me Sam was wearing the bracelet the night

we met her and Grizzly at the National. "Quincy, I don't know what's more unnerving. The fact it's been sixteen years and she never took it off or the fact he noticed. Did she still love him? Heaven forbid, did he still love her?" Something fluttered inside me at the thought, although there was no reason why I should care. I wasn't AJ's keeper.

Quincy's paws twitched. He was running in his sleep.

"And Grizzly? He says he admired Sam but he's a Gaia extremist and Sam followed the science. Something's not right there."

Quincy lifted his head and cocked an eye at the window. Louisa's headlights swept across the glass as she crept down our slippery driveway. The garage door groaned and the dog shot across my legs and raced to the door at the top of the basement stairs, prancing and yipping in anticipation. Once we'd accidently left the door open and he launched himself at Louisa, almost breaking her neck as they tumbled down the stairs into the basement.

"Quincy, back up," Louisa said, slowly opening the door and edging into the kitchen before giving him a proper huggy-pat hello.

"I'm glad you're home," I told her. "You're a much better thinking partner than Quincy."

She lifted both hands in a sign of refusal. "Forget it, I'm exhausted. We're going to bed." Quincy agreed and they marched upstairs leaving me alone, fretting in the kitchen about Sam and AJ and Grizzly.

———

The next evening AJ and I were parked in Sabine's driveway. It was six o'clock, the night was cold and frosty and except for the ghostly uplight shining on Sabine's paper birch trees, her place was dark.

AJ had spent the whole day darting in and out of my office with ideas on how he would pry the truth out of Sabine. I told him not to get his hopes up. As my dad used to say, nothing is ever sorted in the first round.

"I guess we should have called ahead," I said, rubbing my hands together to keep them warm. It had been twenty minutes, there was no sign of her.

"Yeah, and said what? There are holes in your story and we're coming over to give you the third degree."

I glanced at him for a moment, a category five hurricane was about to make landfall.

Something metallic rapped on my side window.

"Jesus!" AJ jerked back in his seat and I jumped so hard my seatbelt cut into my throat. Beaming at me in the gloom was Levi, it was so dark he wasn't wearing sunglasses and it took me a moment to recognize him. He waved a red plaid thermos at me, then tucked it under his arm so he could point at his wrist and then at Sabine's house. "The bracelet?" he shouted through the glass.

"AJ"— I unbuckled my seat belt—"we need to talk to this guy."

After making a shambles of the introductions, I told Levi the bracelet didn't belong to Sabine but to the murdered environmental activist whose body had been buried in the rubble. "It's evidence in a murder investigation."

He stiffened. "Are you sure?"

When I told him there was no doubt whatsoever, he seemed to shrink into his camouflage parka; the hood falling forward to hide his face.

One of the other workers called his name. It was quitting

time, they were going to the pub. Levi nodded absently and said he'd catch up to them in a few minutes.

"Listen Levi," AJ said, "can you show us exactly where you found the bracelet?"

The McMansion site was dark and we used our phones to pick our way along the edge of the foundation excavation. The foundation pour was finished and its footprint confirmed Sabine's suspicion that the McMansion was nothing more than an oversized, uninspiring box.

We crept across the uneven ground in the narrow space separating the concrete from Sabine's garden wall. Someone had taken it upon themselves to shear off the prickly branches of the burning bush poking over the sandstone wall and the hedge was lopsided, like a kid with a bad haircut. Normally that kind of thing makes Sabine livid, but she hadn't mentioned it to me.

About three quarters of the way along the foundation wall, Levi stopped and nudged a clod of dirt with his boot.

"Bud, you sure about that?" AJ crossed his arms, fixing Levi with a cold stare. AJ's voice was firm, not the least bit accusatory. That would come later depending on Levi's reply.

"Levi." I eased past the truncated branches of the burning bush to stand next to AJ. "You didn't find it here, did you?" The image of the bottle picker flapping his umbrella to frighten the crows came to mind. "Levi, you're a scavenger. You search for things at demolition sites and sell them on to scrap dealers and junk shops, right?"

There's no shame in that and yet Levi lowered his eyes and shuffled his feet, making the snow crunch underfoot.

"Look," AJ said as he bent down, bringing his face closer to Levi's, "no one's in trouble here. We're just trying to figure out how you ended up with that bracelet."

"Okay." Levi waved a hand, indicating we should follow him. He opened a gap in the wire security fence and led us out into the alley. Telling us that unlike those other guys, who focus on the big stuff, copper tubing, stained glass, marble mantlepieces, he preferred to scrounge for collectables. The Players cigarette tin he'd shown Louisa and me would sell for fifty bucks, easy, on eBay.

"This vacuum flask"—he held up the red plaid thermos—"could be a hundred years old. They made a Barbie thermos in the nineteen sixties, can you imagine what that would go for—"

He stopped talking, suddenly aware he was babbling.

Levi led us to the concrete apron behind Sabine's two car garage and pointed to her garbage bins. This was where I'd run into the bottle picker who accused me of hurting the crows. Levi was about to say something when one of the garage doors rumbled open. We all flinched as if we were under gunfire.

In the pale light spilling out of the garage AJ looked as if he'd been caught doing something illegal. No doubt I looked the same. I turned to Levi but he was gone, the gap in the security fence was closed and he'd disappeared into the night.

Sabine braked sharply when she caught sight of us. Her headlights were bright and slanted and looked vaguely menacing. Slowly she drove into the garage. We followed in a plume of exhaust fumes and waited for her to turn off the engine.

"What is the matter with you two? You gave me a horrible fright." Sabine opened her door and glared at us, then reached across the passenger seat and slung a large leather handbag over her arm. The garage door made a metallic purring noise as it slowly came down.

"Sabine, wait." I ran to the door. "Can you keep it open? We have some questions about the bracelet."

Her face became a smooth mask. She leaned into the car and touched the remote clipped to the visor. The garage door groaned and reversed course and AJ and I ducked out to stand in front of the garbage bins casting long black shadows into the alley.

"Sabine," I said when she joined us, "I know you recognized the bracelet. You said as much to Robert."

She shifted her heavy handbag from one arm to the other as I recounted Levi's story. "He picked up the bracelet here, in the bin or next to it, the morning Vincent found you with the dead crow. It was Bijoux, wasn't it?"

"Yes." Her voice was tight. "Poor, poor Bijoux. He'd been injured and the other crows were frantic."

"When was this?" I asked.

AJ interrupted, "Where did you find it?" He looked ghastly in the flat LED light.

"When did I find it?" She'd misheard him. She pulled her phone out of her black leather bag to check the date. Her hand was shaking and she couldn't enter her password. After two tries she dropped the phone into her bag and said, "Robert took me to a concert. Marc was working late preparing for his trip to DC—"

"Sabine." AJ's tone was brusque as he cut her off. "Where did you find the bracelet?"

Tears welled in her eyes. "Next to him. Poor, poor Bijoux."

"Here?" I looked at the narrow space between the two bins. "The bird and the bracelet were both here?" I kept my voice calm, matter of fact. "Why did you lie about recognizing it?"

A sob, then another. Oh God, she was falling apart.

The rumble of the garage door startled us all. The LED lamp on Marc's side of the garage flicked to life as his headlights swept into the alley, bobbing through the potholes in the frosted asphalt.

Sabine darted back inside and activated her remote. We ducked under the door, barely making it inside before it touched the concrete floor.

"Enough," she said. The tears were gone. The Black Swan was in control. "Leave before Marc sees you."

His door was wide open, waiting as cones of bright white light raked across the high stone wall on the other side of the alley.

Sabine disappeared out the side door and down the flagstone path that runs through the garden to the back of the house.

AJ took a tentative step after her, then slopped and turned to me. "Do we stop her? Do we stay and talk to him?"

I shook my head. It was too late. Sabine had vanished into the house and I was certain Marc would explode if he saw us again. We hustled down the flagstone path, around the house to AJ's car which was parked in the driveway. Marc would never know we'd been there.

CHAPTER FORTY-NINE

The following evening after dinner Louisa told me AJ and I were becoming obsessed with Sabine and the bracelet. "You two egg each other on. It's not healthy. You need to back off and let the cops do their job." She gave me a hard look before continuing. "Also, why aren't you ready?"

Ready for what? I wondered. That's when I noticed she was wearing her nice wool coat and had already pulled on her leather boots. Louisa dragged my coat out of the closet and handed it to me. And I remembered: Girls Night Out.

Louisa, the social secretary in our tiny family unit had expanded her network and was now the social secretary for the female half of BLV. I don't know how this came about but she's constantly booking Madeline, Bridget and me into events that sound like a great idea at the time but turn into an ordeal when the day finally arrives. Tonight was no different. It was bitterly cold; the wind could rip a car door right off its hinges and we had tickets for the Locked Library event at the Central Library.

At first Madeline and Bridget balked. Madeline said if she was stuck in a confined space with the three of us, she could not be held responsible for her actions and Bridget declared she was claustrophobic and wouldn't survive the night.

Louisa assured them the library wasn't actually locked and they could leave any time they wanted, but she'd be terribly disappointed if they did.

I grumbled all the way into town, saying it wasn't too late to forfeit our tickets. Louisa wouldn't hear of it. "It wouldn't be fair to Bridget and Madeline; you know they can't do it alone. They'll have a much better chance of winning with us along."

I tried not to guffaw. Winning the Locked Library game is a lot harder than it sounds. The last time Louisa talked me into playing we were up against twelve teams in a small suburban library. The only reason we didn't come in dead last was we beat a pair of old ladies from Britain by thirty seconds.

I gave up and parked the car a couple of blocks from the library. The architects claimed its glittering glass façade was inspired by snow drifts and chinook clouds but to me it looked more like a cruise ship or a sunlit iceberg.

We joined the crowd surging around the registration table. There were more than a thousand players in the game tonight. Halfway to the front of the line we heard a piercing wolf whistle. Standing on the stairs leading up to the auditorium was Bridget, waving her arms as if she were signalling a rescue ship from a desert island. Madeline was beside her pretending she'd never seen Bridget before in her life.

Louisa pantomimed that we'd join them in the auditorium, Bridget nodded and Madeline shot me a look that said, *I can't believe you talked me into this.*

We found them in a corner of the auditorium poring over their game sheets and uploading QR codes to access the game website. Bridget appointed herself team captain and started barking out instructions the minute the starting bell sounded.

"Into the elevator. We're starting at the top."

She's a tough taskmaster, which was a good thing because I was transfixed by the sheer beauty of the space—the soaring red cedar walls, the vaulted ceilings and the giant Oculus skylight that allowed a glimpse of a mysterious moon—the architecture moved me in a way I couldn't explain. Marc wanted to evoke the same feeling of awe on a much smaller scale, but when I thought about the Ballet House, all that came to mind was the Sin List.

"Evie, eyes on the prize! Let's go!" Bridget clapped her hands together twice.

We plunged into the crowd and rushed in and out of rooms and up and down stairs, quibbling about the meaning of clues and where the next one might be hidden.

After fifty-three minutes of clue-spotting and code breaking and eavesdropping on teams further along in the game than we were, we raced across the main lobby to ring the finish bell and memorialize our very respectable finish time with a selfie.

Madeline suggested a celebratory drink but after the Barbella experience we begged off. "It's a school night," I explained.

The euphoria of the game lasted until Louisa and I were back in the car heading home. I was still distressed by Sabine's lie. "I can understand why Levi lied about where he found the bracelet. He didn't want to admit he was a scavenger, but why would Sabine lie?"

"You're obsessing again."

"Can I ask you a question?" Louisa sighed, crossing

her arms and slouching lower in her seat. "Was Sabine's delirium and memory loss real?"

Up ahead the light changed to green and I sped through the intersection.

"Yes, it was real, but it was temporary. It would have eased off by the time they released her from hospital."

"So she lied twice. Once when she examined the bracelet at the ballet school and again in my office. Why would she lie?"

"Why does anyone lie?" Louisa replied. "To protect themselves or something they love."

I ran through all the things Sabine loved: Marc, Robert, the ballet, the Prix de Lyon, her status as a leading philanthropist and stalwart supporter of arts and culture.

Which one was she lying to protect?

CHAPTER FIFTY

At BLV we don't believe that loose lips sink ships, in fact we're the opposite kind of law firm. We make a point of leaving our doors open and ensuring everyone is up to speed on everything. Which was why Bridget blanched when I told her I was not to be disturbed for the next thirty minutes and locked my office door.

Last night, just as I was dozing off, I remembered that Sam's bracelet was evidence in a murder investigation and I should have reported it to the police sooner. Given our history, I fully expected Sargeant Pritchard to blast me.

First, I aligned the edge of my yellow notepad with the edge of my desk, then I selected my favourite BIC pen (they're not all the same) and only then was I ready to scroll through my contacts and place the call.

Pritchard picked up immediately and I explained that I'd come into possession of a bracelet that had belonged to Sam and two people had had lied about recognizing it.

There was a long pause. Then his gravelly reply. "You should have turned it in immediately."

"It didn't come into my possession until, um, a few days ago."

"A few days?"

Quickly, I conceded he was right, I was terribly sorry and I'd bring it to him right away.

Soon I was parking the Mini in Pritchard's crumbly parking lot. Every time I come here, there's a long black train rolling across the western horizon and sure enough, there was one there today.

The man on the front desk buzzed Pritchard who appeared a few minutes later and led me back to his office. I passed him a Ziploc bag. He ripped it open and slid the cuff onto the blotter on his desk. As he examined it, I examined him. I've known Pritchard for six years and he hasn't changed a bit. Tall and lean, with thick brown hair and curious eyes; taciturn to the point of being rude.

"Have you made any progress identifying Sam's killer?"

No response.

I tried the question a couple of different ways, hoping he'd drop his guard as he tapped the cuff with a pencil, turning it in the light to examine the inscription.

Eventually he glanced up at me. "Everything the public needs to know, that would be you, is in the public realm." Right, he wasn't going to tell me a damn thing.

Then he asked me a question I wasn't expecting: did I know whether Sam was seeing someone?

"You mean other than Grizzly—sorry—Paul Adams?"

"Adams is just a friend."

"I'm not so sure about that." Whenever Sam's name came up Grizzly, that hulk of a man, fell to bits like an office tower crumbling in an earthquake.

AJ? Should I mention AJ? No, they'd had a relationship sixteen years ago. There was nothing between them now. Sam's bracelet mocked me: *Are you sure?*

Pritchard's eyes never left my face. "Apparently she was seeing someone."

"You mean before she was killed?"

"That's what I said."

I shrugged. "I wouldn't know anything about that."

There was another long pause. Pritchard slid the bracelet back in the Ziploc bag and stared at me, waiting for me to recognize my cue to leave.

With a small smile I said, "If you need my help in any way, please feel free to call." I'd said this to him many times before but this time I actually meant it.

He tightened his lips; was he stifling a laugh or irritated with me because he thought I was being sarcastic. Then his eyes softened. He thanked me for coming in and assured me the police force could function just fine without my assistance.

"Good day, Ms. Valentine," he said as I rose to leave.

"Good day, Sargeant Pritchard."

———•———

When I returned from the police station, AJ followed me back to my office, peppering me with questions before I'd even hung up my coat. "How did it go? What did he say?"

I circled around to my desk, slanting the blinds to soften the glare glinting off the snowy river. The wind whipped through the cotoneaster and its branches scratched the windowpane like fingernails across a blackboard. "Pritchard asked if Sam had a lover."

"Sam didn't have a lover...other than maybe Grizzly. He's been crazy about her ever since our university days." The look on AJ's face bordered on defiant and I wondered how he could possibly know who Sam was, or was not, seeing,

I changed the subject. "It's been almost two weeks since they found Sam's body; you'd think the police would know more by now."

"NEO certainly won't give the cops any information," AJ said with a firm shake of his head. "Most of these people are nomads. Living out of their backpacks and going from protest to protest in their mission to save the world. Half of them will be long gone by now and the other half wouldn't talk to the police if their lives depended on it."

I shivered and went over to the thermostat. Someone had been fiddling with it again. As I nudged the lever to draw more heat I said, "Well, someone must have said something to give Pritchard the impression Sam had a new lover." The fragment of a thought... after all these years could the lover the police were searching for be AJ?

AJ rose to leave, then hesitated in the doorway. "Is Pritchard going to return Sam's bracelet? I'd like it back."

I told him I didn't know.

CHAPTER FIFTY-ONE

This place is no better than the ER," I muttered to Louisa who was clinging to Quincy's collar to stop him from bolting across the waiting room and slaughtering what looked like a very large hamster or a very small cat in a plastic carry cage. Whatever it was, it was making a horrible hissing noise.

It was Saturday morning. Quincy had done something to his ear that left a trail of blood across the kitchen tiles. After much debate Louisa agreed to take him to the vet. Louisa works in a busy neuro ward; she's seen more than her share of suffering but she becomes unhinged at the whiff of a veterinary clinic so I went along for moral support.

"Stop that, Quincy," Louisa rolled up his lead, pulling him tight against her knees. He growled deep in his throat and the hissing creature across from us threw itself against the mesh wire door of its cage. Its owner, a teenage girl with a buzz cut and a diamond nose stud, tsked a few times and pulled a large blue towel out of a droopy black bag and draped it over the cage door. This infuriated the creature which hissed even louder. Not that I blamed it,

I too would rather see my killer coming at me than be taken by surprise.

The vet, a young, gentle-looking woman, called Louisa and Quincy into the examining room. When I rose to join them, she shooed me away saying there was only enough room for Quincy's mom.

The girl with the diamond stud flashed me a sympathetic smile as if to say in this day and age it was entirely possible for Quincy to have two moms and I smiled back.

Voices floated up from the bottom half of the building as I returned to my plastic chair. The clinic was a large two-story structure. The animal care offices were located in the top half, a mezzanine really, with stairs leading down to the bottom half which was a large shop that sold everything from kibble to Halloween costumes for pets, something I'll never understand.

"Put that back, they won't touch that trash."

I glanced over the top of the railing into the store below. Sabine had Robert by the arm and was towing him down an aisle. She plucked a large box of bird food off a shelf and handed it to him, nodding to indicate he should put it in his carry bag. He glanced at it and shook his head.

"No, Sabine. Read the label, this is for small birds like finches and canaries, not wild birds."

She plucked three more boxes of finch food off the shelf and dumped them in Robert's arms. "The crows won't eat. I'm at my wits end."

I was about to call down to them when Robert said, "My darling, that's my point. You can't stay with him any longer. He's driving you mad."

Sabine, who'd been hovering over a sale bin at the end of an aisle, straightened and looked Robert in the eye.

"The only thing that's driving me mad is the crows, even Jasmine misses them."

She moved to the display at the end of the next aisle. Now they were directly below me. I shrank back from the railing, I could no longer see them, but their voices were clear. Something rattled, like pills in a plastic bottle, and dropped into Robert's bag.

"They need vitamins," Sabine said.

"Sabine, you must see it." Robert's voice was firm. "Marc is a narcissist, always was, always will be. You don't deserve this constant humiliation. Come away with me, please."

A woman and a small child entered the other end of the aisle. The woman stopped, took the child by the hand, and turned back the way they came.

"My dear Robert, stop worrying about my marriage— where is the mineral water?—you and Marc are more alike than you care to admit. Always worrying. You worry about me, and Marc worries about everything else. He needs to focus on finishing the Ballet House. I will not lose the Prix de Lyon because he's behind schedule. Now darling, help me find the fortified pellets."

She stepped into view, then returned to Robert when he called her name.

"Sabine, I'm serious. Who squires you around town? Me. Not Marc. He's too busy *working*"—the word was heavy with sarcasm—"who takes you to concerts and runs you home at intermission when you're unwell? Me. Who stays with you in the hospital for days on end? Me. It's always me. Not Marc. He's never there when you need him, but I am. You have no idea what I've done for you, and I'd do it all again in a heartbeat. Please Sabine."

Sabine heaved a loud sigh. I could picture her staring sadly at Robert with her ice-blue eyes. Her voice was low.

Soft and seductive. "Dear Robert. I care for you more deeply than you can possibly imagine, but Marc is my husband. You must accept that. For my sake, please." Was she touching his cheek, imploring him to stop this nonsense?

He coughed slightly, then with a half-hearted chuckle, said, "We can't bring all this bird seed home for the crows without buying a present for Jasmine."

She laughed and when they swept into view her arm was linked through his as she led him into the cat food section.

Behind me there was a commotion at the front desk. Louisa and Quincy were out of the examination room. Quincy's right ear was smeared with something white and he was wearing a large plastic cone that got caught under Louisa's coat, then snagged on a waiting room chair as I took the lead out of Louisa's hand. She added a bag of dog treats (because Quincy was such a good boy) to the already exorbitant bill and we hauled the dog back out to the parking lot.

After we settled Quincy in the back seat of the Mini—not an easy task with that ridiculously large cone catching on the head rests—and headed back across town to go home, I told Louisa about the conversation I'd overheard.

"So what else is new?" Louisa asked as she reached through the space between the two front seats, trying to settle Quincy with a pat. "Every time I see them Robert is trailing after Sabine like a lovesick puppy."

"He wants Sabine to run away with him, I think he really means it. Isn't that sad?"

"Of course it's sad." She pulled a dog treat out of the paper bag in her lap and tossed it into Quincy's mouth. "But Robert is dreaming in technicolour. Marc and Sabine have been together for what... forty years? She'll never leave Marc, the famous architect, for a bit player in the

Symphony, no matter how many women Marc falls into bed with. Those two have an understanding and like it or not, it works for them."

"That's very transactional of you, Louisa." We were in Mission now, almost home.

"Speaking of transactions, how is *ze boyfriend*, AJ?"

"Don't you start or I won't help you get your dog out of the back seat."

She did the 'zip my lip and throw away the key' gesture, but her eyes sparkled. I was never going to hear the end of this.

CHAPTER FIFTY-TWO

When AJ announced he was meeting Grizzly at the Inglewood Bird Sanctuary, a haven for migratory birds just fifteen minutes from downtown, I told him it was a terrible idea. But AJ was adamant. He had questions only Grizzly could answer.

"And if he can't... or won't, what then?"

"He will," AJ replied.

Given that these two couldn't be left alone in the same room without one of them popping the other in the eye. I said I was going with him and he agreed. I'd been the uninvited passenger so many times I think he'd given up arguing with me.

Grizzly's NEO pod was holed up at the Nature Centre for the day. The Ballet House campaign was losing steam. If Grizzly couldn't get it back on track, everything Sam had worked for would be lost. At least that's what he told AJ when they talked that morning. Grizzly agreed to spare AJ fifteen minutes, max. He was sounding more and more like the corporate CEOs he despised so much.

The path from the parking lot to the Nature Centre was slick with ice and we shuffled along like penguins until we reached the safety of the bright white lobby. No sign of Grizzly.

AJ went to the window wall and stared moodily across a thicket of trees while I stopped at the tabletop representation of the park. I love these diminutive dioramas, the tiny green trees and the miniature rocks lining the banks of the acrylic blue Bow River. Along the edge of the table ran an inscription: *If you truly love nature, you will find beauty everywhere.* Maybe not everywhere, but certainly here.

With a bang, the meeting room doors swung open and a mob of NEO activists spilled into the lobby. Grizzly spotted us and indicated we should meet him in the far corner of the room.

"What do you want?" Clearly Grizzly was on the clock.

AJ came right to the point. "The police say Sam had a lover. They're pursuing it as a legitimate line of enquiry. Is this true or are they on a wild goose chase?"

Grizzly rolled his eyes to the ceiling. "Of course she had a lover. Me."

"No," AJ persisted. "Someone other than you."

The colour drained from Grizzly's face. He swayed from side to side. AJ guided him to a chair before he buckled and fell to the floor. Grizzly leaned forward and took a couple of deep breaths before speaking.

"What's it to you? You betrayed her years ago. She hated you AJ. You have no idea how much she hated you." A cruel smile crossed Grizzly's lips. "Face it, man, she duped you, she was using you to get dirt on the Ballet House."

If the words stung, AJ didn't show it. "Be that as it may, what matters is this: If Sam had a lover you need to tell the police, otherwise they're wasting their time and the real killer is getting away."

Grizzly blinked at AJ, then his demeanor changed.

Anger giving way to pain. "Two months ago I would have said I was the only one in her life. We've been together off and on ever since you dumped her back at uni." His gaze drifted outside to the snow-covered hillocks and the naked trees bracing against the wind. "She'd drift away but she'd always come back. It took me a while to understand, but when she returned she had all kinds of inside information we could use to throw a monkey wrench into a project. That was her leverage." He gave a bitter laugh. "Ironic, isn't it, that this time her unsuspecting insider was you."

"It wasn't me," AJ said. "I met her once with you. She wanted to meet again, but that fell through. We all know why."

"Grizzly," I said, gently. "What happened two months ago?"

He continued to stare at AJ. "It wasn't you? You swear on a stack of bibles it wasn't you?"

AJ shook his head. "It wasn't me."

Grizzly gazed past us at the NEO activists chatting and milling about in the hall. I called his name again and finally he turned to me.

"What happened two months ago?" He repeated the question quietly to himself. "We came to town, set up base at the motel and got to work. But this time she was different. Preoccupied. Disappearing at all hours without telling me where she was going or for how long. When I asked her about it, she became defensive and blew me off. I figured it had to be you. She'd reconnected with you. You of all people. But she refused to tell me a thing."

The noise level in the room cranked up a notch as the activists returned from the bathrooms and their mini-sojourns outside. A tall, thin woman called Grizzly's name, then pointed to her watch. He stood up to leave but AJ stopped him.

"Just to be crystal clear, you and Sam were lovers right up to the day she died, but she may have been seeing someone else on the side. One of your NEO brethren perhaps?"

"One of my NEO *brethren*? Do you hear yourself?" Grizzly pushed past AJ. "I don't give a shit who she was seeing as long as it wasn't you."

By the time we returned to the car, we were lost in our own little worlds. The traffic was slow, taillights flickering in a long red line. The mood in the car was fragile. Who knows what AJ was thinking, I couldn't read him anymore. But I was struck by the intensity of Grizzly's belief that AJ and Sam had rekindled their relationship. Not because it was ridiculous, but because it could be true. Despite everything AJ had said to deny it.

CHAPTER FIFTY-THREE

Sometimes I think Louisa working shifts is harder on me than it is on her. Tonight she'd come home from a pick-up shift and was wired. She'd spent the last two hours tearing the basement apart looking for a small wooden footstool.

It was early evening, all I wanted to do was curl up with Margaret Atwood's latest book but Louisa was convinced Quincy was starving to death. He hadn't eaten a thing all day because no matter how he approached his food dish, whether he crept up on it slowly or tried to take it by surprise, his cone scraped the floor and the sound of plastic on tile spooked him. He'd jump around until his cone caught his food dish, flipping it over and sending kibble flying all over the place.

I said she could handfeed him tonight and we'd come up with a solution tomorrow, but she was determined to find the footstool.

After The Great Flood destroyed our basement, we finally understood what it meant to live by the river. Anything precious stored in the basement had to be boxed up and placed on a high shelf. At first, we were diligent, sorting mementos, wrapping them in newspaper and wedging them in carefully labelled cardboard boxes, but over time we became sloppy and our labelling system had fallen apart. *Junk (Childhood)* was not a great descriptor.

Now we were paying the price for our haste, digging through large boxes crammed with graduation photos, elementary school report cards, Brownie badges and Louisa's baby shoes (mine had mysteriously disappeared) looking for a small wooden footstool. Finally we found it. Dad made it years ago; it was so sturdy you could park a tank on it.

Triumphant, Louisa declared it was perfect. She wedged the footstool between the pantry shelves and set Quincy's bowl on top. "Voila!" she said to the dog. "Dinner is served." Quincy approached his dish with trepidation but once he was satisfied it wasn't a trap he accepted Louisa's invitation to dine.

"Aren't you clever," I said.

"I am," she replied.

I was about to make a snarky remark when my phone rang. It was Sargeant Pritchard. I felt a flicker of apprehension.

"I understand you've been busy today." Pritchard sounded irritated and my apprehension grew.

"You'll have to be a little more specific," I replied, while mouthing his name to Louisa who raised her eyebrows.

"Paul Adams says you and your sidekick were hassling him."

"Grizzly said that? AJ and I weren't hassling him, we just talked to him for a few minutes—"

Pritchard interrupted me with a heavy sigh. "You told him you were following up on a line of inquiry, acting like a pair of rent-a-cops."

"Oh please, he's exaggerating." It occurred to me then

that we'd underestimated how much Grizzly despised AJ and how far he'd go to make him, and me, look bad in Pritchard's eyes.

"I want you to stop whatever it is you think you're doing." Pritchard had never welcomed my assistance but tonight he sounded especially aggrieved.

"So what happened?" I asked. "Did Grizzly blow his stack at one of your guys."

"He called the station. Let's just say the suggestion that the police are investigating whether his girlfriend had lovers other than himself did not sit well."

"Yeah, well at least we got him to admit Sam was seeing someone else on the side and had been doing so for months. That's more than your guys were able to do. I'd say you have a solid new lead thanks to us, wouldn't you?"

"Speaking of leads," Pritchard replied, "Mr. Adams says AJ and Sam were a hot item once and may have rekindled their relationship when NEO rolled into town. That's something you didn't bother mentioning when we last spoke."

He had a point. So I changed tack. "Tell you what, Pritchard, we'll back off in return for a favour." Before he could tell me I was dangerously close to being charged with interfering with an investigation, I added, "Have you narrowed down the time of death?"

There was a long pause. Maybe I was pushing our relationship (such as it was) a little too far.

But he relented. "Determining the time of death is both an art and a science. The coroner's best estimate is Sam was killed sometime between midnight and two a.m. on January 17th."

"Does the coroner know how she was killed?"

Pritchard laughed. "One question Evie, that's all you

get. Now stay away from Paul Adams and his friends." With that he was gone.

I set the phone down on the kitchen countertop and turned to Louisa. "The police have narrowed down the time of death—"

"Let me guess," she said, holding up her iPad. "Between midnight and two a.m.?" Displayed on her screen was an updated news story. "And the score is 1:0 with Pritchard in the lead. Evie, you're losing your touch."

CHAPTER FIFTY-FOUR

The garage door at Arts Commons took its sweet time to open and I fidgeted behind the steering wheel anxious to roll down the steep ramp into the parkade. Thankfully it was midmorning, there would be plenty of parking spaces.

I selected a spot close to the elevator and concentrated on imprinting every single turn of the twisty hallways on my brain from the minute I stepped out of the car. The Arts Commons building is packed with so many venues—Jack Singer, Max Bell, Martha Cohen—I'd need a trail of breadcrumbs to find my way back out.

After backtracking out of one wrong turn I finally found myself in the lobby of the Jack. And there he was, right on time. Sabine's devoted plus-one, Robert.

He'd been so cryptic when he called this morning that I expected to find him wearing a trench coat and felt fedora with a copy of the *New York Times* tucked under his arm. Instead he was casually dressed in a black cardigan and khaki trousers. After a hurried greeting, he led me into the concert hall.

"What's up, Robert?" I asked as we walked down the gently sloping aisle. "I was surprised to get your call." Other than that morning at the vet clinic when he professed his desperate desire to run away with Sabine, I hadn't seen him for weeks.

He hustled me to a row of seats near the front of the auditorium. Up on stage, the orchestra's instruments looked forlorn, abandoned by their owners who were on break back in their dressing rooms or outside sucking down cigarettes and quick coffees.

"I don't have much time," he said nodding in the direction of the empty stage, "so let me be direct. I'm terribly worried about Sabine. She's so focused on bringing the Prix de Lyon to Calgary—which, as you know, is contingent on the Ballet House opening in October—that she's lost all perspective."

He bristled. This was Marc's handiwork. "Her husband knows the Prix means everything to her. He's manipulating her, using her good name and reputation to bring in the big donors. It's bad enough that he's overworking her, but he's also feeding her a pack of lies about the Jack, denigrating the quality of this magnificent concert hall."

Here he stopped and pointed to the space above the stage. "See that? That's an acoustical canopy. It's made of laminated spruce and can be raised or lowered to tune the hall, the way you'd tune an instrument, yet to hear Sabine tell it the Jack's acoustics are pitiful."

"Hold on, Robert. Weren't you the one who told me there's a lag in the sound as it travels from one side of the hall to the other?"

"Show me one concert hall that doesn't have its own idiosyncratic acoustical profile."

Given that I'd never heard the phrase 'idiosyncratic acoustical profile' until that very moment I couldn't show Robert anything.

The air quickened in the concert hall as the musicians trickled back on stage. Coughing and settling themselves in their chairs. Picking up their instruments and turning the pages of the sheet music resting on metal stands in front of them.

"Ask any of them," Robert said. "they're perfectly happy with this facility, it has a pleasant green room, nice changing rooms, even a vault to keep the multimillion-dollar violins on loan safe. It's a far cry from some of the dumps we're stuck in when we're on tour. Drafty, dreary rooms with a simple curtain separating the men's dressing areas from the women's are par for the course." His shudder was so intense it was almost theatrical.

"Robert, why are you telling me all this? What do you want from me?"

When he turned to face me, the stage lights filled his black framed glasses and I couldn't see his eyes. "I know she's not doing this intentionally, but she's lying to the people who've always trusted her. They will be livid when they discover they've been duped. These are powerful people, Evie. They'll treat her like a pariah. She's the Black Swan, a pillar of the arts community. If they shun her, it will kill her."

Robert leaned close and touched my arm. In the background an oboe let out a mournful cry.

"It's not her fault, Evie. You've seen her. She's spent. We used to go out all the time. Concerts, plays, the opera, then nightcaps afterward; we rarely made it home before midnight. Oh, how we tripped the light fantastic."

He flashed a wistful smile. "But not anymore. She tries, the poor dear, she really does but she has no energy. Even for things she adores, like the Broadway/Hollywood concert. She had a migraine and we left at intermission. I had to tuck her into bed as if she were a doddering old woman." He turned his eyes to the stage where the violins were running through their scales. "She's changed, She's not my Sabine, not the woman..."

As his voice faded away, my mind finished the end of his sentence, *not the woman I love.*

"What are you saying, Robert? That Marc is abusing her? Physically? Mentally?"

He flinched. "I wouldn't rule it out." Then stood up, break time was over. I told him I'd see what I could do. But as I navigated the maze of corridors back to my car, I wondered whether anyone could save Sabine from herself.

CHAPTER FIFTY-FIVE

What's that?" I stared at the ratty looking thing Louisa smacked down on the kitchen table in front of me. We'd just finished dinner. I'd been quieter than usual, still fretting about my conversation with Robert earlier in the day.

"A gauntlet!" she laughed. "It was in the driveway; I'm assuming it's yours."

"It's a motheaten glove."

"Right, it's a *glove*. Thrown down before you. By me." She wiggled her eyebrows, expecting me to connect the dots. I didn't, and she continued. "I'm challenging you to finish the Scrabble tournament. Best two out of three. I'm going to trounce you like you've never been trounced before. It's a matter of honour."

"Louisa, you're a lunatic, you know that don't you?"

She didn't answer. She was in the TV room fetching the Scrabble game. Shaking the box like a flat castanet, she danced back into the kitchen. "If you fail to take up the challenge you must withdraw to your bedroom, your reputation will be in tatters, your disgrace will be known throughout the kingdom. Quincy here is my second." She ripped open the box and dumped the Scrabble tiles in a clattering heap on the table.

"I think you've got your dueling and jousting metaphors mixed up, but fine." I went to the cupboard and pulled out the kettle. "Anything to stop you from babbling like a demented knight of the realm."

Midway through the game she put her hand on mine. I'd just laid out B-U-G.

"Evie, that's a pitiful word, you've left the U wide open, surely you can do better than that." Louisa has a finely honed killer instinct; it was not like her to be merciful.

"What's wrong with B-U-G, it's six points times two on a double word score."

"You've been playing terribly all night. Even worse than usual."

"Gee, thanks."

"What's wrong?"

The kettle boiled and clicked off. I poured the hot water into the tea pot and brought two mugs and a plate of chocolate chip cookies to the table. Quincy scrambled out from between the chairs, bashing Louisa's knees with his cone, and sniffed the floor in case I'd dropped a miniscule cookie crumb somewhere.

As I poured our tea I told her about my conversation with Robert earlier that day. "He says Sabine is exhausted from all the pressure Marc's been heaping on her. She's not herself."

"That's entirely possible. She had a bad bout of hypothermia and dehydration. She needs time to recover, especially at her age."

"What if it's more than that?" There was something about Robert's tone, fear mixed with vitriol, that alarmed me. Was Marc abusing Sabine? He'd destroyed her career, denied her a family. Had affairs left, right and centre. Their entire relationship was focused on Marc and his needs.

I picked B-U-G off the board and rearranged the tiles on the rack in front of me. Nothing. B-U-G was the best I could do.

Clicking the tiles around I asked, "When was that Broadway musical concert we went to?"

Louisa adores musicals. When the Calgary Philharmonic put on *The Broadway/Hollywood Songbook* she badgered me for days to go with her. 'They're doing the biggest hits from stage and screen. *The Sound of Music, West Side Story, Lion King, Moulin Rouge*. It'll be amazing.' As much as I hated to admit it, it was. For weeks I'd been singing raindrops on roses and whiskers on kittens in the shower.

"January 16," she said, "I know because I traded shifts with Roxanne."

I scrolled through my text messages looking for the one Marc had sent just before he flew to Washington, DC. Please check on Sabine while I'm gone. She's stressed about the house next door.

Marc's words weren't important, the date was. January 16. The day Robert took Sabine to the *Broadway/Hollywood* concert at the Jack. Louisa and I were in the cheap seats way up in the back, but we caught a glimpse of them as they worked their way down the aisle to their expensive seats up front.

The concert started at seven thirty p.m. and was over around ten p.m. Robert took Sabine home during the intermission because she had a headache. That would have been around nine o'clock and tucked her into bed. The next morning Vincent found Sabine wandering around in the alley, delirious, with a dead crow clutched to her chest.

"So what's your point?" Louisa asked after a gulp of hot tea.

"I don't know," I replied.

I picked up my U tile and dropped it in the Scrabble box, hoping to pull something better in exchange. I pulled another U.

"Your turn, Louisa."

As she shuffled her tiles around on her rack I said, "None of this makes sense. Why would Sabine lie about recognizing Sam's bracelet? More importantly how did it end up in Sabine's trash?"

"Do you really want to push this?" Louisa asked. The word BISQUE appeared on the board.

"What do you mean?"

She leaned back and folded her arms across her chest. "Because the one person connected to Sam and the bracelet is AJ. You and I know that but Pritchard doesn't. Do you really want to keep stirring it up?"

I stared at my rack of tiles. Nothing but B-U-G and now the place where I was going to put it was gone. I hate this game.

Louisa reached over to my tile rack, scanned my tiles. "You're doomed," she said, shaking her head.

"Evie, think of how this would look to Pritchard. People don't hold on to matching love bracelets for sixteen years if they don't have feelings for each other. Why did AJ keep his, the damn thing gives him hives."

"You're not suggesting AJ could be involved in Sam's death? Get serious." I picked up U-N and placed it on the board under B.

"Too late," she said as she removed my tiles from the board. "I went out with BISQUE." She swept my Scrabble tiles back into the box and closed the lid.

I watched her jot down our final score, she had 401, I had 133. I picked up the plate of cookies and walked across the kitchen to the sink. "You know, the more we talk about this, the more worried I get."

"About AJ and Sam?" Louisa asked.

"About Marc and Sabine. There's something not right with those two."

CHAPTER FIFTY-SIX

You know how sometimes something is weighing on your mind and try as you might not to say anything, it just pops out of your mouth at the most inopportune time? This was one of those times.

We were gathered in the conference room in our Monday morning huddle talking about the week ahead and trying to outdo each other with *you'll never guess what I did this weekend* stories—Madeline had us all beat, one of her admirers took her out for Babajian, in Monaco—when it slipped out. My suspicion that there was something seriously wrong between Marc and Sabine.

Keith dropped his head in his hands and groaned. Madeline sat up straighter in her chair, and AJ furrowed his brow. Only Bridget had no reaction. She doesn't know me as well as the others do.

When Keith finally spoke, it was with controlled neutrality. "Do not, I repeat, not, become embroiled in this."

"In what?" Bridget asked.

He continued as if Bridget had not spoken. "We've closed the Ballet House file. We've fulfilled our remit and we're out. Marc and Sabine's relationship has nothing to do with us."

Keith was only half right. I couldn't ignore whatever was going on between Marc and Sabine. Their relationship wasn't a legal matter but something my mom, if she were here, would want me to investigate. For Sabine's sake if nothing else.

I tried to reassure Keith that I had moved on. He didn't believe me.

The huddle ended on a strained note and when I returned to my office AJ came through the door right behind me. He sat down and gave me a long hard stare. His eyes are very blue, when you're on the receiving end of his gaze it's like looking deep into the endless summer sky. Finally he spoke. "You're not going to leave it alone, are you?"

I crossed my arms and stared back at him. "You haven't been completely honest about Sam, have you?"

He blinked a couple of times. It was just a feeling, but I knew I was right.

"AJ, for the love of God, what is going on?"

He let out a long breath and started talking about that morning he'd dragged me out in the freezing cold for a walk down by the river.

"Yes, I remember. You said you and Sam were an item in university but broke up after she tried to get you to join NEO." He grimaced when I mentioned the activists. "You also said you'd spoken with her once after we'd met the two of them at the National. But there's more, isn't there, AJ?"

He sighed and said, "There were no more face-to-face meetings, but we did talk on the phone, three, maybe four times—"

"Jesus AJ, what were you thinking? Sam was hell bent

on destroying our client." I rose from my desk and went over to the door, closing and locking it behind me. He wasn't leaving this office until he told me the truth, all of it.

I returned to my desk, sat down and waited. AJ's eyes moved restlessly around the room. After a moment he said, "She said she'd met Marc a few times, just her, not Grizzly, to ensure he understood NEO's concerns. It was part of her negotiation/compromise strategy."

"That's nice, AJ, did she tell Marc that if he refused to negotiate she'd firebomb his office and send death threats to his house? For Christ's sake, AJ, you're a lawyer, you know the ends never justify the means."

"She'd never resort to arson or death threats."

"Well, somebody did."

Fighting the urge to grab him by the shoulders and shake some sense into him, I said, "AJ, answer me honestly, did you give her legal advice or say anything, anything at all, that she could use against Marc?"

"No," he said, firmly. "Never. I told her to go to the regulators if she thought Marc had breached his permits. Because I couldn't confirm or deny anything. That was it. Nothing more."

I said I believed him and his eyes softened.

"Evie, I wish you could have known her in the beginning. The cause burned in her. She was fierce and righteous, like a modern-day Joan of Arc. NEO is up against forces far greater than themselves. Corporations have all power and all the money; the law is putty in their hands."

"I'm sure Joan of Arc felt the same way when she embarked on her divine crusade and look where that got her, burned at the stake."

He looked away, out the window at the frozen woods beyond. Too much sarcasm, I had to tone it down.

"AJ." I changed my tone, trying to sound gentle, and he pulled his gaze back from the frozen woods outside. "Sam may have been fierce, but she wasn't righteous. We have laws, criminal laws, which must be respected regardless of the merits of the cause."

As I said it, I realized what troubled me the most. It wasn't AJ's blind devotion to Sam, but that he'd acted in secret as if he had something to hide from the firm; from me.

Evie, you are such a hypocrite. Considering how many times I'd kept secrets from Keith because he didn't think a situation was as dire as I thought it was, I was the last person to judge.

Looking at AJ I understood his pain. That aching sense of helplessness. I didn't know how to help him.

After AJ left my office I wandered down the hall to the coffee room. And that's where Madeline found me, staring out the window while pouring milk into my mug, oblivious to the white puddle spreading across the countertop.

"Evie!" Madeline thrust a wad of paper towels into my hand and helped me mop up before pulling her own dandelion yellow mug out of the cupboard. She was wearing a robin's egg blue dress and it looked like a fashion accessory.

"What did you mean about Marc and Sabine's relationship?" she asked.

I hesitated; the last thing Sabine needed was the elite gossiping about the state of her marriage. Madeline tilted her head. "Well, are you going to tell me or not?"

"Promise me this goes no further."

She promised and I told her about Robert's insinuation that Marc may have harmed Sabine in some way. "Louisa and I are popping over there tonight to make sure she's all right."

"Of course she's all right," Madeline said with a theatrical eyeroll. "Who do you think wields the power in that relationship?" She smiled at my dumbfounded expression.

"Think about it." Madeline stirred her coffee. "Marc was what, nineteen. when they first met, Sabine was twenty-five. Right there you've got a power imbalance. He was still a boy; she was a woman. A sophisticated Parisian woman at that. Who knows what she wanted from him back then, but it's crystal clear what she wants from him now. The Ballet House and the Prix de Lyon. It's her dream and Marc is moving heaven and earth to give it to her."

I remained skeptical. Madeline was judging Sabine by her own standards. Madeline holds the power in every romantic relationship she's had. Anyone who tried to alter that dynamic fell right out of her orbit.

CHAPTER FIFTY-SEVEN

The McMansion was a grim sight with one lonely streetlight doing its level best to illuminate the flattened lot and a small white utility trailer parked in the corner next to the blue plastic porta-potty. This would be Sabine's view for the next six months.

In the Mini on our way over, Louisa and I debated about Sabine's wellbeing. Louisa thought I was overreacting. "Robert has his own agenda, don't forget."

I said Sabine had no family, just us, and if we didn't check on her, who would.

"Fine," Louisa said as I turned off the car. "You're sure Marc won't be here?"

I was sure, it was not quite seven o'clock. Marc never left the office before nine p.m. we'd have plenty of time for this difficult conversation.

Sabine greeted us with surprise when we rang her doorbell. "Quick, quick, come in from the cold." She hustled us through to the living room and we settled in the armchairs overlooking the garden. The snow covered shrubs were soft melted marshmallows and the garden lights glowed like tiny elf houses. The fire in the hearth warmed the room, a restful place decorated in a tasteful blend of cream, beige, caramel and white.

"Are the crows back?" I asked Sabine who fussed in the kitchen brewing tea.

"I'll bet you don't want them back, do you Jasmine?" Louisa crooned to the cat sprawled in her lap, it replied with an irritated meow.

"Don't let her up onto the furniture," Sabine called from the kitchen. "She's shedding so much she'll be bald soon. If she bothers you, put her on her cat blanket."

"What, that ratty red and blue blanket under your chair?" Louisa asked. It was the only thing that jarred the refined elegance of the room.

After Sabine returned with the tea tray and sat down she said, "To answer your question no, the crows have not returned. They come by sometimes on their way to someplace else, but they don't like it here anymore, not since Bijoux died."

Bijoux. The strange old crow that gashed Sabine's hand.

"Now we have magpies," Sabine said with a tsk. "They're beautiful birds but bossier than the crows. Isn't that right, Jasmine." The cat blinked at her and nudged Louisa's hand. *Scratch me.*

Louisa and I locked eyes. We couldn't put it off any longer. Sabine was perched on the edge of her chair as if she knew this wasn't a social call. Even casually dressed in slim fit black jeans and an oversized white shirt she was intimidating. Her hair was tightly pulled back in a high ponytail and her feet were bare and knobby. Unlike other women who were embarrassed by their bunions, Sabine considered her gnarled toes symbolic of her successful career as a *danseuse étoile*.

Jasmine growled—Louisa had stopped patting her—then sank her teeth into Louisa's arm.

"Jeez!" Louisa yelped and shoved Jasmine roughly off her lap.

"Jasmine! You naughty girl!" Sabine scolded the cat which landed lightly on the floor, then strolled over to the garish cat blanket and began fluffing it into a fuzzy ball.

"It's okay," Louisa said as she pulled back her sleeve. "She didn't break the skin." Then she turned to Sabine and said, "Evie and I would like—"

"Louisa, wait."

She looked at me, confused.

I'd always felt comfortable at Sabine's house, it's as soothing and peaceful as a spa. But tonight something was off, like a discordant note on the piano. My mind went to the McMansion and the body in the basement wrapped in its dusty shroud. And I realized I'd been focused on Sam's bracelet when I should have been focusing on something else.

CHAPTER FIFTY-EIGHT

Everything in Sabine's house was curated. Nothing deviated from her strictly neutral colour scheme: cream, beige, caramel and white. Except Jasmine's garish blanket. A mishmash of clashing colours: reds, purples, greens, and blues. *It doesn't belong here.* It belonged in Jamine's cat carrier, it was the only thing that soothed that neurotic cat on her histrionic trips to the vet.

No wonder Jasmine was cranky. Her favourite house blanket, a soft caramel cashmere throw that matched Sabine's décor, was gone.

At that moment the world cracked. Sam's killer had wrapped her body in a large blanket which had been sent to the lab to be tested.

"Sabine?" My voice shook. "Where's Jasmine's blanket?"

She set her tea cup down on a glass end table.

Louisa shot me a puzzled look. *What's that got to do with anything?*

Sabine blinked, then sat back with her hands resting in her lap. Her eyes flicked to the corner of the room. On the other side of the wall was the kitchen which opened on to the landing leading downstairs to the basement. Cooly, she said, "My little girl was ill. It needed a clean."

Praying my legs would hold me, I walked into the kitchen towards the stairs leading down to the basement.

Louisa followed me. "Evie," she whispered, "what's going on?"

I didn't reply.

Sabine picked up the cat which was purring so loudly we could hear her clear across the room and followed Louisa and me through the kitchen. "Come here, my darling," she whispered into the cat's ear. "I have you."

The basement light made a metallic buzz when I flicked it on. Cheap neon tubes, the utility room look bleaker than I remembered. The washer and dryer were pressed up against the wall at the far end of the room beside the wooden drying rack.

The rack was empty.

Sabine was waiting for us when we emerged from the basement. Her face was drawn and her lips were thin. "If there is something you want to know you can simply ask me, there is no need to prowl around my house like a common thief."

Louisa reddened and suggested we return to the living room where we could have a good chat. "Sabine, Evie and I are very worried about you—"

"No Louisa," I said, "it's too late for that."

Louisa shot me a look, unsure what I was going to say next. That made two of us. We'd come here to offer our support in case Marc was abusing Sabine, but now I was convinced she and that God-damned blanket were mixed up in Sam's death.

Sabine lifted her chin slightly—*suit yourself*—and we

followed her back to the cream-coloured chairs arranged in front of the gas flame in the hearth.

"Sabine." I had to start carefully. "Yesterday I learned that Marc knew Sam."

"Sam?" Sabine looked puzzled. "We don't know anyone named Sam."

"Sam, Samantha, is the woman who was found dead in the basement next door. She was a NEO activist; you may not have known her, but Marc certainly did." I explained that Sam used what she called negotiation and compromise—what the rest of us would call blackmail—to get what she wanted.

The colour drained from Sabine's face. "What could she possible want from Marc?"

"Oh Sabine. Sam was trying to force Marc to change the design of Ballet House to ensure it wouldn't damage the environment, she was especially concerned about the river."

"But that's impossible. Marc could not change his beautiful building. There isn't enough time." Jasmine growled in Sabine's lap and she stopped patting it. "What information could this Sam woman possess to blackmail Marc?"

Sabine listened, impassive, as I rattled off the violations itemized the Sin List. No, she replied, Marc had all that under control.

Then she stopped in midsentence. She put the cat on the floor and crossed to the French doors. Outside, the garage lights came on and a few seconds later the side door opened, casting an oblong shaft of light across the snowy garden.

Marc was home. Early.

CHAPTER FIFTY-NINE

Sabine hurried into the kitchen and Louisa and I followed her. The lock keypad beeped and the back door swung open. Sabine threw her arms around Marc's neck and he laughed saying he hadn't expected such an enthusiastic welcome. He made it all the way to the kitchen island before he realized Sabine was not alone.

In rapid-fire French Sabine chattered at him, smiling tightly and reaching for his briefcase and the long white drycleaning bag he was carrying. She continued talking to him as she carried his things into the foyer, setting the brief case on the hall table and hanging the drycleaning in the closet.

When he tried to speak, she put two fingers to his lips and whispered *shhhh*. Then she pulled our coats out of the closet.

"Thank you girls for coming," she said, handing Louisa her jacket. "I'm afraid it's time for you to leave." When she passed me my coat, I flung it in the chair next to the hall table.

"No, Sabine, we're not leaving. Not until we get some answers."

Unsure of what was going on, Marc put an arm around Sabine's shoulder and said, "Girls, my wife is tired. It is time for you to leave."

"Evie." Louisa slipped into her coat. "We have to go."

"No." I remained rooted to the floor. The minute Sabine embraced Marc something passed between them, a signal in something she'd said. Whatever it was, Marc was taking his cues from her. Madeline was right, it was Sabine, not Marc, who wielded the power in their relationship.

I had to pursue it, but I didn't know where to begin. I decided to start with the lies.

"Marc, would you care to explain why you denied knowing Sam. She told AJ she'd met with you, more than once. Was she blackmailing you with the Sin List, trying to force you to halt construction until you addressed her demands?"

An odd expression flitted across Marc's face. And he did the last thing I expected him to do. He offered us a drink.

Sabine's voice came loud and fast, but she was speaking French and I didn't understand a word of it. Marc gestured at her as if to say, *it's fine, don't worry*. Then walked over to the wine fridge, pulled out a bottle of red, and took four glasses out of the cupboard.

Stunned, I watched him pour the wine and hand Sabine a glass. Moving like a robot, she took it from him and set it on the marble countertop without taking a sip. He poured two more glasses and turned to Louisa and me. We shook our heads, no.

"Suit yourself," he said, raising his glass in an ironic toast and taking a deep drink before setting it down on the countertop next to the wine bottle.

By now Sabine was very pale, holding herself ram-rod straight. She shot a calculating glance at Marc then returned to the living room, suggesting we should all sit down.

When we were settled on the sofa, she sat back in her chair, put her hands in her lap and crossed one long leg over the other. "Evie," she said, "would you like to tell us what this is all about."

I had no choice, I had to lay out my theory, even though it was incomplete.

"Contrary to what you believe," I glanced at Marc, "someone in GCL's office, not us, released the Sin List to Sam. The list confirmed Sam's suspicions that the Ballet House was not the eco-friendly building you promised it would be. In fact it was the opposite. It would cause irreparable harm to the river, the riparian environment, and all the species that live there. Sam had given up on the regulators a long time ago, preferring a new modus operandi—blackmail and extortion.

"When you refused to 'compromise' she torched your office and sent the death threat to your house. Despite this pressure, you refused to stop construction. So, she changed her strategy"—as I said it out loud, I thought I finally understood—"she showed up here to pressure Sabine to convince you to back off."

I turned to Sabine. "What Sam didn't know was that you were on the same timeline as Marc. You didn't want Marc to slow down the construction schedule, if anything you wanted him to speed it up because the Ballet House has to open by October or you'll lose the Prix de Lyon. Sam was here the night before Marc flew to DC. What happened, Sabine?"

Before she could speak, Marc set down his wine glass and said, "No. You forget. Sabine was down with a migraine that night. Even if that stupid woman came here, Sabine would have been too ill to hear her ring the bell, let alone invite her into my house."

From the kitchen came the sharp sound of splintering glass. A moment of shocked silence, then we raced into the room. The white tile floor was covered with red wine and shattered crystal. Jasmine gazed at us from the countertop, her tail flicking back and forth. Sabine gave a small cry and reached for the cat just as it sprang off the counter, she managed to catch Jasmine's hind leg. The cat dangled in the air.

"Marc, help," Sabine pleaded as Jasmine squirmed to break free. Marc scooped the cat up by the belly and passed her back to Sabine. Then crossed to the pantry cupboard, returning with paper towels and a small dustpan. Louisa deposited the larger shards of glass into the bin while Marc gave the tiles a cursory wipe.

When I looked up Sabine was gone. She'd carried the cat back into the living room and was standing at the French doors, staring out into the dark garden.

She turned to face us, slowly rubbing her cheek against Jasmine's furry face. Then she returned to her chair and arranged Jasmine in her lap, blinking rapidly as tears welled in her eyes.

"Marc, please come here by me," she said. As he circled around to stand behind her chair, she spoke to him in rapid French.

He protested, "Sabine—"

"Hush, my darling,"

Louisa and I took our places on the sofa. The room felt strange, as if the barometric pressure had suddenly dropped.

"Poor Bijoux," Sabine said in a whisper. "He was hurt."

She shot Marc a tremulous smile. "You remember him, Marc. He wasn't terribly smart but still, I loved him."

Marc's entire body sagged. He looked as if he could barely stay upright.

Then Sabine told us what happened the night Samantha died.

CHAPTER SIXTY

Your mother was such a lovely woman. Evie, she always said you were a clever girl. Both of you." Sabine graced us with a tiny smile and tipped her head up to look at Marc. Articulating her words very carefully, she said, "Listen to me Marc. Evie is right. Sam came here that night."

He gasped and she patted his hand. "Marc, darling, it's all right. Now, not another word until I finish. Promise me." His head moved up and down. A wooden nod.

She leveled her gaze at me and said, "The migraine tablets weren't working and I was in the dining room pouring myself a drink when there she was, ringing the bell. What kind of person shows up, unannounced, at someone's house at ten o'clock at night?"

Sabine's lips tightened in disapproval. "She sailed into the house. Oh she thought she was so clever, flattering me and cajoling me, asking for my support. But I saw right through her. She knew nothing of art or culture. How dare she meddle with us?"

A big fat tear rolled down Sabine's cheek and dropped onto the cat. Jasmine flicked an ear and jumped out of Sabine's lap. Louisa pulled a tissue from her pocket and passed it over to Sabine. With a grateful nod, she dabbed her eyes then took a wavering breath and continued.

"Sam—what kind of stupid name is that—was there by the window." She waved a hand carelessly in the direction of the terrace. "She said Marc betrayed everyone who believed in him and he had to be stopped."

Sabine glanced up at Marc who was still standing behind her, very pale. "You understand Marc. She must be stopped."

"Sabine," I asked, "how did you stop her?"

She took a deep breath, releasing it slowly. "That ridiculous young woman. She made me so angry with her vicious accusations. I didn't want her here in the house. I shoved her outside onto the terrace. She must have stumbled because she fell facedown on the flagstones, hitting her head on the metal planter."

Marc let out a gasp and bent down, bringing his face close to hers. "Please, Sabine, don't."

She cupped his cheek and murmured it was all right. Everything was going to be all right. By the time she turned back to me, the tears had stopped. .

"And then...?" I nudged Sabine.

"What do you think?" Her tone was one of irritation. "She was dead. There was a dead body on my terrace. I moved it."

Marc sagged to his knees. His head was in her lap and she was stroking his hair the way she'd stroked the cat.

"How?" Sam was small but Sabine wasn't that much bigger.

She sighed. "Poor Bijoux, that's when he was injured."

Marc sat back on his heels, head down, unable to look at her.

Horrified we listened as Sabine described bundling Sam

up in Jasmine's cashmere blanket and dragging her body through a gap in the security fence next door. Something metallic fell onto the flagstones, clinking as it bounced off the metal planter and rolled under one of the wrought iron chairs.

"I should have stopped to pick it up, oh how I wish I had, but I was busy, I would go back for it later."

Sabine hauled Sam's body around to the back of the gutted house, across the threshold into the kitchen—"The locks were ripped off months ago"—to the top of the basement stairs. After that it was easy.

"I pushed her down. It was so dark in there, it's a miracle I didn't go down with her. She made an awful racket bumping down the stairs, then she crashed into something in the wine cellar. Vincent left all sorts of junk down there. There was a loud bang, it scared me half to death, and at last it was quiet."

Marc let out a muffled sob. Sabine patted his hair and stared out through the French doors into the darkness.

"I heard a crow cry out." Sabine's voice caught in her throat. "Silly Bijoux found Sam's bracelet and when... when I tried to take it away from him, he bit me... and I hit him. Just a harmless tap."

Sabine began to sob. "He was stunned, unable to move, and I put him in the secluded space behind the garage by the garbage cans. To keep him safe until he recovered. Oh how I wish I hadn't done that. It was so cold that night. I should have put him in the garage where it was warm, but I didn't want him to fly up into Marc's face when he came home. Marc would be home by eleven. He had an early flight to DC the next morning, he would need his rest."

Louisa touched my arm and glanced at Marc. He was still on his knees, his face pressed against Sabine's thigh.

Shoulders heaving but making no sound. It was time to end this. But I had one last question.

"Sabine," I said, "what did you do with the bracelet?"

"That piece of junk," she sniffed with distain. "I threw it in the trash."

We sat in silence while a clock, its gears and wheels floating in a transparent glass case, ticked slowly on the mantelpiece. It was time to end this. Sabine made it easy. Calmly, she told me to call the police. She was ready to make a formal confession. Marc moaned again and she kissed his ear and rubbed his back while I made the call.

Pritchard's team arrived within minutes.

As Louisa and I pulled out of Sabine's driveway, Louisa began to shake. "Oh my God, oh my God, oh my God." She rocked back and forth in her seat. All I could do was reach over and squeeze her hand.

CHAPTER SIXTY-ONE

The media frenzy following Sabine's arrest brought new meaning to the phrase 'lower than a snake's belly in a wagon rut.'

Her lawyer, one of the best criminal lawyers in town, told his lawyer friends (who told their lawyer friends, which is how we found out) that Sabine had the single-minded obsession of a zealot, totally lacking in any sense of self preservation. She was an obstructive client, but not sufficiently far gone to be certified unfit to stand trial. His only hope was that the combination of alcohol and migraine medication she'd ingested before inviting Sam into her home would help in her defence.

It had been five days since the scandal broke, lighting up our phone screens and tablets, and we were desperate to put the whole ugly mess behind us.

Which was why we were jammed into the coffee room making a big fuss over the sixth anniversary of our firm. Bridget had baked a cake—"It's a Founders Cake"—which looked like a squat pink and white replica of the Tower of Pisa. She declared it was as steady as Plymouth Rock and Keith laughed and said in the 1700s the locals tried to move the Rock, which is much smaller than people think, and it cracked in two.

Nevertheless, it was a pretty cake, sprinkled with edible pearls and gold painted sugar balls and sporting a message piped in pink icing:

HAPPY SIXTH ANNIVERSAY
(BRAXTON) LAWSON & VALENTINE

"Hey," AJ said when he brought the plates and forks to the table, "why's my name in brackets?"

"I should think it's obvious," Bridget replied. "You're not a founding partner, you joined a year after Keith and Evie started the firm, hence the brackets."

"Yeah, but I here now—"

Madeline cut AJ off, "Just be thankful you're on the cake at all. Aren't you the partner who goes around punching people?"

Keith, who'd been squeezing the contents of an apple juice box into a glass—he does this every time because he can't stand drinking juice out of a tetra pack carton—laughed and said, "That reminds me, I've got something for you Evie."

He left the room, rummaged in his office, and returned carrying a teal blue hatbox.

"What's this?" I asked. "If it's a fascinator you're about fifteen years too late."

He set the hatbox in front of me. "Go ahead. Open it."

Bridget served up slices of cake and Madeline poured the coffee while I pried the lid off the box. Inside was a small round bowler hat, like the kind Laurel and Hardy used to wear.

I smiled and put it on. It fit.

"Ooh, it becomes you," Bridget said, reaching for her phone to add me and my hat to her collection of sixth anniversary photos. Madeline chuckled and made the OK sign with her thumb and index finger.

Keith turned to AJ and said, "Yours is on backorder"

"Cool, where's yours?"

Keith pushed his empty plate aside and said, "I don't need one. From now one I'd like you two to don your Laurel and Hardy hats *before* you go off half-cocked and plunge us into another fine mess. If nothing else, that will give the rest of us time to brace for the fallout."

I laughed so hard I almost lost my coffee. For once Keith was right and Madeline was wrong. When AJ joined the firm Madeline said he'd bring me (Tinker Bell) and Keith (Eeyore) into balance. If anything AJ was another Tinker Bell (or whatever the male equivalent was) at my end of the spectrum.

Bridget, eyes down, intent on scraping up the last morsel of her cake, frowned and said, "I still don't get why Sabine killed Sam"—there was some debate in the prosecutor's office about whether Sam was still alive when Sabine chucked her down the stairs and the Crown reserved the right to upgrade the manslaughter charge to murder.

Madeline dabbed a serviette to her lips. She'd barely touched her skinny pink sliver of cake. This is why she's reed thin, the woman has discipline.

"Because Sabine is an extremely ambitious woman, a *danseuse étoile* from the best ballet company in France, the head of a ballet school here, and—let's not forget—the philanthropist who was about to bring the auspicious Prix de Lyon to North America. The Prix agreed to come on the condition it could hold the competition at the Ballet House, a world-class architectural masterpiece. Then along came Sam who was bound and determined to stop the Ballet House and destroy Sabine's dream. So when the opportunity presented itself, Sabine eliminated her."

Bridget, who was sliding slices of cake into Tupperware containers stopped and said, "Well, she's cooked her goose now. They're calling her the murdering ballerina. That will drive the donors away."

Madeline made a delicate *hmpff* noise. "Don't bet on it. Lots of famous architects are dogged by scandal. Louis Kahn had three families. Three! They lived within a few miles of each other and didn't meet until his funeral and Richard Meier was forced to resign from his own firm after a #MeToo scandal."

"How does she know these things?" Keith asked me in wonder.

"Scandal and notoriety," I said, "it's right up her alley."

She tipped her head as if we'd given her a compliment and added, "This scandal will enhance Marc's reputation; he's not the villain in this scenario, his wife is."

AJ was quiet as the conversation swirled around him, working his way through a large slab of cake. Bridget had given him the (BRAXTON) piece. He hadn't said much about Sam since Sabine's arrest.

He set down his fork and said, "In a way the Ballet House is our version of the Taj Mahal."

Keith stared at him. "Yeah, the bizarro version."

"No, hear me out," AJ said. "Sabine wanted to head up the most prestigious ballet school in the country. To do that she had to get the Prix de Lyon to come to Calgary and the Prix wouldn't set foot on any stage unless it was at an architectural wonder worthy of their presence. Marc built the Ballet House as a monument to his wife to preserve her legacy."

"Uh huh," I said, "and the fact that it will secure Marc's international reputation as a starchitect has nothing to do with it, right?"

He gave me a rueful grin. "Yeah, well, there's that too."

Keith caught my eye as he put my bowler back in its hatbox. When he pressed the lid down a poof of air, like a sigh, escaped. He's known me a long time and even though I hadn't said anything, he knew I had misgivings. "Evie, I'm almost afraid to ask: What's your take?"

I shrugged and said nothing. Something was wrong with Sabine's confession, it flickered in the corner of my mind, mocking me, but when I tried to focus on it, it disappeared, as insubstantial as a dream.

CHAPTER SIXTY-TWO

AJ and I strolled into the main lobby of the Atelier later that afternoon. "I didn't think we'd ever set foot in this place again," he said.

I chuckled. "You'd think getting a client's wife charged with manslaughter would strike you off his contacts list forever, wouldn't you."

Up ahead Luke was chatting with a portly security guard. Luke greeted us with a firm handshake and a mischievous grin. He was enjoying this. We hadn't seen Luke since that day at his uncle's place when Vincent received the call saying a body had been discovered in the rubble at the McMansion.

"Ready?" I asked.

"You bet." Luke replied and we stepped into the glass elevator and floated up to the fifth floor where we were met by a pretty young receptionist who settled us in the waiting area.

Ten minutes later Marc's trusty assistant, Barbara Major, appeared looking businesslike in a blue twill suit. She ushered us past rows of busy architects and technicians, all trying not to gawk at Luke—*isn't that the guy Marc fired?*

Barbara put us in the conference room adjoining Marc's office. AJ and I sat at the heavy burl table while Luke prowled the length of a long black credenza covered with photos and plaques proclaiming the Atelier's success. He scrutinized each object with the single-minded focus of a bargain hunter at a rummage sale.

"What are you doing in here?" Luke was talking to a small bronze sculpture, the same way my electrician talks to my light switches. "Aren't you supposed to be propping up the corner of Marc's desk?

"Have you seen Marc's Pritzker?" Luke asked as he peered at the signature etched in its base. We had, the last time we were in Marc's office, the day he accused us of conspiring with NEO.

"It's a limited edition Henry Moore." Luke set the sculpture back down on the credenza. "After Marc won they switched to bronze medallions."

Luke joined us at the conference table and we waited for Marc. It wouldn't be long now. He may have wanted to play the power game, making us wait until he was ready to make a dramatic entrance, but we had something he wanted—Luke—and Marc would come to us quickly, lest we changed our minds and left.

City Council and the big money philanthropists underpinning the Ballet House were very nervous. The bad publicity generated by Sabine confessing to Sam's murder was the last straw. The Ballet House was cursed and no one would risk another penny on the project... unless a reputable third party, someone they could trust, agreed to take over as project manager. Who better than Luke, the bright young architect who had the courage to stand up to Marc even if it meant losing his job.

That put Luke in the catbird seat. He agreed to return as

a consultant if Marc met his demands: absolute authority over the site and a fee that was quadruple what he'd been paid before he'd been unceremoniously fired.

BLV prepared the contract; Marc accepted all the terms. And today Luke and Marc would sign it. We could have used e-signatures but Luke insisted on signing the contract in person. He promised not to gloat.

Marc swept into the conference room five minutes later. Brimming with bonhomie, he shook our hands and made small talk while AJ set four copies of Luke's contract on the table. Marc whipped out a fat green fountain pen and scribbled his signature next to the sticky red arrows. The meeting was over almost before it began.

Outside, huge wet snowflakes drifted out of the steel grey sky as we lingered on the pavement, congratulating ourselves on a perfectly executed meeting. Luke gave me a quick hug and threw AJ a two fingered salute before sauntering off to his car.

As AJ and I picked our way past the traffic barriers—the crater in the middle of the street was getting bigger—he asked, "Don't you think it's weird how Marc is handling this Sabine thing? It's almost as if it never happened."

"That was my impression too," I said, waiting for AJ to unlock the car door before I eased into my seat. "Although when you think about it, it's in Marc's best interests to keep the focus on the Ballet House—it will make or break his reputation—and not his murdering ballerina of a wife."

AJ chuckled. "It's funny you should put it like that. Sabine's lawyer is having a devil of a time getting Sabine to shut up. She keeps telling everyone she had to kill Sam to protect Marc's greatest project."

"What, Marc is a modern day Michelangelo, his artistry must be protected at all costs?"

"Something like that."

Later that evening when Louisa and I took Quincy down by the river for his evening walk I told her about our unsettling meeting with Marc. I found it hard to concentrate because Louisa had a camping headlamp strapped to her forehead.

"You won't think it's ridiculous when it saves your life," she tutted at me. The river path was still shifting after The Great Flood and she was afraid she'd trip and launch herself and the dog into the river. She was adjusting the forehead strap when my cell buzzed. It was Robert and I waggled my fingers at her, signalling I'd catch up with her after I'd finished the call.

"Hi, Robert. How's Sabine?" She'd posted bail and was now at home.

Robert said he didn't know. He'd been touring Europe with the Symphony when she'd been arrested and now that he was back, she refused to see him.

"But you're her closest friend."

"Apparently she's tired of me slagging Marc." He took a deep breath. "Evie, I think I've lost her."

Lost her? Sam was dead thanks to Sabine.

The wind came up out of nowhere, tearing through the treetops and kicking up the snow crusting the riverbank. Louisa's headlamp bobbed farther and farther away.

"Robert, is there something I can do for you?"

"I'm reaching out to all of Sabine's friends. We have to do everything we can to secure her acquittal."

I inhaled too quickly and the cold air caught in my throat. I coughed. "Robert, she confessed to homicide. The only issue now is how many years she'll spend behind bars. There isn't a hope in hell she'll be acquitted." Nothing could save the Black Swan from herself.

"But that's inhumane," he moaned. "They're condemning her to death row."

"She's not going to the electric chair. We abolished capital punishment in this country in the 1970s. She'll get due process—"

"Don't talk to me about due process. These charges are outrageous and should never have been brought in the first place!" His voice dropped and I struggled to hear him over the wind howling in the trees. "Dear God, what have I done?"

I stopped dead in the middle of the path. Up ahead, the fragile light from Louisa's headlamp shone like a tiny beacon in the darkness.

"Robert, what did you do?"

There was a tiny pause, then he said, "Marc was a very cruel man. The pain he inflicted on Sabine over the years was indescribable. It fell to me to protect her. To put an end to the abuse. It wasn't physical, you understand, nothing that would be easy to spot." Robert's voice ached with pain. "This was worse. The constant humiliation. The neglect. Poor, poor Sabine, Marc was driving her mad."

As far as I knew Sabine had never sought counselling and *I have a philandering husband* was not a legitimate defence to a criminal charge. "Robert, I still don't understand what you did."

He rattled on as if he hadn't heard me. "The constant pressure to be out there fundraising, it took a terrible toll"—did it though I wondered, Sabine seemed to relish being the centre of attention, once again the *danseuse étoile* —"and his affairs, so brazen, so cruel. I just wanted him to stop. To stop it all. I, ah, did something that, in retrospect, may have been unwise."

I held my breath so I could hear him over the sound of my heart beating in my ears.

"I, ah, sent him a warning to let him know I was aware of his cruelty. It had to stop. But being the dimwit that I am, I deposited it at his house, not the office. I didn't mean for Sabine to see it. It upset her terribly."

Of course, the STOP IT note. Embossed on stiff white paper. Who else but this prissy little man would send a death threat that looked looking like a wedding invitation.

Robert continued rambling. "Is it enough to acquit her, that I disturbed the balance of her mind?"

It was such an inane question it took me a moment to realize he'd finished talking and was waiting for my reply. Of course that silly note wasn't enough to acquit her, but I told him to tell Sabine's lawyer about it anyway.

"Look, Robert, I have to go." I started picking my way down the path. It was very dark, there was no moon, and the temperature was dropping. I wanted to find Louisa and Quincy and bring them home.

"No wait."

"No really Robert, I have to go."

"She's going to kill me for telling you this."

For a fleeting moment I wondered whether he'd fire-bombed Marc's office as well. No, he wouldn't have the guts. That had to have been Sam who'd risked her life by chaining herself to a sleeping dragon.

Robert cleared his throat and said, "Just so I'm crystal clear here. Sabine confessed to killing Sam in the wee small hours of January 17, right?"

"Yes, after you brought her home from the Broadway/ Hollywood concert. Sam showed up at the house. They had an argument and Sabine pushed her out onto the terrace, she fell and fractured her skull and Sabine disposed of her body in the basement of the McMansion."

"What time was this?"

"Just after midnight. After you dropped her off but before Marc came home."

He made a small sound like a little squeak and said, "Sabine is lying."

"What do you mean she's lying?"

Robert cleared his throat and said, "This is kind of embarrassing."

"Will it save Sabine from going to prison?"

"Yes, I think so."

"Then for Christ's sake, spit it out."

He coughed again, almost as if he were choking.

"Robert, how is Sabine lying?"

And it all tumbled out of him. It was true that he and Sabine had left the symphony at intermission. "Her migraine was so bad she could barely talk. They're triggered by many things, including stress. The pressure she was under due to her miserable husband—"

I cut him off, afraid he'd go down that rabbit hole again. "Okay, severe migraine, you left the Jack around nine o'clock, right?"

"Yes, she couldn't look at the streetlights, she was in so much pain. By the time I got her home she was nauseous and barely coherent. All she wanted to do was lie down in a dark room. I gave her a double dose of her meds and a shot of brandy to wash it down. And I promised to stay until she fell asleep. She doesn't like to be alone when she's ill." His voice softened. "You should have seen her Evie; she was so weak she could barely make it to down the hall."

"Was it real Robert? Could she have been faking it?"

Maybe this was a ruse to gain sympathy from Robert, the poor schmuck who played chorus to Sabine's Greek tragedy.

He made a sound as if he were trying to get something disgusting out of his throat. "It was real. I know it was real, because, well, this is rather embarrassing."

"Robert, please, you need to tell me."

"She won't like it."

"Just say it, Robert!"

"No one came to the house that night and she didn't leave her bed, not once. I know because I stayed with her in her bedroom after she fell asleep..." He paused. "You think I'm some kind of creeper, don't you, because I like to watch her sleep."

"No, Robert. I think you're a loving friend." Actually, as I pictured him sitting in a dark corner of Sabine's bedroom watching her sleep, I definitely thought he was a creeper, but right now I was grateful for it.

"How long did you stay, Robert?"

"Until Marc got home. I cut it pretty close, dashing out the front door just as he came in through the back."

"You stayed until midnight?"

"He didn't get home at midnight. It was closer to 1:30 in the morning."

"And she never left her bed?"

"She was too incapacitated to stand up, let alone kill Sam and drag her body next door."

My heart was beating so fast I could hardly organize my thoughts. Robert fussed at first when I said he had to tell his story to the police. Could I do it for him, he asked. I said I'd call Pritchard the minute we were off the phone to set up a meeting the following day and I'd accompany him to the station but he'd have to tell his story himself.

"I'll be with you every step of the way, Robert. I promise."
Finally he agreed and I hung up.

After I'd left a message for Pritchard, I spotted Louisa
up ahead. Quincy was barking, he'd spotted a small creature in the shrubs and was dragging her toward the river's
edge. Her headlamp bounced wildly, glinting across the
icy river below.

I stuck two fingers in my mouth and let out a piercing
whistle. Quincy stopped in midstride, wheeled around
and raced back to me towing Louisa, panting, behind him.

When he skidded to a stop in front of me, she blew
a frazzled lock of hair out of her eyes and reached up to
readjust her headlamp. "We need remedial obedience
training," she declared as she twisted Quincy's harness
back into place across his powerful shoulders. Her headlamp shone in my face.

"You look like a minion with that thing on. The one
with one eye."

"I'm good," she said. "We're all good, aren't we Quincy.
Isn't it a glorious evening?"

"Indeed, it's amazing." I told her about Robert's phone
call. "This will exonerate Sabine."

Louisa looked thoughtful. "What if she doesn't want to
be exonerated? Evie, think about it. If Robert is telling the
truth, then Sabine is lying. Why would she lie? Because
she's protecting Marc."

Heads down we pushed into the wind, rehashing what
Sabine had said the night she confessed. Louisa tightened
her grip on Quincy's leash, he always speeds up when he
sees the house.

She turned to me and said, "You know what I think.
When you told Sabine that Sam tried to blackmail Marc,
she put it all together. She knew how much the Ballet House

meant to Marc and she knew he'd stop at nothing to save it. Even if that meant eliminating Sam."

"Oh God." I was holding on to my parka hood with both hands to keep it from flying off my head. "When I outlined my theory that Sam came to the house to get Sabine's help to make Marc change the design. I gave Sabine all the elements she needed to concoct her confession."

We trudged along in silence, stunned by the enormity of what Sabine had done.

"Louisa." I stopped on the path. "The drycleaning bag"—that's what had been bothering me—"Marc had barely set foot in the house when Sabine swooped down on him and insisted on taking his briefcase and hanging up the drycleaning bag. She didn't want us to see what was in it, Jasmine's cashmere blanket."

"Yes," Louisa said. "If we'd spotted it, Sabine's confession would have collapsed. If she'd used the cat blanket to drag Sam's body over to the McMansion, it would be sitting in a police evidence locker, not nicely pressed and hanging in Sabine's hall closet."

Quincy was practically galloping up the steps to the front door. Louisa pulled her house key out of her pocket and unlocked the door.

Once inside she said, "Evie, remember how Sabine kept talking to Marc in French when he came home. Usually they speak English in front of company. She talked pretty fast, I didn't catch all of it, but she told Marc to be quiet, saying: *I must do this, let me do this.*"

"She was talking about her confession," I said.

"She was talking about her *false* confession," Louisa corrected me.

I unclipped the dog and he gave himself a mighty head to tail shake that jittered him across the foyer floor.

The look on Marc's face when Sabine confessed. At first, he was devastated and tried to stop her from telling a horrific lie, but by the time Pritchard had arrived and led Sabine out of the house to the squad car, Marc was calm. He'd accepted her great sacrifice, her life behind bars in exchange for his freedom. As if it was his due.

All that would change tomorrow. Robert's evidence would exonerate Sabine. With a little more police work, Pritchard would charge Marc with a horrific crime.

But it wasn't that simple.

CHAPTER SIXTY-THREE

AJ was engrossed in some meaningless file when I barged into his office the next morning. "I can't believe it!" I said, flinging myself into a chair. "I simply can not believe it!"

He cocked an eyebrow at me. "Rough morning?"

"Damn right, it's been a rough morning." I told him about my conversation with Robert and how he'd thrown a wobble this morning when I went to pick him up. 'Sabine will never forgive me if I land Marc in the middle of this,' he'd said. I reminded him she'd grow old and die in prison if he didn't come to her rescue. The knight in shining armour analogy strengthened his resolve and everything was fine until we met with Pritchard.

Last night I'd left Pritchard a message explaining that Robert's evidence would destroy Sabine's confession and implicate Marc. What I hadn't anticipated was that Pritchard would call Sabine to tell her he needed to interview her again in light of the new evidence he expected to receive from Robert.

After Pritchard settled Robert in an interview room,

he listened patiently to Robert's story, then dropped the bombshell: Sabine denied everything Robert had said.

"She's adamant she killed Sam and unless she recants, Robert your story isn't enough. Sabine says everyone knows you're obsessed with her. She says you're a psychotic nutcase determined to frame Marc for murder so you can keep Sabine for yourself."

Robert put his head in his hands and moaned. "Oh God, what have I done?"

"Evie," Pritchard turned his attention to me, "You're a lawyer, you know the prosecutor won't drop the charges against a suspect who's confessed without having hard evidence they've got the wrong person. Calling Sabine a liar simply won't cut it."

By now AJ was on his feet pacing back and forth in front of his window. His face was grim and his movements were quick and sharp. I felt a flutter of unease when the realization hit me: I'd just told AJ that Marc had murdered Sam.

AJ stopped pacing. He folded his arms across his chest and said, "I guess we're going to have to find some hard evidence then."

Which was why, at the end of the day, we found ourselves parked in a long line of cars in front of the Ballet House. AJ turned off the engine and the MGB made a clicking noise as its engine cooled down. A frigid wind buffeted the vehicle and within minutes all the warmth in the car dissipated.

"You should have a blanket in here," I muttered through clenched teeth. "It's a standard safety precaution. I always keep a blanket in my car." Actually it was Quincy's blanket. A piece of fabric covered in dog hair that looked like it belonged on the back of a burro.

"Stop fussing." AJ glanced at his watch. "It's quitting time, the building will be empty soon."

A few minutes later a stream of workers poured out of the building and climbed into their vehicles. Soon there were only two vans and Marc's Mercedes left. We got out of the car and worked our way across the rutted ground to the front entrance.

I shot a worried glance at AJ. "Are you doing okay?" He'd been very quiet all day.

Without breaking stride, he replied, "Of course I'm okay. We're just going talk to Marc, test his alibi. This isn't personal."

Reassuring words, but it sure felt personal to me.

Except for the large glass doors that would be installed later, the exterior shell of the building was finished. The temporary entrance—two makeshift plywood doors covered with safety notices—were, as AJ predicted, unlocked and we walked right in.

Inside, the Ballet House was enormous. The skeleton of the interior was in place but not yet finished and we could see clear down to the far end of the building. The cavernous space smelled dank and cold. Hundreds of utility lights dangled from the rafters but did nothing to lift the gloom. Off to our right a large, thin pool of water rippled under the noisy blast of four drying fans. It was like standing in the middle of an airport runway.

We moved deeper into the building. In the distance came the sound of voices and two workers appeared. A slight woman in jeans and a bulky parka and a roly-poly man wearing a hard hat.

"Excuse me." They stopped in mid laugh at the sound of my voice. "We're here to see Marc Hubert. Can you point us in the right direction?"

This morning Bridget had called Barbara Major who confirmed Marc would be working late at the site. He wouldn't be expecting us because Bridget told Barbara there was no need to give Marc advance notice.

"Head for the main performance stage," the woman said. "You can't miss it. The catwalks just went up. Follow the lights."

"Is he alone?" AJ asked.

If the question surprised them, they didn't let on. The woman confirmed that everyone had left for the day. The roly-poly guy told us to remind Marc to throw the switch on the drying fans when he left. Cold air gusted into the building when they opened the plywood doors and trudged out into the night.

As we threaded our way past high scaffolds and great lengths of lumber sliding off tumble-down piles, I marveled that in a few short months this mess of wood and metal would be transformed into an elegant arts venue. The concrete floors would disappear under sheets of marble, the walls would be covered in exotic woods and the bare bulbs would be replaced by sparkling chandeliers.

A few years ago Keith and I went to New York on a business trip. On our last night we attended the opera, not because we were big opera fans but because we wanted to visit the iconic Metropolitan Opera House. I forget what we saw, but I'll always remember how at the beginning of the performance the chandeliers, twenty-one crystal starbursts, swept up into the dark ceiling like tiny sparkling galaxies. Later someone told me the chandeliers were an accident; the architect dropped a blob of white paint on a drawing and liked what he saw. That's creativity for you.

"Do you see him?" I whispered to AJ as my eyes adjusted to the gloom of the stage.

"Why are you whispering?" he asked. "We're here to talk to the guy, not assassinate him."

True, but Marc wouldn't be keen to talk to us, by now Sabine would have told him that Robert tried to undermine her confession.

In the car on the way over I told AJ we might be able to trick Marc into opening up if we played to his ego. We should allow him to pontificate about his greatest achievement, the Ballet House, and slowly bring the conversation around to Sam and what had really happened on the night she died. He might not take the bait but it was worth a try.

Where was he?

A flash of light overhead. An intense beam overpowered the frail illumination cast by the bulbs dangling over the stage. It cut a swath through the shadows like a lighthouse beacon, finally settling on AJ.

AJ looked away, shielding his eyes with one hand, and called out, "Hey, Marc, have you got a minute to bring Evie and me up to speed on"—he cast around for a specific topic—"the catwalks. I understand they were recently installed."

Marc was standing on the catwalk about thirty feet above us. "You shouldn't be here. You're not my lawyers anymore."

I called up to him. "That's true, Marc, but we represent Luke and he wants us to be up to speed on everything he's doing." That wasn't entirely accurate but it would do for now. "Would you mind coming down?" It was like trying to coax a cat out of a tree.

The beam of the light scanned my face, it was painfully bright. Red splotches clouded my vision. I averted my eyes and gradually the blotches disappeared. Marc was fiddling with what appeared to be an oversized, boxy construction torch. Its beam bounced around in the faraway corners of the hall until he managed to turn it off.

"All right." He strolled along the catwalk with the swagger of a circus performer. Kudos to him. I hate heights; my knees turn to water if I'm more than three feet off the ground.

"These catwalks almost broke the design," Marc said, one hand trailing along the railing. "There was no space for the techs to access the audio-visual equipment for the giant screen, it didn't matter where we put the equipment it always blocked the view." He stopped to look at the blank wall at the back of the stage. "It took months of back and forth with the fabricator to get it right. Even now the catwalk is only fifty millimetres away from the screen. It's tight," he chuckled, "but it works."

His shoe touched the top rung of the ladder leading down to the lower catwalk.

Then AJ made a mistake. "That's good news. One less glitch to add to the Sin List." The list of deficiencies Brianna had sent to Sam and Sam had sent to Marc.

Marc hesitated, then stepped back up onto the bridge and returned to the middle of the catwalk. The construction torch sat dead centre, like the pivot of a seesaw.

"The Sin List. You're here to talk about Sam?" His tone was wary and he hunched over the railing, eyeing us like a giant condor watching its prey.

"Marc, could you come down please?" My heart started to beat faster. "We need to talk."

He gripped the railing on the catwalk and dismissed us with the insolence of a king discharging his subjects. "We have nothing to talk about. I've never met the woman and know nothing about her. Other than they found her body in the rubble next door."

"That's not how we understand it, Marc. A friend of Sam's said she was a new breed of activist. If demonstrations failed to deliver the desired results, she was prepared to break the law to get what she wanted. She was blackmailing you, wasn't she?"

He said nothing from his perch on the catwalk.

"Why didn't you report it to the police? Or at the very least tell us? We're your lawyers we could have helped you and Sabine deal with her."

"Sabine?" Marc leaned over the railing, backlit by a halo of light. "Sam wanted to destroy Sabine." When he pulled back, his face was in shadow but his hands were illuminated, white on the railing.

AJ caught my eye, raising his eyebrows he whispered, "My turn?"

I replied quietly, "Okay, but go easy."

AJ sounded relaxed, almost conversational. "Marc, maybe 'blackmail' is too harsh a word, but Sam had some kind of hold over you, something she threatened to reveal unless you changed the design. It had to be more that the Sin List. Too many people were aware of its existence. It held no power."

There was a long silence, broken only by the faraway drone of the drying fans in the lobby. After a moment AJ continued.

"Did she have proof you'd damaged the water table? That the bioswales were inadequate?" Luke believed this to be the case and had initiated remedial work that could blow through the budget. "Marc, what did Sam want?"

Marc shuddered as if he'd touched a live wire.

"She wanted what all the Sams in this world want." His voice was thick with contempt. "To drive us back into the dark ages. To chop my building to bits and destroy its beauty, its rhythm. She turned her back on the magic of this time and this place. Look around you. This is a place where fairies will dance, where cherubs will sing. People like Sam won't be happy until we're jammed into eco-friendly boxes and live out what's left of our pokey little lives in ugly squalor. That's what Sam wanted."

He hit the words 'chop' and 'destroy' extra hard. There was no point in trying to debate him.

"I'm getting him down from there," AJ whispered.

"AJ, no, give him some time, he'll come down when he's ready."

AJ lifted his eyes to catwalk, then with long determined strides headed for the ladder supporting the far end.

"AJ!" I hissed.

He glanced back at me over his shoulder, his face unreadable. With single-minded purpose he approached the ladder at the far side of the catwalk. Suddenly I knew I had to get up there before he did. I took a deep breath and started walking towards the ladder at my end of the catwalk.

"Are either of you listening to a word I said?" Marc's angry voice rang out overhead.

"Yes, Marc, we're listening." My fingers curled around the rungs of the metal ladder. I made it to the third rung when there was a rustle of movement overhead. Then a blinding flash of light.

CHAPTER SIXTY-FOUR

I clung to the ladder, head down, terrified, unable to move. "Marc," I pleaded, "please dim the torch. It's disorienting." Ghostly images floated in the air beside me, negatives of Marc's brooding figure above. Somewhere on the other side of the catwalk I could hear AJ moving, the rungs ringing as they touched his feet.

"Evie, you okay?" AJ's voice floated across the wide stage.

Marc's beam of light slid away from me and drifted around the stage until it locked onto AJ. He was five rungs higher than I was. I had to move, now.

"I'm good," I replied. The darkness crackled around me as my vision slowly returned. Dragging myself up three more rungs, I called up to Marc. "I'm listening, Marc. Rhythm and magic. Laudable goals in these dark and troubled times."

Across from me AJ wasn't moving, trapped in Marc's beam like a butterfly pinned to a corkboard. His head was tipped down, his eyes squeezed shut. What the hell was that thing? A hand-held klieg lamp?

Finally the light slid off AJ's body as if satisfied he wasn't going anywhere and roamed across the stage, dipping into the orchestra pit, nothing more than a hole, like a basement excavation, then flying up the sloping floor to the lobby. Lingering every so often to examine a rack of scaffolding or a forklift.

Luke was right, the site was littered with machinery and scraps of wood and paper, ready to ignite if someone forgot to turn off a space heater at the end of the day. Marc was so fastidious at home and at the office, a place for everything and everything in its place, how could he tolerate such chaos at the worksite.

"Stay where you are," Marc called out. "I'll be down in a minute."

Mingled with the faraway drone of the drying fans was a high pitched buzz. Marc's torch was overheating, its tiny fans were losing power. Gradually the beam weakened, losing intensity until it faded away to nothing.

What a sight we must have been. The three of us illuminated by the sad little bulbs hanging from the ceiling. AJ and me clinging to ladders at either end of the catwalk and Marc planted squarely in the middle of the bridge, desperately clicking the buttons of the now useless torch.

Without that intense beam, he seemed more vulnerable. The second that light released us; we began to climb.

"Marc," I called out. "My parents never stopped talking about you and Sabine, did you know that? They said you were a tremendously gifted architect. I wish they could have seen the Ballet House. It's stunning. It deserves to be recognized by the likes of Gehry and Pei."

I flicked my eyes to AJ. In the gloom I could just make out the stiffness of his body and the sharp tilt of his head. Was he listening to me? Did he understand why I was babbling about my parents and gifted architects? This was the plan, flatter Marc's enormous ego until he was ready to talk about Sam. But not up here. On the ground.

AJ hooked an arm through the ladder and swung out a little so Marc could see him more easily. "Hey Marc," he said it so casually, "Sam said you ran into trouble with the rainwater capture system, is that right?"

Marc leaned forward, clasped his hands and rested his forearms on the catwalk railing as if he were standing on the deck of a ship with nothing better to do than watch the roiling sea. "She was wrong," he said. "We had everything under control. She couldn't hurt us there."

AJ swung back and continued to creep up the ladder. Moving relentlessly like a soldier behind enemy lines. I had to get up there, fast. I started to climb, clawing my way up one shaky rung at a time while AJ continued to badger Marc about the Sin List.

Three more rungs and I'd be on the bridge, it must have some kind of fancy name, but to me it was just a bridge connecting me to Marc and Marc to AJ. I was climbing to get Marc down. I was no longer sure why AJ was climbing. Or talking. Relentlessly needling Marc.

"Sam said you were having trouble with the on-site water retention system and you were digging temporary holding ponds all over the place. But here's the thing, Marc, there's nothing in the environmental plan that would allow you to excavate holding ponds. You'd need an amendment."

"That would take too long, AJ. I can't afford the delay." Marc released his hold on the railing while at the same time leaning back as if to stretch his spine. That's when he saw AJ standing at the end of the bridge.

He raised a hand, palm up. "Stop right there. Go back. I'll come down when I'm good and ready."

AJ didn't stop.

CHAPTER SIXTY-FIVE

While Marc was focused on AJ, I scrambled up the last two rungs and stood, panting, at the end of the bridge. AJ's eyes glittered in the shadowy light. I couldn't read his expression. Forcing myself to put one foot in front of the other, I lurched along the bridge, clinging the railings on either side, desperate to get to Marc before AJ did.

"Marc," I called out. "Can you help me? I'm feeling faint."

He hesitated for just a second, then made a decision. He would be chivalrous; he turned his back on AJ and strolled over to me.

"I need to get down, right now." Only half of the lady-in-destress act was a pretext. I felt giddy and ill. "Would you go ahead of me, to break my fall as it were." I managed a weak smile.

"Of course, Evie. Of course." Confidently, he eased past me, checking over his shoulder to ensure I was coming along behind him. No worries there, I was practically on top of him, anxious to put as much space between Marc and AJ as possible.

Going down a ladder is always much harder than going

up. You're hanging in space. You can't see where your feet are. I wavered between giddiness and nausea as Marc and I started our descent. Above me, AJ's face appeared. He waited, allowing me to reach the halfway point before starting to climb down.

Marc murmured encouragement with each rung we passed and by the time we reached the floor my heart stopped thumping in my throat and my stomach had settled down.

"You all right?" AJ asked when he joined us.

I nodded. The hard set of his jaw had eased and whatever emotions he'd been wrestling with on the catwalk appeared to have faded.

Marc said it was time to go and we began to weave our way past the bobcats and poly-covered stacks of rough stone and rolled cork.

A long time ago, Sergeant Pritchard told me if you give a suspect enough time, eventually they'll tell you what you want to know. They do it to lighten the burden of the secret they're carrying. I used to think that was a myth, a hackneyed bit of police folklore, but as Marc prattled on about the stone floors and the magnificent chandeliers— yes, he'd heard the Met's white paint blob story—I began to realize there was something Marc wanted to say.

"Marc," I kept my voice gentle, "you said Sam wanted to destroy Sabine. What did you mean?"

Marc slowed his pace. His voice dropped and AJ and I crowded closer to hear him over the drone of the distant fans. "Samantha was a charlatan. Sure, she was clever and very beautiful, but she used her gifts to manipulate people. She duped you, AJ"—it was the same word Grizzly had used—"to get what she wanted."

Here it comes...

"I'll never forget the day she waltzed into my office." He gave a rueful grin. "She was stunning. Beautifully dressed in designer clothes, her makeup and nails immaculate. Even that wild, curly brown hair was perfectly styled. Perfect. That's the word for it. She looked perfect. Even Sabine would have been fooled. I took one look at her and thought she was a future client."

And...?

"She asked me to design a large airy house, a second home on the west coast for herself and her husband. She said he was an oil executive who travelled all the time. Without saying as much she gave the impression she was terribly lonely. Your little friend was such a skillful liar." Marc's voice carried a trace of admiration, almost as if he wanted to give Sam credit for carrying off the deception. "We became very close very quickly."

"Oh God, Marc, you didn't." It slipped out. This was going to be a trainwreck.

AJ glanced from me to Marc. He hadn't put it together yet.

With the vestige of a smile, Marc said, "We had a fling, an affair, if you like."

"You slept with her?" It had taken AJ a moment to comprehend what Marc had just said. "Are you fucking kidding me? She was half your age."

I glanced at AJ. Her age wasn't important. What mattered was Sam was using the oldest trick in the book to wheedle information out of Marc so she could blackmail him. This was how she 'negotiated.'

Marc stared at AJ. "Why are you surprised? You took her when she was much younger. She must have been spectacular back then."

"You bloody—" AJ lunged forward, Marc stepped back and I jumped between them.

Pressing a hand to AJ's chest I said, "AJ, let's hear the man out." If AJ could set his fury aside, he'd realize Marc was dismantling his own alibi. He'd just admitted he'd known Sam. What else would he say?

Impatiently, AJ brushed my hand away and stepped back, his anger in check for now. Marc continued talking as if he hadn't been interrupted. For six weeks, Samantha went through the motions, pretending to be his lover while secretly gathering evidence of their affair: scandalous texts, emails and photos, she kept it all.

Then a week before she died Marc took Sam to dinner at a posh hotel in Canmore. "Right after dessert she laid out her demands: rework the Ballet House from top to bottom or she'd show Sabine the evidence of our affair—it was all there on her phone—and destroy my marriage."

Marc laughed, a mirthless chuckle. "I always forget how parochial this little town is. This wasn't the earthshattering threat Sam thought it would be. I told her she was free to do whatever she liked with her so-called evidence. Sabine knows."

Did she though? Madeline's words came back to me. Sabine would tolerate Marc's affairs as long as they stayed in the shadows. She pretended his mistresses didn't exist, even Diana Barros and Marc's daughter, Alice, were ghosts as far as Sabine was concerned. What would she do when confronted with Marc's testimonials of love and desire?

As we made our way past the orchestra pit toward the lobby we could hear the drying fans, one was making a loud clacking noise that echoed high in the rafters.

"That little bitch firebombed my office"—that's when I understood that Marc saw himself as the blameless victim—"I've had some acrimonious breakups in the past, but that woman was insane. Then she sent a death threat to my house, that's where she crossed the line. I confronted her and she admitted the arson but denied the death threat. Her target was me, not my wife, she said."

"Marc," I interrupted, "when was this?"

Distracted by the clacking fan he said, "the night before I flew to DC."

AJ was staring into the gritty pool of water rippling under the breeze thrown by the drying fans. It was at least fifteen feet across, moving like a whirlpool, picking up McDonald's wrappers, bits of wood, and tufts of pink insulation, drifting around and around in aimless circles.

The date meant nothing to AJ, but that was the night Samantha died.

CHAPTER SIXTY-SIX

You know that moment, that split second before the elevator door snaps shut and you wonder if it's safe to stick your hand between the doors so you can hop on? Marc was standing inside my imaginary elevator, and I had to decide whether I was going to jump in after him or let the moment slide.

I jumped in.

"Marc, you saw Sam the night she died. Where? At your office?"

AJ snapped to attention. *Please don't attack him. Let him talk.*

At first, Marc looked surprised, then he narrowed his eyes and said, "No, we met here at the Ballet House."

"What time?"

"Around nine or so."

"Why here?" AJ asked. "Why meet at all, she tried to blackmail you. She failed. What was the point of seeing her again?"

Marc gave a smug smile and lifted his arms, palms up like a preacher blessing his flock. "She'd only seen the exterior of this place; all those days wasted marching around in circles outside in the bitter cold. I invited her to come inside and imagine what a special place this would become. If nothing else, she would feel better about losing the battle. Her petty concerns were nothing in the grand scheme of things."

The arrogance of the man was breathtaking.

"No." AJ's eyes went hard. "You lured her here to kill her."

When AJ said it, it shocked me. It's one thing to think such thoughts in the dark, nasty corners of your mind, it's quite another to say them out loud. AJ's accusation had no effect on Marc. He just laughed.

"Don't be absurd. You can bring the police down here if you like. Go over this place with a fine-toothed comb. You'll find nothing."

He's too cocky.

Marc glanced from one drying fan to the other, squinting and turning his head, trying to ascertain which one was making the racket.

He turned to me and said, "For all her intelligence, she was pig-stubborn. Nothing I could say persuaded her..." He droned on and on but I was no longer listening.

If he didn't murder her here, where did he do it?

"Such a beautiful woman," he said, "so intelligent yet utterly devoid of culture, no artistic eye..."

The Atelier.

"Marc," I interrupted his rambling recitation of Sam's shortcomings. "You didn't meet Sam here; she would never come here. She hated this place. You lured her back to the Atelier. What did you do, tell her you were changing the design to accommodate her demands and you wanted her approval of the new drawings?"

"She came here," he insisted, his eyes flicking from

fan to fan, seeking the one making a loud grinding noise. "Christ, the damn thing is going to short out." He shot me a look of frustration and strode off to unplug the fan. Skirting the large, rippling pool of water. Squeezing between piles of lumber and large, dusty bags of something white and chalky.

When he reached the closest fan, he bent down to its base, picked up the thick red cord and followed it back to a wall socket hidden behind a stack of insulation near the plywood doors. Two of the fans whirred into silence when he unplugged them, but the defective fan continued clacking even louder as if it were trying to compensate for the two that had been silenced.

Marc flung his hands in the air in exasperation, then crawled over a small pile of lumber, catching his foot on a two-by-four and knocking it off the pile.

He's such a meticulous man, I thought, a place for everything and everything in its place. At least as far as his home and office were concerned. How could he stand the mess of this place?

He found the thick red cord and followed it back to a tangle of cords plugged into a socket screwed into a large post. Finally the blades of the fans stopped whirring and silence fell like a soft blanket.

Marc gave a satisfied nod, then dusted his hands together and brushed the chalky white grit off the front of his coat, smearing the residue even deeper into the cashmere fabric. He sighed and began to make his way back to us.

The frustration of a meticulous man. *A place for everything and everything in its place.* That small, tidy gesture gave him away.

Pritchard told me that without solid evidence, Robert's

story was not enough to overturn Sabine's confession. "AJ," I whispered as I reached into my pocket and pulled out my cell. "We've got him." With one eye on Marc inching around the edge of the filthy pool and the other on my contacts list I dialed Pritchard's number.

Marc stepped over a stack of lumber and knocked another two-by-four onto the floor. It made a loud ringing noise as it bounced along the concrete. He was almost upon us.

"Quick, AJ." I passed him my phone. "When Prichard answers tell him I found the evidence he's looking for."

"Where?"

"Tell him to get a squad car over to Marc's office and seal it off. No one is allowed in."

"What?" AJ squinched his eyes the way he does when he's confused.

"Go, it's ringing!" I gave AJ a little push to shoo him away. He opened his mouth to speak, then Pritchard's voice came on the line and he turned away, striding off in the direction of the plywood doors, head down, talking quietly into the receiver.

"Where's he going? I'm locking up," Marc said, hooking a thumb in AJ's direction.

I needed to stall him for a few more minutes. "She was telling the truth." I watched AJ out of the corner of my eye. He nodded a couple of times, then hung up and started walking back to me.

"Who?" Marc asked.

"Sam. When she said she didn't send the death threat to your house, she was telling the truth. But you didn't believe her. I can't say I blame you. She'd deceived you with the fake mistress act, she firebombed your office and tried to blackmail you. No one in their right mind would believe her."

AJ joined us and handed me my phone. "It's done. He balked at first but he's sending a car to the office. He says you'd better have a damn good explanation."

Marc's eyes bounced from AJ to me. "The office? Whose office?"

"Your office," AJ said.

"The Atelier? Who's going to my office?" His voice, usually rich and full, tightened. "Why?"

Ignoring Marc, I looked at AJ, "Did Pritchard give you an ETA?"

"Twenty minutes."

"If he doesn't get here fast enough, I'll need your help, but promise me, you won't lose your temper."

"Pritchard?" Marc asked. "The police?"

AJ smiled at me. "Okay, I won't lose my temper."

I gave AJ a hard look to indicate I was dead serious, then turned to Marc. "Sam must have been livid when she showed up at your office and discovered you'd deceived her. There was no new design for the Ballet House. There was nothing, only you, telling her to use some common sense. You accused her of making death threats, she denied it and you turned on her. What happened? Why did you attack her?"

My question caught Marc off guard. He stammered that he hadn't touched that deranged woman.

I remembered the last time we'd met at the Atelier. Barbara Major put us in the conference room adjacent to Marc's office. While we waited, Luke poked though the mementos arranged on the credenza, unimpressed until he spotted a small Henry Moore sculpture. The Pritzker. The Nobel prize of architecture that once sat on the corner of Marc's desk—a place for everything and everything in its place—which was now relegated to the mess of lesser trinkets he'd been awarded over the years.

I wondered how far I could push this before AJ blew up. "That's not true. When Sam refused to admit she'd sent the threatening note, which she didn't, you snapped. You'd been under a lot of pressure for the last six weeks and you flew into a rage. You grabbed whatever was close at hand, the Pritzker bronze sculpture, and struck her with it, cracking her skull. I don't know if you meant to kill her, but you did."

AJ exhaled sharply, as if someone had punched him in the gut. I grabbed his arm to steady him but he shook me off. He straightened and took a long, slow breath, saying nothing.

Marc drew himself up to his full height, his arms loose by his sides, and stared calmly into AJ's eyes. Waiting. Biding his time.

Where was Pritchard? I kept talking.

"You cracked Sam's skull. She was lying on the floor, dead. Now you had a problem. Two actually. You had to get rid of Sam's body, but first you had to get rid of the murder weapon."

Beside me, one quick, smooth movement, and AJ had Marc by the lapels and was shaking him so hard I thought his head would snap off.

"AJ, stop, you promised!"

Outside came the whoop of a police siren. A minute later Pritchard and another officer charged through the plywood doors, scanning the dark lobby trying to locate us.

AJ froze. A look of disgust crossed his face and he flung Marc away from him, like a child tossing away a broken toy. Marc went down hard, falling on his back in the filthy water spreading across the concrete floor. Knocking the air right out of him. He gasped and wheezed struggling to breathe, while AJ towered over him, impassive.

I hollered at Pritchard, waving my arm to get his attention. "Over here. We're here."

Out of the corner of my eye I saw AJ reach down and haul Marc roughly to his feet. The back of Marc's coat was soaked with grimy water. Ruined.

Pritchard directed his partner to take Marc and AJ over to the plywood doors while he 'had a word' with me.

"Okay, Evie, let's hear it." He'd used my first name, which was a good sign because when he's really angry with me, he calls me Valentine. Pritchard confirmed his team had secured the Atelier, sending home two employees who were working late. There didn't appear to be anything amiss. "Why are we there?"

"The Pritzker prize." I Googled *Henry Moore Pritzker Prize*. "They'll find it in the large glass conference room next to Marc's office. East corner of the building." I showed Pritchard a photo of the sculpture and emailed it to him. "It's bronze, roughly ten inches high and twelve inches wide. Marc used it to bludgeon Sam to death."

Pritchard's eyebrows shot up—the only indication that anything I'd said was of interest—as he forwarded the photo to his team lead. "Right, now they know what they're looking for." He continued to gaze at the photograph. Then whistled under his breath. "Valued at $162,500? For that little thing. No wonder he didn't want to throw it in the river."

I glanced at the photo over his shoulder. To me, the sculpture looked like a sightless alien creature wriggling on the ground. Marc would rub what its head when he was stressed, making the bronze gleam nicely.

"Forget the dollar value, Pritchard. To an architect, it's like winning the Nobel prize. Marc's was extra special because that bronze sculpture was the end of a limited series. It's the last of its kind."

The thought intruded. Sam had no family; she too was the last of her kind.

Pritchard walked over to a stack of rough stone blocks and sat down. "I assume you have some thoughts on what happened. Care to share?"

I glanced at the plywood doors where Marc, AJ and the police officer were standing. Marc was gesturing at AJ and the gritty pool. AJ leaned against the wall. Arms crossed, watching Marc with contempt. The cop was scribbling in his notebook. I joined Pritchard on the stack of stone blocks. Ready to share my theory.

"Marc admitted he knew Sam and he saw her the night she died. He says she was blackmailing him. Which was probably true. And sending death threats to his house. Which was not true. That was Robert. Marc lured Sam to the Atelier and they had an argument. I believe he lost his temper and crushed her skull with that sculpture.

"It was late, the office was deserted. He wrapped her up in a woven African carpet and carried her down to the parking garage where he stuffed her into the trunk of his Mercedes.

"But not before he cleaned off the sculpture—there was no way he could throw it away, it was too important to him—but he couldn't leave it on his desk, a constant reminder of what he'd done. So he put it in the conference room with the rest of his awards and prizes. Hiding it in plain sight."

Pritchard raised his eyebrows but said nothing. "When he went to DC he left instructions with Marcie, his assistant, to redecorate his office in his absence. A neutral palette. Everything had to go. The change was so radical no one would notice the African carpet was gone."

Pritchard watched me thoughtfully, then said, "After which he drives home and dumps the body in the basement of the McMansion, then goes to bed as if nothing happened."

I glanced at Marc who was now demanding to speak to his lawyer. "He would have gotten away with it but for Kenny, the guy who operates the excavator. Kenny loves his job and is so good at it he can pluck copper tubing out of a pile of concrete and set it aside for the salvage guys. Kenny picked his way through the debris and instead of destroying Sam's body, he pulled it out of the rubble intact."

Pritchard's phone rang. He pulled it out of his pocket, listened for a few minutes, then hung up.

"They got it," he said with a satisfied smile. "The bronze sculpture is bagged and on its way to forensics."

A few minutes later Pritchard cuffed Marc and deposited him in the back of his patrol car. AJ and I followed in silence. The night air was frigid, the stars looked blurry high above.

AJ pulled out his car keys. It was cold in the MGB. It's an older model and didn't have a fancy start button like the Mini. His hand trembled and it took him a moment to insert the key in the ignition. He waited while the engine warmed up. Then slipped the gearshift into reverse and yanked the steering wheel hard to make a U-turn.

"How are you doing?" I asked.

"Okay, I guess." The MGB bumped in and out of the ruts, the steering wheel twisting in his hands. "We got him, Evie. That should give me some satisfaction, but it doesn't."

He glanced at me, his face pale in the streetlights, and

shook his head. "You've known them for twenty years. How the hell could he kill Sam and let his wife take the blame. How could they do something like that?"

How indeed. The first time I'd met Marc and Sabine they were Anthony and Cleopatra. I had no idea who they were now.

CHAPTER SIXTY-SEVEN

SEVEN MONTHS LATER

It was an unseasonably hot Sunday evening in early October and the air was thick with humidity. Rare for these parts. The smoke from the summer forest fires had lifted and everyone was looking forward to what promised to be a brilliant fall. Louisa and I hustled across the gravel parking lot, keen to see whether the Ballet House lived up to expectations.

Louisa pointed to the sign—*Sidney Foster Hall*—and said, "I'll bet Sabine isn't too happy about that." Originally Foster had demanded a bronze plaque in the lobby but after the scandal he pushed for naming rights. The City, eager to erase any connection between the Ballet House and Marc and Sabine, quickly agreed. And it didn't cost Foster a dime.

"We'll never know," I replied. Like Robert, Louisa and I had been banished.

As we walked through the arid garden landscape I wondered when Sabine began to suspect Marc of murdering Samatha. Was it when Sam showed up at Masters Gallery—Robert recognized her from a newspaper photo as the belligerent young woman he'd sent away—or later when I told Sabine that Sam was blackmailing Marc? Was that when Sabine realized the only hold Sam could possibly have over Marc was their affair? An affair that refused to stay in the shadows.

Either way, Sabine concocted a false confession which would have been airtight but for the besotted Robert who lingered at her bedside, watching her sleep, and Marc who refused to part with the Pritzker prize. The police found traces of Sam's DNA on the bronze sculpture and in the trunk of his Mercedes. The brutality of the attack made me shiver in spite of the heat.

"Don't tell me you're cold," Louisa said as we wandered through the elm and aspen groves shielding the Ballet House from the baking sun.

"Just thinking," I replied. The evidence was irrefutable and Marc finally admitted he'd lured Sam to the Atelier. When Sam realized she'd been duped, she stormed out of his office, threatening to tell Sabine that Marc loved her and she had the evidence on her phone to prove it. What could Marc do? He'd almost lost Sabine after Alice was born; he wouldn't risk losing her again. When Sam refused to see reason, he flew into a rage and bludgeoned her to death. What choice did he have?

"Louisa." She was lingering in the terraced garden. "Get a move on or we'll miss the final performance." I didn't want to attend the Prix de Lyon, but Louisa, the little girl who cried because she couldn't be a popcorn kernel in a dance recital, said I owed her one.

According to the lawyer's rumour mill, Sabine was more horrified by Marc killing Bijoux than anything else. After Marc dumped Sam's body in the basement he returned to the garage and found 'that stupid crow' picking at Sam's bracelet in the snow. It must have slipped off her wrist when Marc hauled her body out of the trunk.

He reached for the bracelet and Bijoux fought him for it, gashing Marc's hand with its razor sharp beak. Furious, Marc crushed the bird with his fist, breaking its wing and leaving it for dead in the freezing cold. He washed up and went to bed, rising at four a.m. to catch his flight to DC.

"Wasn't that clever," Louisa said, interrupting my thoughts. She pointed to a prickly prairie rose. "All the vegetation is drought resistant." She saw the troubled look on my face. "Oh, don't tell me. You're obsessing about Sabine again."

How could I not? Sabine's actions were so bizarre. When she awoke to the sound of crows screaming in the back alley she rushed out in her night clothes and found Bijoux lying dead next to Sam's bracelet. She tossed the bracelet in the trash and cradled Bijoux to her chest. She thought she was protecting him from the mobbing crows when they were trying to protect Bijoux from her. And a couple of hours later Levi pulled the bracelet out of the trash intending to sell it on eBay.

"Louisa." I held the door open. "Get in here." Ten little girls in tiny pink tutus fluttered in the door followed by Louisa who flashed our passes at the attendant and picked up two programs. Twenty dancers had made it to the finals, one would win the Grand Prix.

The thought of running into Sabine, who'd kept a very low profile since Marc confessed, filled me with dread.

The auditorium was large and cool and packed with dance students, their teachers and proud parents, all here to be inspired by the best of the best. The chandeliers sparkled overhead like stars in an inky blue sky as we worked our way down the aisle to our seats.

Louisa flipped through the program, stopping at the second to last page. "Evie, look, the past prize winners." She underlined a name with her fingertip. "Sabine Scoffier, Grand Prix winner, 1975."

Nineteen seventy-five, not quite a decade before she met Marc. Not quite fifty years before he murdered Samantha.

Marc and Sabine. Their relationship confounded me. Sabine loved Marc so much she was prepared to give up everything for his happiness. He accepted her sacrifice, and yet, for a brief moment, begged her not to go through with it.

Let me. She'd said it a number of times, caressing his cheek and touching his lips. And finally, he did.

A young man in a white shirt, black pants and black suspenders bounced across the stage to the sound of techno music. Louisa glanced at me. "Not your typical ballet, is it."

Up front there was a ripple of movement. A silver-haired Sabine made her way down the aisle. She held her head high and clutched a small black bag close to her chest. It matched her sleeveless black dress which hung loosely on her frame. The light reflecting off the stage made her face look gaunt and her cheekbones sharp. An elderly couple hobbled down the aisle right behind her. The woman stopped, touched the man's arm, and nodded in Sabine's direction. They waited until Sabine took her seat, then moved to the row on the opposite side of the aisle. Sabine was quiet alone.

The next dancer, a small girl with round arms and dimpled knees, appeared on stage. The sound of an insistent flute filled the air. She raised her arms like a baby bird and took flight.

I've been thinking about scandal a lot lately. Sabine lied to protect Marc and her reputation was ruined. The city's greatest fundraiser couldn't get herself invited to a bake sale now. Whereas Marc's reputation was enhanced. Everyone was talking about the architect who murdered his mistress to protect his artistic vision.

"What's the matter?" Louisa tapped my arm with her program. "You look like you swallowed a sour lemon."

"This is so messed up. Robert wasted twenty years of his life pining after Sabine. Sabine tolerated Marc's affairs as long as she didn't have to acknowledge them, and Samantha was murdered because she didn't understand the rules. I keep thinking about something Grizzly said. He and Sam had been together since university. Sam would drift away but she always came back. But this time something was different. Grizzly thought Sam had gone back to AJ; do you think she actually fell in love with Marc?"

"Dear Lord," Louisa popped open her purse and passed me her keys, she's always losing them. She rummaged around until she found a hard candy, Werther's, Mom's favourite, and handed it to me. "Evie, you know what your problem is? You're a romantic, like those people who rewrote the ending of Swan Lake."

"Someone rewrote Swan Lake, isn't there a law against that?"

"Don't ask me, you're the lawyer. Swan Lake was written as a tragedy. Odette, the swan, and her prince are supposed to die. But someone decided that ending was too tragic and rewrote it so the swan and the prince live. And it's switched back and forth ever since. Live, die, live, die."

On the stage a slim young woman was halfway through her performance. She was wearing a beige body suit and leaping and twirling all over the stage to the beat of tribal music. Two hours and many dancers later, her name was called. She'd won the Grand Prix.

Sabine leapt to her feet in joyous applause. Glittering confetti fell from the ceiling, covering the stage and the finalists with shiny bits of coloured paper. Parents and teachers rushed up, crying and hugging the contestants. In all the commotion I didn't see Sabine slip away.

Soon we were back outside. It was cooler now that evening had fallen. Behind us the Ballet House glittered like a crystal palace, its light blotting out the stars. I opened the car door and took one last look at the translucent building. It wouldn't matter what they called it, the Ballet House would forever be Marc and Sabine's legacy.

Louisa glanced at me and said, "Come on. I'm going to buy you an ice cream cone."

"What flavour?" I asked.

She laughed and said she'd take care of it.

ACKNOWLEDGEMENTS

I've said it before and I'll say it again: one of the coolest things about being a writer is all the wonderful people you meet who are more than happy to share their expertise with you, even when you tell them it might end up in a novel.

Special thanks to Rob Pashuk, a wonderful architect who introduced me to the world of starchitects, and Mike Schuett, a percussionist, who shared his experience as a member of the Calgary Philharmonic. Neither of them are anything like their counterparts in this book.

I'd also like to thank Jeff Fox, who can tackle any electrical problem no matter how big or small, Wes Weiss, the king of the slapshot, and Cole Jorden, the nicest plucky accountant I know.

Thanks also to the crew working on the McMansion down the road who really can flatten a house in a couple of hours.

Despite these experts generously sharing their time, mistakes creep in and they are all mine. Also, this is a work of fiction, so while the story is set in Calgary the problems facing the Ballet House (if it existed) are fictious, the Pritzker Prize is real but the last Henry Moore limited edition sculpture was awarded long before Marc won it, and while many international ballet competitions exist, the *Prix de Lyon* is not one of them.

I'm grateful to my friends at Crime Writes of Canada and Sisters in Crime—Canada West, for their endless support.

As always, a big thank you to my sisters who are the inspiration for Evie's relationship with Louisa, and my family, my husband Roy, the best first reader ever, and my daughters Kelly who played a huge role in getting this book published and Eden who was there to answer odd ball questions at all hours of the day or night.

Lastly, I'd like to thank you, my readers, I'm so grateful for your support.

ABOUT THE AUTHOR

SUSAN JANE WRIGHT lives in Calgary, Alberta. She studied anthropology before she became a lawyer. She worked as a litigator at a national law firm before going in-house with a multi-national corporation. Her career has taken her from the boardrooms of Houston to the streets of Beijing.

Murderous Dreams is the fourth book in the Evie Valentine mystery series. It follows the bestsellers *Fortune Favors the Dead*, *The Glass Lake*, and *Box of Secrets*. Her books have been finalists for the Crime Writers of Canada and Canadian Book Club Awards.

She lives in Calgary, Alberta. When she's not writing she's travelling with her husband and two daughters. Her favourite vacation was a trip from Prague to London on the Orient Express. One day she'd like to take the train from Venice to Istanbul.